T0065615

Maidens of
Trafford House

Maidens of Trafford House

Eight Stories

Harsh Vardhan Khimta

PARTRIDGE

ISBN: Hardcover   978-1-4828-4152-7
             Softcover   978-1-4828-4151-0
             eBook   978-1-4828-4150-3

To order additional copies of this book, contact
Partridge India
000 800 10062 62
orders.india@partridgepublishing.com

www.partridgepublishing.com/india

Contents

Dedicated to you,

the reader,

for investing Time and Money in an unknown author

1

Caroline

I find it pleasantly surprising that even towards the end of August, I should smell of April; an April that smells of marigolds, of snow, of the river and that mountain ... an April in me that smells of Caroline.

While sitting on a wooden bench at the Barog railway station, waiting for my train to Shimla, I can't help sinking into the memories of a recent past. I am going home, to Shimla, on a ten day vacation from my college in Delhi. It might seem unusual to abandon the bus, walk down to this railway station fifty kilometers short of Shimla, and measure the remaining distance homeward in a hill train that is bound to take longer. It is unusual, but to me it seems just about perfect.

I notice the change in seasons. Autumn shall soon arrive at a place where I saw, not long ago, spring in its abundant glory. The platform already has yellowing green leaves strewn about it. Monsoon humidity has replaced the crispy air of April. What shall yet not change, nor wither away like seasons, is my memory of her.

Caroline was French. It was her e-mail that my travel manager friend Ketan had forwarded to me. When I met him in his office that morning in April he looked helpless. "She had enquired a month ago and we confirmed a few days back. I have even received the advance payment and done all the further bookings. And now this," he complained as if he'd been cheated. He handed me the print of another mail written by someone from the French embassy in Delhi. I read it aloud:

Dear Mr. Mehta

I am writing to you on the behalf of Caroline something something. *She tells me that she is over with her tour of the South of India and now looks forward to coming to Shimla for a few days just to unwind before she can return home. She tells me that she has a booking with your agency Amazing Heights. Now that most of the others in the group have left for France, she is anxious about her stay in and around Shimla since she cannot communicate in any Indian language including English. We feel sure that you shall make the necessary arrangements so that her stay can be made not just comfortable but also enriching.*

Yours

Some damn body, I hardly cared to read.

I looked at Ketan, and he seemed to have pratfallen from some really amazing heights.

"So what's the problem, man?" I said.

"We have no interpreters for French. Who do you think will handle it?"

I wondered why he should be so much worried at such a simple thing. I pretended to be more serious.

"If it is so difficult, why don't you pass her on to some other agency?" I said, offering the most valuable and genuine advice I could bring to my mind.

"Lend a customer to one of these, just because we can't handle someone who doesn't speak any of the familiar tongues! You don't realize the sort of ridicule we will be subjected to, even though any of them will be as rattled as we now are. It's the loss of reputation my dear. The loss of face. And they'll make sure we actually do that. And we can't allow that to happen."

I felt Ketan was exaggerating. All I was trying to do was to ease his situation a little. That is the least I could do to help a friend who had given me a chance for professional exposure while I was half way through my graduation. I really wanted to rescue him from that linguistic whirlpool.

"You could ask one of these Khans to escort her. If they can speak English with all the tourists they could easily humor her for a few days."

Ketan smiled for the first time during the conversation.

"Khans only know English sufficient enough to escort tourists to the hotel rooms. They run out of it as soon as they have counted their commission."

"But their English anyway sounds like French. By the time she finds that out she'll have got over with her unwinding."

The smile disappeared from Ketan's face, which unexpectedly turned into a decisive one.

"Fine, boy! *You* take that up. Isn't that precisely what you have come to Shimla for? Truly professional, and what an exposure!"

My disappointed ears couldn't believe what they'd heard.

"But, I am accompanying that Norwegian group to Khajurao."

"Don't worry darling, that'll be taken care of."

"No man! At twenty you just can't deprive me of watching those great performers in the dark caves. Just imagine meeting those tireless ones face to face. What a great experience that would be."

"Look man! I am in a real fix. If we don't handle this French thing properly I could end up ruining a good deal of my business from that part of the world. You know how news travels these days. In fact this booking of hers must have come my way due to some favorable word of mouth. I have a lot at stake in that continent."

He made me feel that the European Union would disintegrate if she were sent to some other agency to unwind her exhausted self. I couldn't even tell him to forget it. Though Ketan and I were old buddies, a professional relationship demanded more seriousness. That's why I willingly conceded a one step higher pedestal to him.

Well, if he thought I was the most suitable person available to him to do a task that prevented not just his *Amazing Heights* from getting a bad name, but also an entire continent from humiliation, or linguistic molestation, by some unscrupulous and semi-educated travel agent of any of those…the *Everest View* or *Plains from Shimla*, or even that bloody *Muzzer Park*; what a name by the way, I wondered which damned tourist would ever guess it to be the name of a travel agency; then I had better make my services available to the dame, who could choose to use them in any way she wished.

"When is she arriving?"

"Tomorrow."

"Fine, I am leaving now. I'll let you know in the evening."

"There is nothing to let me know. You know that. You are the most suitable one for this job, and you know that. Don't you? Imagine how useful such an interaction is going to be for you. Your career I mean. Just think man."

He was beginning to sound contrived. He had probably rehearsed that. I wondered if he would have accepted the assignment, if I weren't around.

"Fine. I'll do it. I will do it. I will reach the office in the morning and let me know if she conveys to you how she intends to unwind."

Saying goodbye to Ketan I left the office. I finally made up my mind as I was getting down the stairs of the *Amazing Heights*.

I reached home and found something to eat. It was beginning to get hot. I took a bath and went to sleep. Within a few minutes my phone began to ring. It had been ringing earlier while I was in the bath. I ignored the phone till it rang once again, almost stubbornly. I looked at the screen. It showed five calls that I had failed to take. They were all from my girl then. I sent her a message that I was sleeping and would speak to her later. I had hardly slept for a few minutes when the phone began to yell yet again. I answered it.

"Where have you been?" she screamed.

"Hi."

"What are you doing?"

"Hi, Shubra…"

"Where are you? Who's with you?"

"Hello, man, hello. How are you Shubra?"

"What exactly have you been doing boy? You can't even answer a call in time."

"I was sleeping."

"Doesn't look like you've been sleeping. You sound rather fresh and excited. Did you sleep-text me?"

"What?"

"Did you write that message while you were sleeping?"

"No. Yes. Of course, I wrote that message but…look, I was sleeping earlier, and then I was watering the plants." Her nagging had turned me into a reluctant liar.

"Whaatterrig the plants? At three in the afternoon?"

"Yeah, it's …beginning to get warm here in Shimla. How's life by the way?"

"Are you sure you actually have flower pots at your place? I don't remember any. Anyway, forget it. My training is getting over a week before scheduled. That means I'll be home sooner."

"That's great news."

"When are you leaving with that group for Khajurao? Next week, isn't it?"

"No. It was to be this week, but Ketan might just change the plans."

"Change? How? But why?"

"I may not be going at all."

"Any other tour he's given you?"

"Well… no. Not really but something might just crop up." I was at it once again.

"But then why aren't you going? You wanted to, didn't you? You said that would help you learn about tour management."

"I can't help if Ketan finds someone else for the job. That's good in a way. You come to Shimla and we can be together. That'll be fun," lying yet again.

"Fine, man. That's just ten days away. Won't you ask me why they are allowing some of us to leave earlier?"

"Oh, yes. You hardly gave me a chance to ask. Why?"

"Because we completed our designing projects well in time. The others will stay longer. All right man, you've wasted all my afternoon. Bye."

"Bye."

"What bye? Why are you so eager to say bye?"

"I just said it because you wanted me to."

"As if you do all that I want you to."

"I try to."

"And why don't you respond to my text messages? And the jokes? You could send some too."

"I will."

"All right then. Bye. Don't get lost among the flower pots. And …I want to see how many of them you have anyway. Bye."

"Bye."

I waited for her to disconnect the phone, so that I wouldn't be seen as eager to end the conversation. God, what a conversation!

I hadn't met Shubra for good three weeks then. Actually, felt good about it. Relieved. Emancipated, indeed. Now she was following me to Shimla. Terrified by the nags that would follow, I tried to sleep.

I got up early the next morning. I went for a jog. After breakfast, my mother took me to a temple; she always did, before I left home for even a day. At the gate of the temple,

I saw the old man whom I remember having seen since childhood. As usual, he reminded me how he used to carry me inside the temple on his shoulders. My mother gave him food and a few clothes, which is what she always did. On our way home, my mother asked me, "Have you done your packing?"

"Yeah. Done."

"How many days is this tour?"

"I have no idea. It's not a long one. There's a French woman whose companions have left. She wants to travel around here for a couple of days."

"A woman? French? How old is she?"

"I have no idea."

"Is she married?"

"How on earth do you think I could know that? Or, even care? How does it matter anyway?"

Just then the phone rang. It was Ketan.

"Bastard, you are late. What the hell are you up to?"

"I am in a temple."

"Temm...ple? A temple? Who dragged you there? Now look, our guest is already here. Get here in two minutes and don't ruin my reputation further."

"Okay."

"Boy! I know you'll fly. You won't like to miss even a minute. Lucky bastard."

"Okay. Thanks."

We reached home quickly. I satisfied mother's inquisition as well as I could. I received her countless instructions absentmindedly. They were just the same as on numerous other occasions in the past. She kissed my forehead and I rushed into my father's study to say goodbye to him.

Carrying my rucksack I panted into Ketan's office. I waved at the receptionist, shook hands with Ketan and then smiled at a woman whom Ketan introduced as Caroline.

"Raman," I uttered, smiling.

"Caroline," she smiled.

That was the only comprehensible word I was to hear from her for a long while.

As Ketan was giving me the details of the program, I could see from the corner of my eye that Caroline sat like a statue and the receptionist was staring at her desktop. Ketan explained to me that Caroline wanted to visit the old railway station at Barog, for some odd purpose, and then spend a night at Kasauli. We were to return the next day.

"God, why did she travel all the way to Shimla? She could have finished off with that Barog and Kasauli thing and then come to Shimla. It's on the way. You should have told her in the beginning."

"Caroline would you like something to drink? Tea, coffee, or something cold perhaps," Ketan said to her, without answering my question.

She looked at him blankly; smiling in embarrassment.

"Caroline, coffee? Tea? A drink?" he repeated, with gestures.

"No, no," she replied.

Turning to me Ketan said, "You duck, she didn't crawl all the way to Shimla. She flew from Delhi. Now let's get on with the job at hand. Two rooms have been booked for you at the Kasauli Resorts, where you will reach by the evening."

We boarded a taxi. I sat with the driver. I didn't know what to say to Caroline. I tried to play the guide; showing her the Shimla airport at a ridge where she had landed that morning and a famous temple down the hill. She just smiled at me; nodding, approving. I was sure she understood at least the basics of English which most European tourists did.

Half an hour later, we stopped at a little waterfall. It gushed out of the rocks barely twenty feet above the highway and was considered clean enough to be drunk. The driver and I got off, not just to drink some water but to fill a few bottles too. Before jumping off, I said to her, "Would you like to drink some water? It's fresh, I can assure you." Unconvinced; she smiled, nodded, and seemed to approve. I handed to her the first bottle of water I had filled. She smiled again, shook her head and uttered a syllable or two pleasantly, which I didn't understand, but translated to myself to mean that she thanked me for being so kind and hospitable but since she wasn't thirsty, she wouldn't drink a drop, and that I had better stop those explanations and gestures since she just didn't understand, and that I needn't waste any time so that she could get over with her business at the Barog railway station and move on to Kasauli before it got dark, as getting late could make life difficult for the two who could neither understand nor abandon each other. That I could infer so much from a couple of syllables shows the power of the unspoken speech, something both of us would have to rely upon heavily over the next couple of days.

A few kilometers before Barog, we took the link road that wound down the hill to the Barog railway station. I had no idea what she wanted to do there. I simply looked forward to reaching Kasauli. I was quite excited about staying at the lovely Kasauli Resorts. Our car stopped at the Barog railway station. It was an important railway station on the Kalka-Shimla railway line and the campus was too impressive for a railway station. Caroline took out her mobile phone and started talking to someone. I began to explore the Barog railway station. A few lines carved upon a stone platform read that the sixty mile railway track from Kalka to Shimla was opened for public use in 1903.

After some time she gave the phone to me. I didn't know who was on the other side. I was confused but still managed to say 'hello'.

"Hi. My name is Stephanie. I work at the French embassy in New Delhi. As I had written in the email, Caroline doesn't know English at all. By the way, she's a student of theatre. She says there is a theatre at the railway station that you are at right now. Help her find that. She'll do her job. Just be around."

"That's all right. We'll try and find it, if there's one."

"Thanks. What could I call you?"

"Raman."

"Thanks Raman, bye."

"Bye."

Now that was an awful task; to find a theatre at a railway station that saw just a few trains cross everyday. I handed the phone to Caroline.

"Who told you there might be a theatre at this place?" I asked her.

She smiled.

I didn't know where to start. I looked around for the station master's office. I was led into it by someone I later came to know was the guard of the station. The station master was delighted to see us enter his office, owing especially to the company of a young and a white woman. He almost got up from his seat, welcoming us both. He was at loss for words, and all he could say was, "Welcome, welcome. Please welcome." The guard felt privileged to have showed us in. He smiled above our heads as we sat on the sofa and withdrew slowly, almost dragging himself involuntarily. I said, "It's a nice station, sir. Almost a picnic spot. I wonder why I've never been here before though I've lived in Shimla all my life."

"You're right. Wonderful place really. We have a lot of tourists getting down at this station, spending some time here and then catching the next train to Shimla or Kalka."

The elaborately decorated name plate behind the station master's head announced rather loudly: T N A Aiyer M Tech, in a single breath, without separating the man from the accomplishment. The excited station master addressed Caroline most of the time, looking at me only occasionally. Caroline continued to nod, smile, and, of course, approve. She would look at me from time to time, begging me to rescue her, while I was enjoying the lecher's hopeless adventures.

Looking at her he said, "Is this your first visit to India, ma'am?"

Caroline smiled, as I might say, most graciously. Encouraged, he went on, "How do you find our country ma'am? I mean, I know you peoples are very cultured ma'am but how do you find our cultures? We are very ancient also." Caroline looked at me helplessly and smiled at him sheepishly. T N A Aiyer M Tech took that to be an approval by her, probably, that he was both, cultured and ancient. While he shot another question at her I continued to sit along unattended like a dusty bush on a busy highway.

"I am very fond of your country madam. It's a very beautiful country madam," he said looking at her very affectionately.

She continued her polite gestures.

"I have been there once. To your country. Beautiful really."

"Which country is it sir?" I intervened.

"England, England. Of course." He said that abruptly, without looking at me as if my question were broadcast through radio.

Caroline's nodding pleased him immensely.

"I like your football also very much. In fact I watched a club match in London. I forgot the outcome of the match but I cherish the memory very much, though here in India, we prefer other sports more. Do you like cricket madam? Of course, we learnt that game from you people only."

She nodded.

"Do you like cricket madam? Or football?"

She smiled when her nod would have been more useful. The absence of any answer made him a bit nervous. He shuffled in his seat and tried his luck once more. Till then, he'd probably been too excited to note that she hadn't uttered a word.

"Are you going to Shimla or to Kalka ma'am? What's your program by the way?"

Caroline almost nodded and looked at me.

"Please wait a minute madam," he said, pulling a nice looking book from his drawer and handing it to her he continued, "Madam this is a lovely book on the Kalka-Shimla railway line. It is written by Raja Bhasin madam."

I then said to the stationmaster, "Mr. Aiyer, she does not understand English."

"Doesn't understand English?"

He was shocked, as if I had suggested that she was a ghost.

"You should tell me that earlier."

"Indeed, but I have been with her only for a couple of hours. I am yet to find out how much she does not understand."

T N A Aiyer M Tech pressed the bell under his desk as hard as he could. A fat middle aged woman with unmanageable breasts and an open mouth entered, looking clueless. He ordered tea for three. She departed as cluelessly as she had entered.

"I am sure you are here on a purpose. Tell me what can I do for you?"

"Thank you, Mr. Aiyer. She is Martha. She is a German," said I, taking charge. I felt very pleased with myself for lying to him. It gave me a satisfaction of having scored a point over him.

"I am her guide, from the *Hill Park*, Shimla," said I, scoring yet another point. I continued, "As I have been told, she is a theatre student in some college in her country. She says there is a theatre at this railway station. She'd be highly obliged if you permitted her to visit it."

His mouth was open and he sat as if I had hinted there was a bomb under his chair.

"A theatre at this little railway station? Are you sure?" He said in a tone intending, 'are you mad?'.

"She is," I said looking fondly at her; at her cocksureness, and her madness.

"Well!" he said, taking a deep breath, "I just joined a month ago only. I am still a stranger to this place. I found this place quite interesting because it has a library I am told. I have not visited it still. I like reading also but no time."

He could not resist occasional glances at Caroline who pretended to be listening to him with attention. I was pleased to be the centre of his address.

"Well in that case we could call it a day. She must have been misinformed. She could do something with the Gaiety theatre in the middle of the Mall Road in Shimla. That's the only one I know of in and around Shimla. Very old too," I announced.

"Just a minute. Just a minute," he said, pondering at something. I knew he wouldn't give up so easily, even for a visibly hopeless rendezvous with a mute company.

He pressed the bell again, this time feebly, looking at me, confused.

The guard who had shown us in, entered.

"*Huzoor*," he nearly pleaded, this time not looking at us at all.

Since the guard understood only Hindi, I was asked to address him.

"Is there any theatre around here? I mean, at this railway station," said I, with a curious and a doubtful expression on my face.

He shed his timid posture in a moment and hovered smilingly above our heads like a benevolent deity.

"There is," he glowed.

"Is there?" exclaimed T N A Aiyer M Tech.

"There is. Do you want to see it, sir? I will fetch the keys."

"Yes. Do that," said I.

The guard departed and the middle aged woman entered with the tea. Her perplexity had turned into perspiration. While we were having our tea, T N A Aiyer M Tech jumped from one topic to another, throwing glances at Caroline, probably hoping that she might understand something. His affectation irritated me. I am not sure if it was because he was trying to impress her. She seemed to have got tired of smiling unnecessarily. She focused on her tea while I looked him straight in the eye.

After the tea, the four of us were walking along the railway track. To me the little station looked more like a sanatorium. It had as many flowers in its many flower beds as the bricks in its about three small buildings. We headed towards the last one. I stuffed myself between Caroline and the station master. We were first shown into the ground floor. It had once been a library and was later converted into a guest room. The bookshelves covered all the four walls of the room. The guard explained to me in Hindi, which only he and I understood. The entire building belonged to some Taylor, an Englishman who left India much after the Independence in 1947. I explained that to the station master in English, which only he and I could understand. Caroline would have to wait, though I had already gestured to her that we had found her theatre. She went aside, pulled out her mobile phone and began talking to someone, probably Stephanie, which none of us could understand. She must have informed Stephanie that we had found her theatre after all.

The guard explained to us that the guest house hosted visiting railway officials occasionally. The theatre that we had come looking for was upstairs. As we were walking up the old iron spiral staircase, I made a polite gesture to T N A Aiyer M Tech to lead so that he could not stick too much to Caroline. Before we could enter, there was an urgent call for him at the office and he had to leave but not before inviting us to lunch at his place in case we stayed long.

Relieved that he had left I asked the guard his name. It was Ram Sukh. He was relieved too, I could sense. As the door opened we were able to see the theatre at once. The entire space was not more than thirty feet by twenty. Old and abandoned, it had huge windows with faded curtains and some old paintings on the walls. Caroline sat silently on a chair while Ram Sukh and I stood by. On one end was a little stage and the rest of the room had arm chairs for the spectators, twenty five in all. While Ram Sukh drew the curtains and opened the windows, I stood under a huge portrait and Caroline still sat pensively on one of the twenty five armchairs.

Malcolm Stanley Taylor, read the inscription at the bottom of the portrait. Ram Sukh walked up to me and was waiting for me to ask him something. He looked very satisfied, though humble, about his growing importance to us.

"Who is this gentleman? What about this theatre?" I asked.

And then he began. "I have been working at this station since 1960 *Saab*. As you can see I am an old man now. My father worked here all his life. Taylor *Saab* was *angrez*. I don't remember him vividly, but my father told me a lot about him. He was a great man. May God give peace to his soul for he must be long dead now."

I looked at Caroline. She was sitting still, staring into nothing. To me it was just a strange thing in an absurd place. To her, it must have been interesting.

"Shortly after the Kalka-Shimla railway track was built by the imperial government, Taylor *Saab* settled in a farm near here with his wife. They reared cows and poultry. As my father told me, the Englishman would spend all his days in his reading room, especially after his wife died."

"Did he have any children? What else did he do?" I asked.

"He had two daughters, who would come to meet him sometimes. He had a few local servants working on his farm. It was a big farm," he said, spreading his open palms and opening his eyes to their maximum.

I nodded.

"He had been in the army before he began living here," Ram Sukh continued.

"What about this theatre?" I asked.

"It was he who built this structure. One floor for the books, and this floor for the *natak*."

"Who performed here?"

"*Angrez log.*"

"Can you tell me something more about it?"

"No more than I know *Saab*. Yes, after the *Memsaab* died, Taylor *Saab* would go to her grave every evening and sit there for long. After many years, when Taylor *Saab* had gone to his home in England, my father would sometimes go to the graveyard and probably remember them both. I should be leaving now. *Saab* might get angry."

It was just Caroline and me in the room with the bearded Taylor looking at us both. I looked at her but she was looking elsewhere. I sat on a chair beside her. The theatre resembled an extended attic. It seemed like a little room on a cloud where a few people performed on the stage and just as many watched. Who were those players? Who were the performers? Who were their spectators? And why at a railway station? Ponderingly, I looked at Caroline. She looked at me. Then we walked around in that little theatre. Caroline drew the curtains of the stage. It was a little place where a few characters could play comfortably.

Caroline spoke to someone on her phone and then handed it to me. It was Stephanie. I explained to her whatever little I knew about the theatre and Taylor. Then she passed that information onto Caroline. Again the phone was in my hand and Stephanie conveyed to me, "Caroline wants to find some documents about the theatre. They might be in the library or somewhere in the theatre. She may need to copy some of that matter. Would you please be of some help to her? She is prepared to pay extra for your efforts."

Caroline smiled at me. I was literally helpless. I didn't know what to do with the theatre or with her. I had no idea how to help her out. It was lunch time and I was hungry. Just then Ram Sukh entered. He had brought tea for us. He was quite glad to inform me that the station master had left for Shimla to attend an emergency meeting. I relished the tea. When I told him about the problem I faced, he took me backstage and showed me a box.

"I don't know what this box contains. I don't even know who has the keys. But if it serves your purpose, I can break it open. It does not belong to the *firangi sarkar*, nor our *sarkar*. Taylor *Saab* is long dead. It belongs to those who can see his things, appreciate them and pray for his soul."

He broke open the latch of the wooden box. It contained costumes for stage performers.

"Should I take them out and see what else is there?" said Ram Sukh. I nodded. The costumes occupied more than half the box. Caroline looked keenly at the heap of those colorful garments. The next to come out was an old leather case. It was not locked. I opened it and saw that it was full of photographs. They must have been in hundreds. She sat down and started looking at the pictures with great interest. Caroline got lost into the photographs while Ram Sukh and I continued to take out the piles and bundles of very old papers. By the time we emptied out the box I saw that she had piled the photographs into a few sets, though I didn't know on what basis she did it. I started shuffling through the ones she had kept aside. Ram Sukh gazed for a while and then took our leave, not without mentioning that we would be served lunch in half an hour.

I categorized the papers into three piles; first, the scripts of the plays that were handwritten; second, the notes written by various people; and the third one comprised of pamphlets of various plays.

We had lunch at the station café. Caroline and I had long conversations with Stephanie, one after another. She explained to me that I was to make a general note of the entire situation. It involved making a list of the plays, the writers of those plays, the names of the actors and where they came from. I was also to deduce from the available information about the reason why a theatre should have existed at such a place and what role Taylor played in this entire endeavor. Lastly, I was to gather as much information about Taylor as possible.

Caroline and I got back to the theatre. I began to go through the plays and the cast of characters. Col. Sheldon played the role of a Venetian musician in a play titled *The Early Songs of Dawn*. The beloved in the play, a singer by the name of Venessa was to be played by some Dorothy. Who were those people, I thought, and where did they rehearse before they played here? I copied down the pamphlet as it was:

The Early Songs of Dawn

By M S T, Esq.

The cast:

The Venetian Musician	Col. Henry Sheldon
Lady Venessa	Dorothy Seany
The Molestor	Augustus Drake
The Duke	His Highness *Mian* Teg Singh of Chogal
The Notary	Samuel Jones
The Big Pigeon	Richard Howard
The Royal Gardener	Ben W. Charles
The Fairy	Catherine Taylor
The Housemaid	Dianne Taylor
The Lawyer	Duncan Seam
Chorus	Mary James
	Dickie
	Suzan
	Charlie
	Mohan
	Jenny

The Hill Chamber 28 March 1938

That was the only printed pamphlet I found there. There were numerous other beautifully handwritten pamphlets of as many as fourteen such small plays. I noted down the titles and the cast of the plays. Then I went through the heap of papers of the handwritten notes. I gathered there were several pieces of information worth noting. It was a laborious task to accomplish. Late afternoon Ram Sukh entered with tea. He informed us that we could stay the night at the guest house in case we needed to. I told him we would finish off in an hour and leave for Kasauli. He told me I could leave the keys under the window at the bottom of the spiral staircase and not give it to anyone and that he would be leaving in a few minutes. He was amused to see the heap of papers and photographs on the floor.

Just before six that evening Caroline made a call to Stephanie who explained to me that for the moment a copy of the titles and cast of the remaining plays would suffice and that Caroline would seek permission to obtain either photocopy or the original handwritten scripts of those plays later. She didn't, however, miss to tell me that a brief note about the plays would be required. Stephanie also told me that Caroline was anxious to leave before it got late. I could understand that it was beginning to get late but my task was going to take time. I began to copy down the contents in her notepad in earnest. She kept herself busy with the photographs. Just before seven I said to her, "There is no way we can finish this today."

She looked at me blankly. I could understand the futility of my effort. I said it simply, pointing to my watch, "Time, time. No time. Late. Very late. Kasauli. Now. I will find a taxi. Get ready."

I left the theatre and went down straight to the platform. There was hardly anyone around. I enquired and came to know that there was no train to either Shimla or Kalka. There was no taxi. I called up Ketan and he gave me the phone number of the local taxi union. I told him we would be leaving for Kasauli soon. I went up to see if Caroline had packed her stuff. I was surprised to see her still in the same position, going through one of the scripts, as if reading. She smiled on seeing me so anxious. I sat down on the floor beside her and told her, "No train. Calling up taxi...taxi," I emphasized.

In her most decisive step till then, one that truly surprised me, she took my mobile phone and switched it off. Yes, switched it off. Then she picked up hers and switched it off. She did it superbly. She did it magnificently. She did it so dominantly, single-mindedly and so convincingly that it almost turned me on. The simple act of switching off both the mobile phones and conveying her decision to me with a smile; a smile that to me seemed to be capable of amalgamating mere stray thoughts into an uncontrollable desire, an abandoned attic theatre into a palace of promises of pleasure, a dusky darkening surrounding into a galaxy; thought I to be an invitation - to the inside of a heart that knew no familiar tongue; to a comfort in a night, in an obscure corner of the globe; to a pair of arms that would break open all the barriers.

I understood then that we were to spend a considerable time at the *Hill Chamber,* copying down the details of the long forgotten plays, enacted by the probably long dead amateurs. She had her own share of the scripts to be copied. They were painstakingly handwritten. Each one ran into more than twenty pages. The little bulb backstage that had illuminated that darkness so meekly during the day now glowed gloriously. We didn't switch on more lights since that could have attracted attention of the outsiders. In that delightfully inadequately brightened darkness, Caroline and I sat for hours. She was much slower than me in copying down the contents. It was then that she showed me the typed pamphlet of *The Early Songs of Dawn*, at the back of which was a little note written in hand. I noted it in her notepad as it was:

> *Colonel, I am not sure if we would see each other soon or ever after. I am leaving for England on April 20th. I'll go back to Kasauli by the morning train. Come to the church on Sunday. Just listen to me once. You may take your decision later. I shall wait. Do come.*

The note was not signed by anyone. I put it away in a hurry.

The titles of the plays were:

1. *The Pomegranate Farm*
2. *Hearts of Marble*
3. *Many More Such Days*
4. *The Priest of the Hills*
5. *The Early Songs of Dawn*
6. *The Next Train on Sunday*
7. *Who Shall Now Sing Those Songs!*
8. *The Kasauli Constable and His Men*
9. *Till the Seasons Next*

10. *Mary Hornbush and Her Lovers*
11. *Mighty Arms and Haunting Eyes*
12. *Of All The Glory That Was Ours*
13. *Castles of Sand*
14. *When I First Looked Into Those Eyes*
15. *Farewell To A Life*

All the plays were signed by M. S. T., Esq. Each play ran into an average of twenty to twenty five pages. Immediately after the title page of each play was a two odd page outline story of the play. It was these pages of each play that I had been copying faithfully. She could have sought permission to have the entire thing photocopied but for that purpose the manuscripts would have had to be taken to the nearest town and that would have attracted a lot of attention. It probably suited her that Taylor's legacy and her efforts remained out of trouble.

After I had put the papers away uninterestedly, I suddenly felt struck by the solitary personal note addressed to the Colonel that I had noted earlier. I pulled it out of the heap of papers and read it; each word, each line. I read it over, many times. It dug deeper into me each time I read it. While I was reading it, Caroline's eyes were fixed on me. It began to haunt me the more I read it. It should have been too ordinary to haunt anyone such as me but it seemed so different given the circumstances we were in. Since it was penned anonymously, no one would ever know whether it was Dorothy, Catherine, Dianne, Mary, Dickie, Suzan, Jenny or any one of the audience. It could also have been written by Taylor's wife, or just someone. Anyone. I began to somewhat worry, whether the woman ever got to talk to the Colonel. The writer of those lines could not have been a man, of course. Was the Colonel married? Or, the woman?

Did Caroline want to know what that note meant? I turned towards her. Against all commonsense I attempted, "Caroline, this means that there was a woman, I am sure she was a woman, who was in love with the Colonel. I believe she was Dorothy or someone. But there was a problem. She probably could not have spoken to the Colonel openly about her feelings. She may have been somebody's wife. Oh, God! May be the Colonel was a married man. I had not thought about that." I was looking at and off Caroline. She seemed interested. May be that was merely to oblige me. After all, I had done her a service for almost an entire day. I felt an irresistible desire to impress something upon her. I had no choice but to go on with my soliloquy and give everything a vent. I continued, "I don't know about their marital status but one thing is sure - there was love between them. It was not something they could have easily displayed in public life. There was some social obstacle that they could not have overcome, some social obligation that felt obliged to be acknowledged or there could be no other reason why someone should be so nervous about expressing their feelings. The Colonel playing the lead role of a Venetian musician in a play titled so romantically, suggests he was truly worth somebody's secret longing. Did they ever meet that Sunday in the Kasauli church? Did Dorothy tell the Colonel how much she loved him? Did the Colonel respond? Or had he had his fling and was waiting for Dorothy to sail to England? No one shall ever know. Or, maybe no one can ever know anyone who could know what happened."

While I said all this to her she attempted well to maintain an interest in the babble. She had a faint smile on. Having said that to Caroline, I felt relieved of a burden in my heart. Was it the burden of the Colonel and Dorothy that I had acquired lately? Was it the consciousness of bearing the unbearable feeling of not being in a passionate relationship that not only did justice to the age and blood but also showed a window to the future? Or, was it the burden of Caroline and me that I was afraid I would be the only one to carry; may be, intolerably for a while, and just faintly for longer? That the lonely darkness of a night in a colonial building should induce in me such longing and nostalgia was unbelievable. But I believed it. I loved believing it.

It was ten at night and we had finished most of the work.

It was then that I realized I was hungry. I gestured that to her. She understood it, partly because she too was hungry. I ejaculated the words to her compartmentedly, "I-aam-going-ouut-too-find-some-theeng-too-eet." The loud words were accompanied by exaggerated gestures pointing mostly to the mouth and the stomach. She smiled. She and I could understand why she was smiling. She waved a goodbye as I was leaving the little theatre. Acknowledging the goodbye I felt as if, at wide sea in a wrecked ship, leaving my beloved behind, I was venturing out in search of an island. I stood atop the steel spiral staircase and saw that the entire railway station was quiet and dark, sparing one lamp post that dimly lit the track. At first, I decided not to go down lest someone get suspicious. But soon, overwhelmed by hunger, I descended the staircase and strayed into the little platform. There was not a soul there. The tea shop, the offices, the place where we had lunch that afternoon, the office of the station master, the ticket counter, and everything else, was shut. I walked back and nearly stepped upon two dogs sleeping near the tea shop. I walked up the spiral staircase, glad not to have been noticed. There probably was no one to notice. Before entering, standing upon the old steel platform of the staircase with my back to the gate and facing the dimly lit villages and partially visible fields under the moon that had partly begun to be seen above the hills, I wondered what the night had to offer the both of us. Why did Caroline choose to stay back? We could have come back the next day to finish the remaining job. Was it because she was afraid the station master wouldn't oblige? Or, did she take his absence to be the least cumbersome occasion to accomplish her job without having to answer many questions? In the inner most corner of my heart, I had begun to entertain some vague thoughts whether her decision had something to do with me. A pleasant chill went up my spine. Was there some conversation that she wished to do with me, a conversation that needs not the tongue to be trained in any particular script? It need not be the script of love. It could just be the language of a particular moment, the language purely of flesh and blood; a script devoid of innocence, yet free of guilt.

I entered the theatre like a loose sack; loosened less by hunger and more by desire, by the fear of losing the opportunity, the fear of losing my moment among the stars. I saw her sitting in a chair in the middle row. I indicated to her with my empty palms that I had returned with nothing. She understood at once and smiled. It was a smile that could satiate a lifelong of hunger but ignite an unquenchable desire on a disproportionately magnified scale. I noticed that she had drawn the curtains of the little stage and the light from the backstage illuminated the room faintly. Neither of us wanted more light. It was the first time since that morning that I noticed Caroline and our surroundings so minutely. There were three rows in all. The first row had five chairs, and the other two had ten each. She was sitting in the middle row. I sat down near her, leaving only one chair between us. I didn't look at her. After some time I asked her, "Are you hungry...Caroline?" She said not a word. I was certain she had understood that I had just uttered her name, loaded with anxiety. Silence had consumed a long time, before I turned to her and said, "Caroline...Caroline, I hope we don't go down the Colonel and Dorothy way. I don't know about them, but this is our moment. This is our moment...Caroline. This is our moment." Unable to say anything further, I continued to look at her and settled back into my chair. This is the closest I had got to saying anything resembling my desire. Of course, she didn't know what I had said but to me it gave a relief of expression along with the embarrassment of having propositioned. She stared at me without any expression. Did she notice that I had uttered her name many times, in such desperation? I did notice, with attention; her clothes, her earrings, and the chain she was wearing around her neck. What did she make of my suggestion? That I might be willing to go down to the nearest village and wake up a gentleman and fetch my guest a roasted lamb or that I could take the next available train to anywhere, and returning by another, get my sleeping damsel a meal before the stars begin to fade, or, did she get it right: that it was time to worth a remembrance for the rest of our lives? Caroline Caroline Caroline! I could have crushed my thighs in frustration. Gripping them fiercely, I rose to walk away when I saw her hand stretched in front of me saying, "Raaman." My heart flushed into my mouth and I stretched mine in her direction. I noticed that she was offering me a cigarette.

I helplessly responded to her smile with mine. I sat down, this time leaving no chair between us. She lit my smoke and I gushed my first puff into the air. She smoked calmly while my lips were on fire. I blew my smoke in her direction. She smiled and continued to smoke calmly. I breathed out the next puff so close to her that she couldn't have inhaled without taking in a part of my breath! Her smile spread like our mutual smoke. My happiness floated in those little misty cloudlets that glided about us. The haze of the smoke made it clearer for us to see each other in a new uninhibited way. My lips were quivering. Then I took another puff and blew it softly on her face and hair. She smiled and continued to smoke. I knew the cigarette had to be smoked meaningfully, or it would burn out on its own. I knew the night had to be lived purposefully, or it would sleep away on its own. I puffed again and, leaning forward, breathed it out into her lap. That prompted her to draw her thighs closer. I sucked in a long puff and, looking at Caroline, blew it softly across her bosom, on one, and then, on the other. At that moment I wished my breath could blow endlessly. I saw the smoky flames of desire rise up, like dense fogs rising above the hillocks on misty monsoon mornings, as if in emancipation, after fulfillment. I moved closer to her. I thought she would blush and that would be it. She didn't. She looked rather perplexed. But she didn't look away.

That forced me to a halt. It took me ages to withdraw slowly into my former position. I smoked the rest of the cigarette in silence; not that it was not silence already, now it was silence absolute: in the absence of any thought. The same smoke that had glowed through the unfamiliarity between us seemed to have darkened the blaze of desire. I held the cigarette butt in my fingers. I didn't look at her and she did not seem to move either. I could feel her next to me. I could still feel the fragrance of her garments but not her body. We sat like two ghosts in a closed graveyard. The theatre of desire stood in front of us, and in my view, was mocking us. We sat buried into our chairs. I began to regret my comment on 'going the Colonel and Dorothy way' though I was fully aware that it was not planned or affected or even exaggerated; it was a candid expression of a true feeling. It was an expression of a true fear; a fear, the repercussion of which now seemed imminent. But I truly regretted saying it. I knew she would never know what I had said. The sad part was, I knew what I had said. Well! The sadness was also because she would never know what I had said. How I wish she did!

It got messed up and that put me off. On what ground could I have compared our situation to that of the Colonel and Dorothy? Who knows what Dorothy went through? Who knows what sacrifices the Colonel may have made in order to play a role in *The Early Songs of Dawn* by an obscure playwright, enacted in a lowly attended theatre by a railway station, may be only in order to meet Dorothy? The Colonel played the Venetian musician, and must have held in his hands a violin, instead of his gun. It must have been cold that night, March 28th 1938. It also means the Colonel never got the note. Otherwise, he would not have thrown it away to be found by an imposter like me decades later. Oh my God! Did the Colonel never get to read that note? God! Did Dorothy leave it somewhere she hoped he would find, whereas someone mindlessly threw it away? Or, did the Colonel drop it before he could read it alone? Did they ever live together or was the Colonel killed in the Great War that followed? How could I have said that to Dorothy? I mean Caroline!

I was sitting there; with a stranger, in an abandoned theatre on a desolate railway station, curtains opened after decades, as if watching a performance of *The Early Songs of Dawn*, without applauding. We had all along been thrown into silence by unfamiliar tongues and now rendered almost immovable by inexplicable circumstances. Wasn't it all my fault? Now I needed no language to apologize. I could say it anyway and she would understand. She was an intelligent girl. I tried to move towards her but I felt I could not move my back or lift my legs and arms. I had been still for a long time. I flickered my eyes, took a deep breath and moved towards Caroline. Before I could decide about how to apologize, I saw that her eyes were shut and she was asleep. I then realized that a very long period of time had passed since we had lit those cigarettes. At first I thought I could apologize in silence. I looked at her calm face that was clear to me in the light of the lamp dimming backstage. When I saw her hair shining faintly, I noticed the dim moonlight that had begun to filter in through the old curtains that were too coarse to resist any such gaze of nature.

Upon the peace that rested on those closed eyes; the eyes that I could see under the dim light, and the scattered rays of the moon; I pondered over my decision to apologize. Should I apologize to her? And say what? That I was sorry to have felt like a man, towards a woman? And that it was inappropriate for me to have nourished the thought of memorablizing a night, that comes disguised in obscurity once in a lifetime, if at all! I would rather I were a sinner than apologize for my blood, and be a greater sinner! No apologies, Caroline! None at all! None for an honest man's unrequited passions! So what, if they rose only to be buried into themselves; I would not dishonor them by either disowning, or by a meek submission of an apology. You should apologize, I thought, looking resolutely at her serenely closed eyes, if one is to. Thus emboldening my gaze, I drew closer to her face that was emanating not just fragrance and warmth but also, what to me seemed, apologies. I could feel it. I condescended upon that ever more beautiful face, and close distantly touched her cheeks with my quivering lips to mark the occasion, to immortalize the moment, and to say to her, that she had been forgiven!

I huddled into my chair and hours must have passed before I was woken by a cool breeze touching my face. I rubbed my eyes only to see that Caroline was not in her chair. When I looked in the direction of the breeze I saw her standing by an open window. The boldness, that had possessed me while she was asleep, had withdrawn. It vanished completely on seeing her awake. She was barely a few paces from me. I got up and walked towards her, very slowly. She sensed that I was approaching. I saw her shuffle a little. I stood inches behind her. It was half past three. I looked at with awe what she had been relishing for a while. It was a full moon right above the hill, and beneath its radiance we could clearly see the thick forest, open fields, and trees of various shapes around a village of about ten to twelve little houses. I felt that nature had put up such a display only for the two of us. It was at that time that Caroline looked back, at me, and, with a smile. I didn't know how to read it. I smiled and could just manage to utter, "Caroline! This….is extraordinary." I did not know what was more overwhelming; the night, or that we stood so close and she greeted me with a smile. That invigorated me to an extent and I went closer to her. There was hardly any space between us. She did not move forward. We continued to look out at the gleaming landscape. Since it was a low window, I felt we were swaying over the hill. I was overcome by an uncontrollable feeling; that I was going to lean forward and fall upon and slide down her back helplessly, that I was going to disintegrate into nothing by just rubbing onto her, that I was going to be unable to reclaim myself from the lifelessness I had slowly slipped into as I was going to melt and subsume into her. I could, for the first time, smell her hair. It must have been fragrant, for nothing else can explain the numbness that it caused in me, by the mere virtue of its proximity. Fresh in my mind, her smile, raised my previously doused spirits to new heights, and with unmistakable conviction, I leaned forward upon her. I, did, lean, upon, her; my shins, my knees, my thighs, my groin, my stomach, my breast, my nose, my cheeks, my eyes, my forehead sank into her from the back. My arms stretched down along hers, and my palms clasped the back of her hands. Moments married into minutes, and the blissful absence of space between us drained out from my consciousness any sense of the passage of time. I shut my eyes for I didn't want to attempt to see anything. The cool breeze of the early April morning was beginning to contrast against a thin layer of warmth that existed inescapably between us. I moved my face forward along her neck and she leaned backward so that our cheeks met and I slowly folded our arms beneath her bosom. A slow warm fire was beginning to rise within me. I could feel it in my groin. The fire that emanated from there was slowly inflaming my entire body. The overwhelming consciousness of my groin pressing against the most prominent part of her back rendered it an irrepressible deep current of excruciating unbearability. I had never imagined, never known, never felt the way it was then; Caroline and I, wrapped in those moments that had ceased to pass, breathing in unison, frozen in fire!

The first drops of sweat then dripped from my armpits. I was being consumed in soft fire. I had never felt being melted away; slowly upon her back, like a layer of cheese on a warm toast, feeling that she would soak me in. With my wet shaking lips I touched her on her neck and began, very slowly, to eat her away while she sighed. My palms released her hands. They moved elsewhere. My lips were eating into her mouth, my groin found a moment broken of all frozenness and in the midst of all this were just Caroline and me. I quietly drifted her away from the window. There, leaning against that wall…we kissed to eternity.

Minutes later, it was a cockcrow from a nearby farm which announced to us that it was time. We heard it clearly, as if it were outside our window. We smiled looking at each other, slightly embarrassed. She buried her head between my left cheek and shoulder. I stood leaning against the wood-paneled wall, with Caroline upon me; her breasts upon my breast, and thighs upon my thighs.

When the early golden sunlight upon the nearby hills had turned silver, when the cockcrows had given way to the chirping of the other birds, and when the chilly stillness of the April morning had conceded to the warm noise of dreary movements of life, Caroline and I, sitting on the benches on the still desolate platform, could hear the whistling of the first train arriving from Shimla. She didn't know where I was taking her. I had no idea where she was taking me. We were simply waiting for the train. The train arrived. We prepared ourselves. She had been running her fingers through her hair. The little train stopped ahead of us and we walked up to the first available door when suddenly our eyes fell on Mr. T N A Aiyer M Tech. He hopped out of the door. As we saw him, our combined reaction held us back. Neither Caroline nor I, for some reason, wanted to run into him, and the only way we could avoid him was to retreat completely which we did. Pulling her away and crossing the railway track behind the train we jumped down the hill. We took a narrow path that led us into fallow rice fields. We rested on the parapets of those fields. We saw the little dust clouds that we had raised behind us. We burst out laughing, partly at having avoided being seen by the station master, and also at the childishness of the entire act. Laughter needs no language. Dodging the station master occurred to us almost as soon as we had seen him. That was thinking along.

Having laughed out the station master's encounter from our memory, which was now a combined one in the absence of any speech between us, we threw glances around us to see which direction would suit us the best. I gestured her to follow me along the same path down the track till we reached a little fenced farm with a house in the middle. A woman emerged from the cowshed that was a few meters from the house. She was carrying a bucket of fresh milk. She smiled at us. We responded to her goodwill warmly without betraying that we did not know where we were heading. Caroline seemed at ease. The woman asked us to tea. I accepted the invitation and both of us sat in her little courtyard where a lamb had been tied to a lemon tree. A dog came wagging its tail and sat at my feet. The woman went into her house. I saw that it was the only one around. It was half past six. Caroline was looking around curiously. While I continued to laze in my little bamboo chair, she got up from hers and went around exploring the courtyard. She touched the neatly painted mud walls and the paved courtyard. Then she touched the wooden pillars that supported the roof, as if to confirm they really did.

The woman appeared once again, carrying a tray that had two cups of tea and homemade cake. She was followed by two little children, a boy and a girl, who seemed to have been woken up by her to see strangers. The boy was rubbing his eyes and seemed unimpressed while the girl, barely six, smiled and walked up to Caroline who stretched out her arms inviting her. Caroline sat the little girl in her lap. The woman asked us who we were and where we wanted to go. I was not prepared to tell the truth because I did not want to shock the poor good woman out of her long cemented sense of propriety. I told her we were tourists from Delhi and had arrived by the morning train from Shimla. She was good enough to guess that the woman was not an Indian. I told her she was right. Before the woman asked us whether we were married - which would not have been difficult to answer as I could have simply lied to her for her own sake - I asked her, just to keep the discussion in safe area, whether she knew anything about Taylor.

She had nothing to add to what we already knew except that Taylor had auctioned his main farm and that his house no longer existed since a new house had been built instead by the new owners. She also said that her father-in-law had served in the Taylor household and that particular farmland had been gifted to him by Taylor before he left India. I passed all the information to Caroline through Stephanie later in the day. We had finished our tea and wanted to leave. The woman said her husband was in the fields and we could wait for him if we wanted to know more. I did not. We thanked her and walked downwards. Later I gathered from Stephanie that Caroline had given her to believe that we had spent the night at Kasauli. I had no problem in accommodating that little harmless untruth into my arsenal of lies and blunders.

What followed, was a quiet little trek through a countryside that had never been very far from where I had spent the most of my life. Yet so different it would be to my existence, I had not known. A lamb tied to a lemon tree, open palm shaped old trees, into the upwardly open finger shaped pruned branches of which farmers stacked dry grass; little caverns not more than a few feet in depth- where the folks had lunch or a little siesta when tired of their labor, and then a rivulet that we could see below us. That I should ever get to beat down this path, following the steps of a stranger of a woman I now considered beautiful, seemed to me, to be a very extraordinary experience.

We washed our faces at the rivulet and then walked uphill till we reached the main road. We boarded a bus to Dharampur, from where we hired a taxi to Kasauli. The first thing we did was to check into the beautiful Kasauli Resorts, where we had a reservation for the previous night. The manager showed us our rooms and wondered why we could not make it the previous night. "A slight change in the program. Anyway we will check out before twelve," said I. After a great bath I waited for Caroline in the restaurant where she came a little later. After an extremely prolonged breakfast we checked out of the hotel and spent some time at the Kasauli church where I took Caroline on purpose. We sat on the old cemented benches of the church lawn. I tried to imagine that Sunday in the same lawn many years ago. I looked at Caroline. She was unimpressed but happy for her own reasons. I gave up on her and tried to dip into those thoughts on my own. Then, out of the lately sad and melancholic lanes of my longing mind, the Colonel and Dorothy appeared in front of me. They appeared to be together and yet separate. I looked into their eyes but they looked elsewhere. I asked questions and they seemed not to hear. I wanted to touch them but they were too airy. They provided me the two extreme possibilities that may have resulted that Sunday many decades ago. Both, the Colonel and Dorothy, were unwilling to tell me which one was more probable or true. I didn't give much thought to how Caroline felt about being in that churchyard where, many decades earlier, the Colonel either kept a date with destiny, or broke into many pieces a maiden's heart. I was certain that she could not indulge into this world of the Colonel and Dorothy as she could not read the letter at the back of the pamphlet of the *Early Songs of Dawn*, nor had I any way to convey that to her. They appeared before me not merely because I could read Dorothy's note but because I was smitten, by it, by their condition, and, by my own happy circumstances.

We walked around the streets of Kasauli and I helped my companion buy a thing or two. I felt less like a tourist guide and more of a newly-wed, not just because there were many of them around us. I knew how couples go about the streets of little exotic towns buying souvenirs. I bought two big identical hats; the sun was all over us, and I did not want to run into any acquaintance who would peep into the spell that bound Caroline and me.

We walked down a few kilometers from Kasauli before taking a taxi to Dharampur. I had this idea of taking a train to Shimla instead of travelling by road because I knew too well that the hill train took much longer. Fortunately we were in time for a certain train to Shimla. It had passengers whom I could easily identify as people in groups from Bengal, Gujarat or the south of the Indian peninsula. We sat in the last compartment in that small train which we in Shimla affectionately call the 'toy train'. It moved slowly through the low hills. We sat opposite each other. There were many tunnels; some not long enough for me to move closer. The nearly invisible bond that the tender threads of the night had weaved between us seemed to fade in the clear daylight. I tried to enter into it, but could not. I noticed two children, peeping into our direction mischievously through the glass door. I smiled at them, and they vanished.

My instinct to talk out my heart's content was growing. I wanted to tell someone; someone who would keep it a secret. I could just speak it out of the window and vent into the fresh air of the hills and no one would ever hear or ever know. But that would not satisfy the impulse to share. It had to be shared. Shared with someone. Someone. There it was. Shared with the one. Who better than her, it dawned upon me. She won't even reveal it to anyone, not because she was a partner in the experience, but because she wouldn't get a word of it.

Looking out of the window I said, "This could easily be the most extraordinary experience of my life. Dear traveler please tell me how one is to describe it."

She did not respond. She was not expected to.

As if talking to the winds, I continued, "Please help me regain myself, my companion. I seem to be drowning. How I wish I could spend more time with you."

She did not say anything. She was not expected to either.

I looked at her and then resumed my talks to the winds, "Let these trees and this fresh air be the witness that there was once a time when you and I traveled together on this railway track, in the toy train."

The train entered a tunnel. I spoke rather loudly into the darkness.

"The darkness reminds me of the night. What a night. Sometimes I feel we wasted the night. Sometimes I feel we lived the night."

She began taking interest. She was looking at me as she realized she was being addressed. She did not say anything.

"O dear! How sorry I am that it came to an end. Aren't there some nights that never come to an end? Couldn't we have entered such a one?"

She felt intrigued for I wasn't talking to the winds anymore. She knew I was talking to her because I looked at her as I spoke. She smiled curiously. It was because I was supposed to remember she could not understand what I was saying. Then she broke the shell that the unintelligibility of each other's tongues had induced upon us. She smiled very convincingly.

"Let me tell you, you have an enchanting smile. In the beginning I had not noticed that magic. Now it seems to be undoing me, slowly and irretrievably. Either douse these flames that rise within me or just do not do it to me."

She said something with a smile. It was in a strange tongue. The one that she spoke to Stephanie in. Must have been French. Of course, I did not understand a word of it. I could not utter anything because it shocked me to hear her speak which made me feel, for a moment, that she had understood me.

"Did you say something to me?" I enquired nervously.

She said something much longer than I had asked, with a body language that did not reconcile with the answer that would've been appropriate. She sat back into her seat and said something more that seemed to me to be a curious proportion of confusion and conviction. May be that is how you feel when you hear strange language being thrown at you, by someone who is as strange to yours.

"I hope you are not hungry. Is there something you want to eat?" I said this to change the course of my earlier conversation because I wanted to guess the answer to these questions by the means of body language.

She said something that I didn't understand, but she did not answer it with either an earnestness that confirms agreement, or with the satisfactory disgust that expresses disagreement, nor with a courtesy that conveys gratitude; earnestly, or satisfactorily. And, she continued to speak.

Calm settled upon me. She had guessed the game of uninhibited, though polite, conversation that I had started. She seemed to be enjoying it. I began to enjoy it too. I rendered my heart out. She must have been doing the same. We chatted a long way. A time came when we talked as if we could understand each other's tongues perfectly, yet chose to speak in our own. We were alone in our compartment. I noticed the train was merrily slow. It was not meant for regular commuters; it was for tourists, and those at leisure. It was much different from travelling to Shimla by road; something, I had done all my life.

Her reactions of smile, surprise and sadness did not always coincide with what my remarks had necessitated. That assured me further that our conversation was truly one sided but comforting both ways.

Here was a game on. I spoke out my heart's true feelings. She would speak as I ended my sentence. Then I waited for her to complete hers before I would start again. The largest part of my confession included my disgust and frustration with her at the beginning of the journey, my jealousy of the station master's attention towards her, my inability to appreciate the futility of the effort involving the copying down of the manuscripts, our stay in the theatre, and feeling about the entire journey till then. I told her in detail that her switching off the mobile phones was the turning point. I asked her whether she had started fancying me by then. She spoke as much as I did; even more than me, at times. What she told me shall remain unknown forever. We spoke spontaneously, smiled at each other, laughed looking at each other, all in the manner of a smooth conversation. It was great till it lasted.

At a little station somewhere, a woman accompanied by her three children entered our compartment. At first I felt utterly disgusted with the intrusion. It was one indeed. Why should they have come to our compartment when they could have sat anywhere in the huge locomotive? Her eyes popped out on seeing a man alone with a woman in a compartment. The children ran around, none of them more than seven years old. The woman was looking at us. Our conversation came to a conscious end. I greeted her, though I thought it was stupid of me. She responded enthusiastically which frightened me. It even threatened that the good times were over. What surprised me no end was her first question, "No children yet?"

My first reaction was to give her an answer which would end any prospect of a further conversation between us, without having to worry about offending the feminine sensibilities of my partner.

"No," I said with all the politeness I could conjure. I felt my earlier loquacity had lost its venom over the last two days.

"*Achha achha*. Honeymoon." She said the word in English since it was so common.

"*Jee*." I acknowledged. My efforts to understand the intruder's linguistic capability soon convinced me, a few sentences later, that she did not know English. French was out of the question.

Looking at Caroline I said, "She is not entirely wrong. May I even wish it were true. Sort of." I recovered my comfort with her now that our intruder had settled our relationship.

Caroline picked up from where we had left. She said something, which, I hope, only she understood. I began to respond quickly. The conversation continued. The intruder felt left out. She began to yell at her children who were all over the compartment. When the speakers could not understand each other, the silent listener stood no chance. She shifted her glance from one of us to the other. I felt Caroline and I sounded the same to her. She probably had no chance to imagine that the entire conversation was as meaningless to her as it was to each of the speakers.

Carrie and I spoke spontaneously, though slightly embarrassedly, which could have been due to the content of the conversation. Possibly due to the presence of the woman between us, at least my side of the conversation was more toned down to everyday things like interests, life, studies, plans and parents. But throughout the conversation, I wondered what a time an invisible listener, who could understand both English and French, would have, listening to the both of us; marveling at the hopelessly incongruent matter and body language with which she and I responded to each other; marveling also, at the same time, how two individuals reveal their true feelings to each other when they are uninhibited by the barriers of the possibility of comprehension or revelation.

It was not long before one of the children almost jumped into Caroline's lap. Another one came and sat in mine. The eldest of the lot sat beside her mother. It was the woman who had quietly instructed them to occupy the laps as that was her only way of getting back into the group and be spoken to, or at least acknowledged. After a token rebuke which the children did not even notice, the woman relished the sight of a child each in our laps before remarking, "You will soon have your own ones in your laps. May the Lord Hanuman bless you with many. I am taking these children to *Sankat Mochan*, Lord Hanuman's temple in Shimla. You should visit it too. There is another one on the Jakhoo hill but there are many monkeys there. And they are pampered. I have three like them of my own. Can't take a risk even if their parents are along. One can seek blessings anywhere."

Caroline was running her fingers through the child's hair when the train entered a tunnel. We had come through several of them but this one was really long. I was to know it later that it was the longest tunnel on the entire route. Being alone with Caroline would have been a real blessing. It was easy to identify the tunnel because as we emerged from it we came to the Barog railway station. She smiled at me. It was a smile of remembrance of a shared past that had not been so long ago. I looked into her eyes for a long time. Before the train moved, our compartment was full of passengers. I thought it best to give our conversation a break, for it would be too tiring and futile to attempt to know people's capability to understand English; for, if someone did, my side of conversation would not only be understood but could even be laughed at. It could also shock some. I did not want any such intrusion, no matter how passive.

When the woman saw the passengers flooding into the compartment, she left her seat and sat with us. She shared Carrie's side. All three of us had a child each in our laps. From the slight disgust on the woman's face, I could feel that she had felt intruded upon by the passengers. She tried to revive the conversation with us. She asked me how we had met and how long we intended to stay in Shimla. I baked my answers with great ease as soon as she provided me with the raw material of questions. She looked at Caroline as much as she did at me. Carrie obliged the woman with smiles and blushes, and, of course, approval. Oh, have I been saying Carrie? Not Caroline? Well, she was beginning to be familiar.

The woman was bursting with the enthusiasm to talk to both of us. I could feel her frustration at not being able to do so. Suddenly she came up with a solution. She said to me, "Ask your wife," and then she became stiff as if interrogating, nervously, "Do you like our culture?" I translated that into English and passed it onto Carrie, who, since observing us keenly, seemed to have readied herself for the occasion. She appeared to me, to have begun to enjoy this whole mess. She gave a polite reply in French. I manufactured her answer in my own way, into something that the woman expected to hear, and passed it onto her in Hindi. With her numerous questions to Carrie and my very suitable answers on her behalf, the woman grew very fond of her. Then she asked me to convey something to her which I did as it was: "Look daughter, you need to plan a family very soon. See these are my grandchildren and I know that I don't look that old. Get over with this honeymoon thing soon. It does not last forever. Don't be like many of our girls these days. And now Carrie, this is from me - you must be a good actor really. I mean theatre and all. You manage all this too well. This is a compliment." I gestured and winked at her, while the woman drew satisfaction as Caroline smiled at her with approval.

As our train meandered into the hills on the way to Shimla, I saw that the woman and Caroline were beginning to feel sleepy. The children in our laps had already been sleeping. The one in my lap had his thumb in his mouth. I woke up the woman as the train approached her station. She was surprised how I had guessed it right. She did not have the time to make further enquiries. She gathered her grandchildren and before disembarking said to me, "Take good care of her. She will take time to adjust into our society. She is a lovely girl. Oh God! I wish you had woken me earlier. We could have had a longer chat." Caroline waved a goodbye. I could sense some pain of a parting company in the gentle woman's heart. I wondered how someone could end up being so fond of strangers in so less a time. My own experience, then whispered politely into my ears, that it was possible. It brought a sad smile on my lips. Very soon, within a day or two, I would be waving a forever goodbye to Caroline. I felt a strong affinity with the fond woman who was by then out of my sight.

Shimla was a few miles away. The train approached Jutogh and Summer Hill. I was dumbstruck how this part of the train journey to Shimla was so breathtakingly beautiful. I had spent the most of my life in the town but never taken the joy train route. The oak forests, lit up by the blossom of the rhododendrons, rendered an almost mystic air to the whole atmosphere. With those vast forested hills, the fresh air of April and bright sunlight, it felt like chugging into a paradise, into a valley of flowers and yellow green leaves.

The sense of arriving in Shimla only dawned upon me once the train had crossed the tunnel number 103. Only upon seeing Shimla and the crowning Jakju hill above it did I remember to do something: to switch on my mobile phone. I showed mine to Caroline, in order to remind her. She took out hers and switched it on casually. Had she kept it away all this while not to be disturbed by anyone? Was it normal for her or was it an out of the way effort due to some other compelling reason, as it certainly was in my case? By now the screen of my mobile phone displayed messages: the important ones and the sundry. The number of calls that had been attempted was one hundred and forty eight in all! My heart began to sink. I opened the folder. There were three from home and four from Ketan. The rest, one hundred and forty one, ranging from eight o'clock the previous evening to eleven in the morning, were from a temporarily and pleasantly forgotten source, Shubra.

Caroline and I reached Shimla at three thirty in the afternoon. I was sure I looked like a pale ghost. Such mad attempts at my privacy and my life; my life, were more frightening than annoying. I became stubborn. I informed mother and Ketan but not Shubra. I also told Ketan that I would be taking Caroline for lunch. We walked up the hill that led to the Mall Road and not far from the office of the *Amazing Heights*, Caroline and I sat for a late lunch at one of my favorite restaurants, the Fascination. I ordered food that was least spicy. Caroline could sense I was not in the best of moods. I switched off my phone once again. I made a few attempts to smile, to assure her that nothing was wrong.

Waiting for the meal, Caroline and I had a good time together, looking at people walking on the Mall, through the half-drawn curtains of that upper floor restaurant. At that time of the day when most of Shimla had had their lunch and it was too early for tea, there was, much to our mutual bliss, just one more table occupied by a teenaged pair, who had no time to spare on their surroundings. I played the guide, "Madame, these are the humble citizens of my town." She smiled at me, knowing well that I was back to the usual play. She said something immediately, looking at the humble citizens of my town. When I said something again, pointing out with my finger, she knew it was now a play that did not require much initiation. I spoke my heart out, "Some of them will go home drunk, some will buy something for their family; garments, vegetables or anything. And there is one among them, sitting with you, who will go home and sleep with an aching heart, without the least hope of any kind. I fail to understand why I should feel so nostalgic about the time we have spent together. It is not love. It is not love making. Even then I long to spend that time again. I am glad to know that so crazy could be one among the humble citizens of my town." She smiled back in a manner that I took as approval.

Looking out of the window, on the other side of the road, I noticed the renovated Gaiety Theatre, the oldest Shimla had. Right in front of where we sat, on the other side of the Mall road, was the municipality Town Hall, on the large and many marble stairs of which sat young men and women, some of them tourists. Some people were walking up and down the marble stairs which connected the Mall Road to the Ridge above. Among the people walking up and down the stairs, I noticed, to my horror, Shubra Sandhu. walking not up and away, but down, and in our direction. My balls flushed into my mouth. I am not sure if Carrie could read that on my face. She crossed the Mall Road and headed straight into Baljee's, the restaurant on the ground floor, a floor below the Fascination. In a few seconds, she would storm in. I began to count. Five. Four. Three. Two. One. Come, boy, come. Come. Come. Let's have it out. Let's get it over with now. I am sick of being hounded anyway.

She took a little longer to reach us because she must have taken a while to search the restaurant on the ground floor. And then she entered. I got up from my seat to embrace her with an exaggerated surprise, "Hello, Carrie, my dear! Shubra Shubra. Sorry. Great to see you, Shubra." I could not have committed a greater blunder. Addressing Shubra as Carrie was the most unforgivable slip of tongue. A lot happened over the next five seconds: Shubra threw nasty glances at both of us, Caroline smiled nodded approved and looked at me nervously. I was trembling. Shubra pulled a chair away from an unoccupied table like dragging a hapless woman by her long hair and sat down at the head of our table. "Hi Caroline," she flung a salutation, "or, Carrie, may I say?" She smirked at me. Carrie smiled a 'hi' at her. I wanted to know who told her Caroline's name but all I managed instead was, "I am so pleased to see you Shubra. But you were supposed to return next week."

"Disappointed to see me?" she retorted.

"That's not the point, of course."

Looking at Caroline she said in a sharp tone, "I hope I have not come at the wrong time. I know I shouldn't be disturbing. Both of you must be truly tired."

"She does not understand English at all."

"So kind of you to tell me. I know it. So will you explain it to her in your own sweet way that I shouldn't be disturbing but I give it a damn." She threw another nasty glance in Caroline's face which hurt me.

"What are you trying to say?"

"So, you were busy all night? No time to answer my phone."

"Oh I forgot to tell you. I have lost my phone. Truly…I mean really."

She gave me the worst expression I had ever seen on a woman's face and said, "And you found it half an hour earlier to call Ketan up."

The bearer entered with a huge tray. He placed all the dishes on the table. I requested him to bring another plate which Shubra refused saying, "No thanks. Let the bastards eat alone." The bearer, a humble looking middle aged man, gave me a subdued look, and retreated meekly.

"Why are you talking like this?" I said, trying to look angry and in control.

"Even she lost her phone I guess," she said with a sarcastic smile. It means she had found out everything from Ketan.

I requested Caroline to start the meal. She served herself with trembling fingers. That made me feel so sick. I offered Shubra once more before I put some into my own plate. She refused very loudly and I could see that the teenaged couple had found it interesting enough to look in our direction. I had hardly begun to eat when she asked firmly, "Where did you stay last night?" My God! The bitch knew even that. I still preferred to take a chance, and said, "We stayed at Kasauli…"

She did not let me complete when she thundered, "You did not check into the hotel there and…," and without caring to complete what she had in her mind she gave me such a hard kick that I felt my ankle fall off. I got down nursing my wound, and looking up at her screamed, "You stop behaving like a mad woman and just listen to me."

"There is nothing left to listen you swine. I know what plants you've been watering. You were always a dog Raman. And this bitch anyway looks like a whore." She got up and picking up Caroline's cold coffee, splashed it on my face with such force that in that cold I felt my cheeks had sunk into my bones. She stormed out of the restaurant, cursing the dog and the whore. As soon as she left, the bearer entered, apologizing and helping me with things. Caroline and I were standing and the teenaged couple looked away as if to share our embarrassment. Caroline uttered a few syllables which comforted me. The bearer offered me a cloth to wipe my face with. I was sure I looked like a dog who'd just come drinking from a muddy puddle.

When we finally sat down to have our lunch I felt a very relieved man. I had my meal with Caroline like a man who was having his first meal since release from captivity. I knew it was over and I wasn't going to pursue it with Shubra anymore. It was not that I would be free of guilt; I have never carried that burden upon my shoulders; it was a freedom from nags, controls and policing. I could not have shed Shubra at my own convenience. I was almost grateful to her for having rid me of her own self, no matter how. With Shubra it could not have ended any other way. My initial disgust towards Ketan for providing Shubra information had now mellowed into pure gratitude.

During the meal, I spoke a great deal to Caroline. I spoke to her without any borders. There never were any. It was a mixed jumble of apologies, description of some of my past adventures, and varying repetitions of my feelings of the previous night. I spoke to my heart's content; I spoke more than I ate during that meal. Her inability to comprehend what I said provided a sort of immunity against any offence; for most of what I expressed, should have, for the sake of a universal virtue, gone uncomprehended, even though for me it was as necessary to have spoken. Having been free lately of all the tiresome clutches of affection, I relished the meal which was followed by coffee and another coffee. We left the restaurant at six. I happily paid the bearer a lavish tip.

I walked Caroline to her hotel which was on the other end of the Mall Road. It was a walk that was sure to last long in memory. All this came at a little price; even though the ankle had received a slight bruise, it had stood its ground. I tried not to limp at all. I looked either at Caroline, or down on the road. I didn't look at people; as if they just did not exist. Many may have noticed me walking with the woman. I didn't want to share hellos with anyone. We reached her hotel in thirty minutes. Woodville Palace leaves me breathless. I always loved coming to the magnificent hotel for weddings and parties. To be there with Caroline was most special. The parting would have been a bit sadder, had I not known that she still had a day or two to spend in Shimla.

At ten that night, I received a call from Ketan. He wanted to know a lot of details about the trip. I disguised it neatly into an innocent package. He informed me that the tour was not over. To my utter surprise, though extremely welcome, he told me that I was to accompany Caroline on a couple of days tour to Kinner Kailash in Kinnaur; two hundred and thirty kilometers north of Shimla, along the banks of the mighty Satluj and not far from the border with China. Trying to conceal my excitement, I asked Ketan if someone else could accompany her because I was tired and not too keen either. He was prompt: "Bastard! Six in the morning. Lucky dog. Goodnight."

Next morning at six, at the Woodville Palace parking, I was keen not to betray any excitement. She was either not excited at all or too good at concealing it. I nearly felt that the last time we had met was in a dream, which, by now, I remembered only hazily but felt all over me. I understood at once. It was indeed a tour to Kinner Kailash. Within hours we were miles away from Shimla. I sat in front with the chauffeur. He gave me a paper packet in which Ketan had sent a detailed guide map and an English-French dictionary. I turned over the pages of both the books. Crossing Kufri, Fagu and Theog, we reached Narkanda. We stopped for breakfast. While we were having our food, I remembered a story I had read at school. It was *Lispeth*, by some Kipling. She was a native who had been raised as a Christian by the missionaries at Kotgarh, not far from there. She had unwittingly fallen in love with a travelling Englishman. After the Englishman left, Lispeth, though intended Elizabeth, left the missionary heart-broken and went back to her 'dirty' people and lived a ripe old age to tell her sad tale. I had my breakfast heartbroken. It was such a contrast to the previous day's meal at the Fascination. The chauffeur's presence made her feel a stranger to me.

Beyond Narkanda she started reading some book, the title of which I could not locate even in the dictionary for it was marred by too many commas hanging from the top. Trying to reclaim the intimacy that had been there between the two of us not so long ago, I said, "Caroline please forgive me but you must not waste your time reading. Look around. You may not find it this way so easily in many other parts of the world. You may be travelling a lot but do not miss what you can experience here." She smiled as dumbly as she always did. I opened the dictionary and blurted out the French words for 'sorry', 'read no more', 'enjoy', 'this time'. She laughed out loud. That was the turning point in the journey. She threw the book aside and folding her arms leaned forward towards me, said something in a loud voice, probably to beat the roar of the vehicle. It was still French to me. It was a similar situation. We could not understand each other, and, the chauffeur, neither. He and I spoke from time to time in Hindi. But I wanted to get started with Caroline to make the tour more enjoyable.

Suddenly she snatched the dictionary from my hand and began to look for some words. She attempted with a smile, "Tell me." "Places." With useful inputs from Mahesh, our chauffeur, I pointed out a few places to her: "Kumarsain"…. "This is Kingal…We shall see Satluj soon…" She smiled dimly and reacted approvingly when I named a place, for she needed not a dictionary to find out its meaning. Many a happy mile was travelled merrily. I spoke to her about many things; the ones that were seen outside, and those that were felt inside. Before reaching Rampur I noticed that she had fallen asleep.

We stopped for lunch at Jeori, around thirty kilometers beyond Rampur. A little distance further from Jeori we entered the district of Kinnaur. We saw steep and rocky mountains above, a gushing Satluj below, and a few and far flung villages thrown about here and there. A short distance from Bhavanagar we came to the famous goddess temple on the rocks of Taranda. Mahesh told us that travelers usually pray at the goddess temple before proceeding. We got down and walked up to the temple. I wondered whether I should enter the temple with her or the chauffeur. Before I could choose, she entered the temple and I stood with Mahesh at the gate, ringing the huge temple bells. The road cut into the rocks at Taranda was breathtaking. At Wangtu and Karchham we saw huge hydel projects where the ancient river rattled into the dams like a reluctant serpent. The river Satluj seemed to be in a perpetual hurry and constant fury. It was chocolate in colour. There were many points at which the road went through what appeared to be narrow passages with steep rocky slopes on both the sides desperately striving to embrace each other, with only the furious river drawing a separating line between them. For most of the journey the river was our only companion. I thought of Shubra, her pernicious tentacles and my freedom from them. It was like a journey to celebrate my newly liberated soul, into a region that was exotic.

We reached Kalpa at around four in the afternoon. It was a few kilometers above the district headquarter at Reckong Peo and stood in compelling peace at more than nine thousand feet above the sea level; face to face with the snow covered peak Kinner Kailash. We checked into Hotel Apple Cart which was in an apple orchard. It was a double storey structure with lovely large windows. I saw that the orchard was in full blossom. Numerous pink buds and countless white flowers, against the backdrop of the spotless snow of the Kinner Kailash mesmerized me. I didn't know how she felt about it but I had begun to feel enchanted. Almost intoxicated. Our rooms were on the top floor. We checked into our own rooms and Caroline took the dictionary with her. I thought I needed it too.

I called up the travel agency which had planned our trek to the Kinner Kailash the next day. He informed me that we were part of a group of around twenty people and all would leave Kalpa at seven in the morning. We were to be driven all the way down to Powari, a few kilometers below Reckong Peo, go across the Satluj and then begin to trek all the way up. He told me that the trek took many hours and ended at the massive *Shivalingam* of stone. Less than half of the path had snow. What I found interesting was that we would have to spend the night in a cave on our way back.

I had a long bath, followed by a nap. I woke up at seven and ordered some tea. I had tea sent for Carrie into her room. How I longed to have tea with her! I wandered about the corridor with my cup in my hand. It was nice to see Caroline at her door as she walked out with hers. She smiled at me which I took to be a good omen. We sat in the little balcony. We had tea in silence as we gazed in awe at the lofty peak. We could see many houses in the surrounding areas, mostly in apple orchards. From our balcony we overlooked the black road among green trees, like a lifeless snake in soft green grass. This ancient village, said to have been established around 1100 AD by a Buddhist monk, was now much more than a village. It had hundreds of houses, hotels and tourist camps. Satluj, miles below where we sat, continued to flow. The wind carried a chill in it, probably straight from the cheeks of the snowy peak in front of us. I could see Carrie's eyes narrowing against the breeze. Her cheeks and the tip of her nose became prominently pink.

Below our balcony, all over, were huge apple trees in full blossom. That prince of all fruits, that Royal apple that we relish in great summers, goes through this courtship here in the Spring, in this valley of flowers. I was so lost in my thoughts that I almost missed something she said.

"Speak," she had said in a soft tone.

I stared at her, as if in exalted insanity, with a smile that stretched across my cheeks uncontrollably. What was it? Speak? Yes. Speak. The first complete, voluntary, natural expression of hers to me. Speak! It was a sound sufficient to fill every corner of the silence of a century of an entire graveyard. It seemed to me a request that I could not turn down, an order that was too sincere to be defied, a calling impossible to ignore, a judgment too lofty to be questioned. Speak. The word resonated in the corridors of my mind like a whisper; of a fairy that I could not see, of a wind that I could not feel; the emotion of an unfathomable thought that even my mind could not decipher. Speak. It was the longing of a blind companion to be shown around in syllables, of a deaf soul mate to be sung soothingly away from dreadful silence, of a crippled darling to be swayed in postures.

'I shall speak, my dear, I shall. I shall speak.' I only thought.

It was the first thing of its nature. It was the first imperative between us.

'What shall I speak?' I thought, my vision blurring into the vastness of the snow of the peak.

Speak, I had heard her say; speak, I shall; and, what shall I speak, I had replied. Shall I say once again that this is the most extraordinary time of my life? I don't know if I am happy or I am not. I am not sure enough whether I am happy that the moment is here or that I am already beginning to feel the sadness since the moment shall pass.

The snow peak loomed large over me.

"What shall I speak?" I said as if speaking softly to myself, without looking at her. "I don't even know how I am to feel about it." Overwhelmed by the timelessness of our surrounding, I continued, "Please forgive me if that hurts you but I feel proud of it." Belittled by the very forgettable existence of my being seen against the all encompassing mount, I huddled into my chair, "I fail to explain how I feel about this whole thing. I can't explain how I feel about you." Driven wanton, I felt, by the dim glow of the moon, now blossoming to its full, and lonely, I clenched my fists and, called forth by the temple drums that were beating in the distance possibly for evening prayers, I said, "How sorry I am that this too shall pass." I shut my eyes for they were moist. I felt embarrassed for this sentiment, even though concealed. I just hoped she had noticed nothing of it. Flickering my eyes to render them dry I looked at Caroline to say something that she may find comforting, or by merely hearing me speak. I opened my mouth but failed to push through any word. It was probably the meaninglessness of the uttering that left her amused. The sound that comforted her did me no good except to make me restless. 'This too shall pass,' I knew for sure. It saddened me, not because I said it; it saddened me, because it was true.

I could feel and see that Caroline lifted her hand and cupped the back of my hand. It felt like an attempt to trap the passing moments into that inescapable touch. I rubbed the arm of the wooden chair warmly. She continued to press my hand gently. She looked into my eyes. I saw in her eyes not the usual approval or bewilderment or even interrogation. I could feel the warmth of the touch percolate not just into my palm but deep down my spine. I could feel the shiver in my thighs. I could sense the perspiration on the immeasurable vastness of my tongue. I could not resist the rub on the back of my hand. I could look into her eyes no more for my eyes began to burn. I looked at the cool mount which had begun to blaze under the ever glowing moonlight. When the moonlight made me nervous again I looked at Caroline who had closed her eyes while her palm continued to rub the back of my hand softly. These were the syllables of silence. They needed no interpretation.

Moments later it got cold and I do not remember how late it was when we finally walked back. We stood at her door. She entered. I stood at the door. For a moment I was afraid I would stand there for the rest of my life; I wouldn't move, nor would the moment pass. She held her hand out and pulled me slowly across the door. She bolted the door and holding my palm let me in. In, to the room; in, to the unguarded corridors of sensuality; in, to the final destination of desire. Neither of us showed any hurry for we knew that time was lazying at our window, naughtily smiling, with his head resting on his folded arms, too intoxicated to move on. The garments that prevent our human bodies from their natural introduction to each other, that necessary evil barrier to safeguard human virtue, slipped on their own, to be forgotten on the floor for another day. Carrying her around the room in my arms, I felt as if I had embraced warm mist that sank into the pores of my skin. Our mouths smoothened within the confines of the lock that bound them together. It was too long before we lay on the bed. Our bodies were moist and smelling of perspiration. I had thrown the curtains wide apart and moonlight ushered in through what was a pair of window panes for an entire wall. The exalted peak with its valleys of white snows shining under the yellow moon appeared to be so close to the window that we could have touched it through that crystal clear glass which made it look clearer, nearer and more beautiful. I licked the perspiration that formed upon her throat and all the way down, down and about, down, down. She exulted in conversation with my palms and mouth, under the bright gaze of moonlight. That moonlight was our constant and solitary companion, from the theatre at a railway station to this theatre of love above the Satluj, across the mount.

Such was the oneness of the experience that I felt ours was just one body making love to itself. She moaned beneath me. That is the most beautiful sight of a woman I have known. That breathless propelling of mine across that string of writhing sighs that mixed inextricably into mine was the immortalization of satiated desire. But such was the hunger caused by the fulfillment that it asked for as many more replenishments to quench. It was a never ending fever. I licked the moisture that exuded down her cheeks, throat, neck and bosom. That most irrepressible core of mine that nearly had my entire being melt upon her back in those early hours of that morning in the theatre, was now restless to surge into her. Deprived of food and speech, nurtured by yearning and patience, and threatened by the passage of time, this was emotion at its purest; the emotion of making love. Far away, on top of the mount Kinner Kailash, full moon in its most radiant form beamed with the celestial light; it shone brightly like the burning sun that warmed the vast frozen snows of the mount, and melted it into tiny tricklets of silver all the way down the many chasms where the thirsty Satluj leapt at it with her thousand tongues.

I had never lived a night like that. There was no part of her body that my tongue did not savor, that my senses did not smell, that my eyes did not see. She sat in my lap, and we beheld the moon shining above the Kinner Kailash. Before we fell asleep in each other's arms, I could see a thin layer of cloud that had made the moonlight a little hazy. The moon had now travelled a little from the lofty peak as if it had walked away from the scene reluctantly, carrying away with it the radiance of its deep yellow light.

I can't remember vividly the dream I saw that night. I was dozed into a lull like an infant in the womb, who will later know that he was once there but won't remember how it felt. Towards the morning, as the dim brightness of the April morning reflected through the window, I could feel, despite the numbness of my consciousness that it was drizzling. The hum was evident through the tin roof. I saw that Caroline and I had huddled into the blanket as it had got cold during the early hours of the morning. I called up the local guide and he said that the trek had been postponed due to the weather. At the prospect of an unexpected holiday, I threw my phone away and got into the blanket with her. I parted her sleepy lips with my tongue and she responded warmly even though she wasn't awake. I only know that we woke up at around eleven. It was bright and sunny.

We made love once again before getting out of bed. After bathing each other we had lunch. Laying in bed we fell asleep and woke up at five. We went for a walk through the Kalpa bazaar. The sky was clear but it was misty in the bazaar. Fog had filled the apple orchards in full blossom. We took the little path that shot off the main road and led up towards the Buddhist monastery that faced the mighty mount of Kinner Kailash. It was cold and the road was wet. Little shops; serving soups, noodles, drinks, tea, coffee and snacks and none higher than ten feet of wooden structure, marked both the sides of the narrow but well paved path. Men sat over drinks, and a solitary white man sat in one, smoking. We walked up the few stairs to the monastery. Standing at the door of the monastery I threw a glance at Kalpa and the surrounding villages. Houses were scattered all over. Apple flowers twinkled through the mist. We walked further up and sat at the back of the monastery. We witnessed the most overwhelming view of the snowy mount. It seemed to be very close. It was like a huge pineapple cake on a plate in front of our eyes.

We had smiles on our faces but neither of us spoke anything to each other, no matter how unintelligible. We walked back through the narrow path, peeping into the glass windows. Most of the shops could seat just around ten people. *Lama Chowmein Corner. Tea and Coffee. Sapna Food Place. Sangy Tailor. Fresh.* Some of the shops smelled of smoke and some of soups. We wandered on the roads of Kalpa and strayed into some of the apple orchards. Beneath one such tree in a dense orchard, amidst wandering fog and forgetful fragrance of the blossom, I held her in my arms and kissed her as deep as I could. We ambled back to our cottage when it was dark.

Time got wings then. It passed mercilessly. The Night undressed us too rapidly. Scarce, it seemed to me, had we indulged in its magic before it was chased into invisibility by the first penetrating rays of the dawn. By six in the morning we were driven all the way down to the banks of the Satluj, and crossing over the large bridge we were trekking up the hill to the *Shivalingam*. We were eighteen in all; including twelve foreigners. Everyone introduced themselves. I took little interest in anyone as I was too occupied with my company of Caroline. I hardly counted her among the foreigners. By nine in the morning we had reached a spot from where we could see the entire region above the Satluj on the other side of the river: Powari, a few feet above the Satluj; Reckong Peo, further up the hill; and Kalpa, at the top, crowned by a mountain range that had no vegetation. We located the monastery and our cottage among the blossoming apple trees.

We were provided meals on our way up. We split into smaller groups. Caroline and I held hands. It was like an endless tiring walk. It appeared to me that we could reach the moon by the evening. She shot a lot of pictures on the way. The trek was worth it.

We reached an erected rock that people believed to be a *Shivalingam*. It was four in the evening. We were somewhere near the base of the mount Kinner Kailash. It was an open space with a few inches of snow. Only highly trained professionals trekked further. We were provided tea and snacks. An hour was given to us before we were to gather for the downhill trek. We again split into familiar groups. Carrie bit the snowball I had thrown at her. We ran around like children. I gripped her waist and we rolled on the pristine snow cover. I threw soft snow all over her. She blushed. It was a blush that could have melted away valleys of snow.

We began to trek downhill when it was six. We reached an almost open cave half way down and there we were to stay the night. Caroline folded her scarf and filled it with lovely wild marigolds she plucked on our way down. Those lovely flowers of varying shades, along with many other wild flowers, grew strewn about our path in countless number.

After dinner, we sat around a bonfire. The mood inside the cave was purely magical. The light reflecting from the fire made me aware of people around us. The elderly white bearded Spanish gentleman with a husky voice, who repeated that he was Antonio, played guitar. A Portuguese couple played another instrument. People sang songs; sitting with their companions in blankets. The three bearers who accompanied us slept at the entrance, guarding it in some way. Caroline and I slipped into our sleeping bag, the inner sides of which Caroline had sprinkled with lapfuls of petals of marigold. That gathering of ours in the cave gave it a very medieval air. Men and women, from Latin America, Europe, Arabia and the Indian subcontinent, sipped beer, whiskey and gin; smoked full cigars, and sat and sang around the fire. I zipped the bag. Our heads were lurking out. Caroline smiled at the seducing air as she unzipped each of us. The Portuguese ended a very melodious song. So many songs in as many languages were all enjoyable even though not understandable. It was the sheer power of music and the universal rhythm of poetry. An Irish couple then took to singing English country songs among others. Amid the magic of those songs, Caroline and I, with the heap of coals shimmering through the ash on the periphery of the fire at the center of the cavern, making soft silent love, and later, under the spell of *Up Where We Belong*, happily losing our consciousness among marigold, unawarely slid into the all forgetful lap of slumber.

We reached Reckong Peo at noon the next day. Caroline and I strolled through the market place and little shopping complexes. We reached Kalpa after lunch. Then followed what was usual: mutual bath, lovemaking, lunch, lovemaking and then a siesta in arms that lasted till almost five in the evening. I looked at myself in the mirror. I had not known the shape that my face had assumed as a result of a smile that had not left my face for days. At six we found ourselves facing the great mount, sitting at the back of the monastery. I was overwhelmed by Caroline's growing fondness for me. She held my hand, and rested her head upon my heart even as we beheld the great cake of ice. She looked sharply into my eyes as if searching for something inside me. I was not sure if I had something in there. What Shubra had always looked for, unsuccessfully alas, was possibly beginning to assume a shape.

It was as clear as any sky can be before the sunset. The sun set on the other side and it threw light almost red on the snows of the peak. Caroline and I were in absolute awe, aware that this mount, the full moon and the setting sun had been inseparably linked to our destiny; all trapped in the warmth that was between the two of us.

The next morning my heart ached to leave Kalpa. I was not used to entertaining such emotions though. Throwing our luggage into the taxi, I threw another glance at the cottage, the apple orchard and the monument of ice. I wondered whether I should sit with the chauffeur or at the back seat with her. She pulled me in with her. I packed the French dictionary that had not been opened ever since our arrival.

On the way I thought of how we had needed to speak verbally just once with Stephanie and not at all with Ketan. Caroline and I hardly spoke to each other, not even indulgently. Our road ran along the Satluj for much of the journey. One town followed another; Powari, Karcham, Tapri, Wangtu, Bhava Nagar, Jeori, Jakhri, Rampur - like beads of the towns on a string that was the river. Caroline slept most of the way as she was tired after the trek, her head mostly resting on my chest. I was not too keen to strike much conversation with the chauffeur, just as much as I thought was necessary to keep him from dozing. During our lunch at Matiana I could feel the agony of parting weighing upon Caroline too. She tried to ease that through smiles. I wanted to wander with her into the forests of Narkanda and meet Lispeth, whom I surely knew to have died decades ago. The rest of the journey to Shimla was heavy, knowing that it would end her tour. We rubbed each other's moist palms as if escorting the other to an operation theatre.

We reached Shimla in the evening. I didn't call Ketan. Her program was known to each one of us. She was to leave Shimla at eight the next evening. We drove to the Woodville Palace and I said goodbye to the chauffeur. We walked to her room on the first floor. I was too much with my own self to notice the magnificence of that imperial structure and the estate. We reached her door. I did not stand there but entered it. I embraced her, leaning against the window that offered a magnanimous view of the best part of Shimla. It was my Shimla. For those moments I was overcome by the strangest of emotions. Caroline and Shimla became inseparable. There were no kisses this time. There was no love that was made. Only anxiety shared, holding her as if she were an hour glass. I caught sight of the Shimla airport, miles away on the ridge of a hill in Jubbar Hatti, its lights winking at me, saying that it was over. We had coffee in silence. Then we walked to the door. While she leaned against the wall, I closed the door after me.

It was the longest walk home. I was indifferent to the cool April breeze that kissed my cheeks. I was no longer bothered by the monkeys who blocked my path. I was not intrigued by the sweet girls who crossed my path.

My mother seemed to be more excited to see me home than I had been depressed to have left Caroline behind. Father seemed very pleased too. While talking to them, I felt an unease in the mouth as speaking is one thing I had not done in days. I talked out the experience of the past days, barring the most essential parts of it; only, how I had escorted a French tourist around without the advantage of a common language. I informed them that I had had enough professional exposure for the time being and would leave for Delhi that very week.

I did not want to talk to anyone. I had ceased to feel any need for the spoken language. It seemed so unnecessary. I had started to feel the richness of a quiet life. The spoken word was such an aberration into the profound rich silence of the existence of life that I had begun to see lately.

Next day I informed Ketan that the tour was over and I would report to him after escorting Caroline to the airport in the evening. I drove her to the airport that evening in my father's car. I tried to be cheerful. She was cheerful. I confess that the absence of even a mild sadness in Caroline made me feel lonely. It meant I was alone in feeling that way, knowing that we would never meet again. Shouldn't that make one sad? Her cheerfulness made me harder. I thought I should forget the whole thing. I thought it was just the thing to do. A journey such as this deserved a farewell thus cheerful. Then I looked at her. Seeing her radiant face my temporary hardness was gone. It was soft sadness once again. Stopping a mile before the airport we kissed passionately. It lasted minutes. Later, outside the lounge, I said to her, "Caroline! You gave me the most memorable time of my life. It is only natural that you should make me so sad as you now leave. How I wish you could understand me. I want to tell you that the intimate moments I spent with you, form the greatest treasure of my life." I pecked a kiss on her cheek and slowly pushed her away. Before she left, she took out an envelope and put it into my pocket and said, "Look…later," in the manner of our broken and single worded dictionary conversation that we had on the way to Kalpa. She waved a goodbye, and so did I. I soon lost her among the many shapes that walked about her. On my way back I stopped at a little temple. I sat behind its wall. The last rays of the setting sun fell on my face. I looked at the little airport in front of me. It was not a busy one anyway.

The sun had set on Shimla. It must have set on Kalpa, on Delhi, Amrtisar and Multan. While preparing to set on Kandahar and Tehran, it must be having men and women readying for tea on the banks of the Bosphorus in Istanbul, and lunch further west of the Mediterranean in Barcelona, Gibraltar and Casablanca. The same sun would be wished good morning in Washington while it earlier sang to sleep those in Seattle and Vancouver. But the sun had set on me, and it had set on that part of Caroline that was mine.

I had almost forgotten about the envelope that she had put into the pocket of my jacket. I opened it. It was written in hand and it was written in English. It read:

Dear Raman

> *I don't know where to start. Well let me try from here. Now concentrate. I am the great granddaughter of Malcolm Stanley Taylor. My mother married a French citizen, and has lived in France since. Therefore you are right. I am a French citizen. But I know as much English as my mother. I have spent half my life in England. I have been doing a course in theatre in Cardiff for the last two years but my time spent with you was the most phenomenal theatre training and performance of my life. I could never thank you enough for it. It was a special programme I had designed for myself but I had no idea I could ever have had a guide like you for it. You make an inseparable part of this training. I remember each moment spent with you. It is as special to me as it might be to you. Even for me… it was the most extraordinary time in many ways.*

I feel sorry for what happened between Shubra and you. I don't know what I should say about that. But I have no regrets about what happened between you and me. I am sure neither of us had planned it that way. I sympathize with your initial frustration at accompanying me. I hope you can forgive me if I say that I really enjoyed it. You could be a great judge of my performance. I hope you shall understand the task of an artist who has to enact a character different from their own.

About my great grandfather! He died peacefully in Derby many years ago. It never crossed your mind I guess that he did not use his military title. He left the army after the Great War. He was a very warm man. My mother told me about the railway station theatre of his. I was just a child then. When I finally took up theatre I thought it was time for me to find out more about it. Our task is not over yet. About the Colonel and Dorothy, I know nothing. If there's any clue I get from my mother or anyone, I'll let you know.

Let me tell you I enjoyed every bit of my time with you. Since I knew my plan, you had my sympathy from the beginning. The part with the station master was very interesting. The night at the theatre was both interesting and memorable. The morning tea in the nearby village was very special. I shall fondly remember the journey to Kinnaur and the snowy mount of Kinner Kailash. I have admiration for the Satluj and sympathy for its reckless exploitation. The time spent at Hotel Apple Cart and its surroundings has become an inseparable part of me.

Raman dear I will come back in November. It's going to be a much longer tour. You make the arrangements. No travel agency between us this time.

I hope you aren't hurt by the revelation. If I may say, this has been the most extraordinary time of my life.

I had reached the end of the letter. I believe my smile spread wider. I didn't know how to feel about the whole thing. I could almost see her smiling. I thought I should call her but didn't. I didn't want to ruin by intelligible speech what had so dreamily been webbed by silence. Not now. I waited on the steps behind the temple till the solitary plane took off. It was eight and darkening. The lights twinkled. I waved at them. When the plane disappeared, I turned towards Shimla. The moon had appeared on top of the Jakhu hill. It was the same moon. I knew it too well by then. As I drove back, I felt the taste of Caroline in my mouth. I knew I would not have that till long. My spirits were rejuvenated now that I knew I would meet her again. I did not know how to feel about it though. I lamented the loss, though, of innocence, that speechlessness and silence had nurtured between us.

I told my parents that I had had dinner. I did not brush my teeth that night. I wanted to preserve her breath within me. Thereafter, each night before going to bed, I could feel the same taste evolve in my mouth. I hoped the freshness of that breath could induce in me a sleep wherein I would be lulled into dreams of Caroline.

The train is once again nearing Shimla. While I cross the leafy surroundings of Summer Hill of August, I imagine how it will be when Caroline and I travel again along the same route in November. It would be autumn then. There is a similarity in spring and autumn. Both have the same chill in the air; spring has that chill in its last breath while autumn in its infancy; but chill nonetheless. Both are hauntingly enchanting; with joyful apparitions, now appearing, now disappearing. The leaves, the petals, and the scent that hang in the airs of spring, will then be freshly laid on the grounds of autumn.

It's an April in me that has stood through the heat and dust of May and June, the rains and mists of July and August. An April in me, that shall perhaps, stay forever.

I have my task cut out before Caroline arrives in November. There will be a railway line to Kalpa. I'll have the railway platform and the theatre built behind the monastery, in the open ground of the primary school. The trek route to the *Shivalingam* shall have roses and jasmines on both sides. On the open pasture I'll have snowflakes descend upon us despite a sunny day. I'll dismantle all the dams along the Satluj so that she can drink the pure snow of the mount and flow freely along her age old path. In our living room the theatre, there will be a picture of Dorothy and the Colonel, and Lispeth and the Englishman. Caroline and I will understand that it is essentially our portrait because we are not in it.

2

The Dying Letter

Mrs. Mehra returned from Delhi last week. This morning she was sitting in the little garden in front of her two storey house. It was a late morning. She saw that the flower beds had not been tended for over a month. The morning newspapers were spread on the little table, along with the cup that still had tea that she had brought for herself but forgotten to drink. The few newspapers that Mr. Mehra and she had subscribed to for years had not been opened. Sitting there, she imagined herself to be a cloud which hovered amidst two carpets; of green grass beneath, and the blue sky above. She spent most of her morning trying to figure out what to do next. The last people she and her husband had visited were the Thakurs but that was more than three months ago. The last visitors she had were Mrs. and Mr. Chauhan. It was three days ago. People are reluctant to come on their own to help her with their company. At the same time it wouldn't be quite alright to invite people so early or even visit some. Also, not many were possibly aware of her return from Delhi.

At eleven, the postman came. He was known to almost everyone in this little town. He opened the white wooden gate of the garden slowly. The noise stirred Mrs. Mehra from her drowsiness.

"Good morning, ma'am."

"Good morning, Rattan. How are you?"

"I am fine, ma'am. Thank you. I hope you are well."

She readjusted herself in her chair.

"Sit, boy. I haven't seen you for days."

"I dropped your mail in the box. I saw you sitting here today, so I thought I could meet. You haven't collected it?"

"No, I haven't. These days people drop in through the letter box or phone. I'm not interested. Even you didn't come. Is it that you didn't know what to say to me? Did you think it would be awkward to console me?"

"I didn't want to disturb you, ma'am. I didn't see you outside. I thought you would be taking rest."

"That's the only thing I've got to do now. It's just that I don't know how to go about it."

He opened his bag nervously.

"Are you in a hurry, son?"

"Not at all, ma'am."

"Tell me in case you really are."

"No, ma'am. Really. In fact, I don't have much to deliver. And, I have the entire day to myself."

"You have your entire life to yourself, child. I hope you live long."

She started piling up the newspapers and he glanced at a few headlines while trying to comprehend the meaning of her good wishes under the circumstances.

"And yes, that's not just to deliver other peoples' messages. Enjoy life, and be around long enough for your loved ones."

He sat timidly in his chair, shuffling his bag.

"There is a registered letter for you, ma'am."

"I see. So that's what brings you here."

He opened his bag and handed it to her.

"Later dear. Let me bring you a cup of tea. I had been thinking of that for some time." She walked towards the door. The postman continued to be stiff in his chair and could only plead, "Oh, no, ma'am. There's no need." He got up.

"Please, don't bother yourself, ma'am."

She turned around and asserted, "Sit."

He settled into his chair as she entered her house. He noticed the frail gait that hadn't been so till a few months ago. He busied himself with the newspapers that he was not much used to reading.

Mrs. Mehra was back in minutes with two cups of tea and some biscuits. Rattan dropped the papers and sat straight. He realized he lacked the ease with which he sat on the same chair on his earlier visits. But there would be two people sitting with him then. They began to have tea.

"What post is it?"

"A registered letter, ma'am."

"All right…." she said looking at him and then at his bag.

He continued to have his tea, sitting stiffly. Realizing that she might want to see it at once he moved about suddenly and said, "Do you want to see it now?"

"Yes," she smiled, throwing glances at his bag.

He took out a yellow envelope.

"There is something I want to tell you, ma'am. It is addressed to Mr. Mehra. Also, as you can see, it says that the letter be returned to the sender if not delivered to Mr. Mehra. It involves risks now that Mr. Mehra has passed away. I thought I should seek your opinion before sending it by the return post."

"When did it reach?"

"Yesterday."

"What is the risk?"

"In case the letter were indeed to be opened by him alone, there could be an inquiry about who it was delivered to, incase the sender comes to know later that Mr. Mehra had died three months before the letter was even posted. Since the sender is from Dehra Dun and he posted it now, means he does not know you too well to know that Mr. Mehra is no more. I thought it might concern you."

"If that is how it is let it go back. His official obligations have more or less been taken care of. If there is yet another one then so be it."

"That would be the safest thing to do. I thought I owed the two of you at least this much."

He put the letter into his bag. He finished his tea and seeing that Mrs. Mehra had finished hers, he got up. She escorted him to the gate and as he was about to leave she had a second thought and said, "Can I have a look at the letter?"

"Most certainly, ma'am." He showed her the letter.

It was marked *Personal*. She noticed that there was another envelope inside the main one.

"Could we take the risk, Rattan?"

"As would please you ma'am? Open it in such a manner that it is not detected. We could post it back tomorrow."

"Help me with it then."

They went back to their chairs. She saw that it was from some Arindham Mehra. The postman opened the envelope for her. There was a letter to which was stapled another envelope. She read the letter before opening the smaller envelope. It read:

Dear Mr. Mehra

I write to inform you that my mother passed away two months ago. It might be of little consequence to you except for the fact that she left behind a letter to be sent to you. In respect to her, it has not been opened. In fact it has been posted to you in a manner she had desired. Should you have something to convey to me, you could let me know or even pay a visit. I would be obliged. I must admit I find it rather queer that my mother should have something to be conveyed to someone immediately, and only, after her death.

Mrs. Mehra didn't know whether to let the postman go away to come back later or just get over with it. He opened the other letter for her with a blade. She saw that the letter was handwritten. She forgot about the postman and began to read. It was dated a few months ago.

Manji

I was supposed to have died this Monday morning. I didn't. It is now in the evening that I thought I should write to you.

These years have been longer than I had ever imagined. I had decided never to get in touch with you. Now it seems inevitable. I am dying Manji. Now that you are reading this letter I could safely say that I have left. Doctors had given me a few months. They differ about how much time I have. Sometimes I don't know whom to oblige. After I left Dalhousie I didn't know where to go. I decided against going to my sister's because I thought that would be too much noise. I stayed a fortnight at my parents house before joining a school in Dehra Dun. Arindham was born less than six months later. Other than my nose he has inherited everything yours.

I don't know how it feels to know in your sixties that you have a son who's now almost thirty and doing well. You need not worry about him. He is doing really well in life.

I'm writing to you because it makes it easier for me to die. I have lived all my life with a guilt. I don't want to die with another. The guilt of disappearing from a father who would never hear of his child, of giving birth to a child who would never know his father. I can ask you for a favor. Please read this letter with sympathy.

My life changed drastically after I came to know that I was pregnant. It had been okay till then. I know you couldn't have married me. I know it would have been unthinkable for you to turn your back on Maya. She was your wife. And, you loved her too. She deserved much more of your affection and my consideration. I felt like a witch teaching Punya in the class while I knew I was carrying her father's child in my womb. Days later when I saw Maya and Punya buying a birthday present for you I broke down in the same flower shop. I hugged the child and wept bitterly, lying to your wife that I had lost my mother recently

*and that seeing them together reminded me of her.
That was when I decided not to see you again. I left
two days later.*

The letter was not over but Mrs. Mehra could not
read further. She looked at the postman and thought of
him a phantom from the past who had come to wreck her
sorrowful fragile world. She suspected that he could see the
horror in her eyes.

"Can you come back tomorrow, son?"

"Certainly, ma'am."

He left and closed the white wooden gate behind him.

Mrs. Maya Mehra slowly sank into her chair. Her
thoughts, shiveringly emanating out of the shuddered mind
of hers, strayed upward like clouds of fine dust that rise
out of the wreckage of a gigantic locomotive that falls off a
steep gorge and bangs upon a stony surface. Like a stubbed
lunatic, staring cruelly into an equally cruel unfathomable
and intangible reality that now engulfed her staggeringly,
she tried to remember Punya's school days. Thankfully there
was just one school Punya had gone to. She tried to think
of her daughter's teachers. There were so many but would
not come to her mind vividly. She tried to remember the
female teachers. That meant majority of them. She tried to
figure out the ones who were not married while her daughter
studied there. It all seemed such a terrible task to accomplish
since it was her husband who took care of their daughter's
school matters as it was on his way to office and Mrs. Mehra
travelled a great deal to her workplace in another part of
Dalhousie. She didn't even know Punya's teachers so well.
Manji was so good to take care of it all. He was so good at it.

He went a few steps ahead though. Was this woman almost a step mother to her daughter? Was Punya aware of it? Had she been too busy with her business that she was found wanting in her duties towards her daughter and husband? Was that the reason that she never opted for a second child? But she loved Manji so much. So so much. Wasn't just to love enough?

She was angry. Bitterly. But she didn't know what to do with it. She didn't know how to handle it. Anger is soothing when you have a target. Manjiv Mehra, her husband, who was Manji not just for his widow but also for his one time and now deceased lover, needed to have been alive to provide her that target. Without him around, that anger would consume her into a blank. She knew that. And she wouldn't allow that to happen to her. There were many questions that she sought to be answered though. But was there any use really? Would those answers help her in any way to cope? Who would provide those answers?

She leaned her head back and closed her eyes. Was there any such day when she and her daughter were in some gift shop when a stranger came and hugged Punya on the eve of Manji's some birthday? She found it awfully difficult to locate. It was all more than thirty years before. She didn't even remember the gifts she had bought for her husband. It was clothes, perfumes, tennis racquets or some music albums. She had bought books too. Her efforts frustrated, she sat up and opened the letter once again. She started from where she had left. It seemed to her that completing reading the letter was the most difficult task.

She carried on, nervously, as if serpents would strike out of it:

Sometimes, I realize I shouldn't have done it. I mean just disappearing. But then there's so much we shouldn't have done in the first place. It took me years to console myself about the whole thing. By the way I found a job before Arindham was born. Oh I've told you that already. He grew up as a normal child whose father was given to be in the merchant navy. My parents had no choice but to accept me and my destiny as it was. Months later my parents, Arindham and I went to Delhi where, the neighbours in Dehradun were given to believe, Ary's father was coming on a weeklong break to see his son. Two years later his father was made to drown somewhere in the Arabian Sea. I wept bitterly that night. It was because I could no longer talk to Ary about you as alive. For the world it was an imaginary father but to me it felt like a real loss. For the first time in life I felt Ary would be orphaned should something happen to me. Papa was a real support. Mother took a little longer to accept. Ary was twelve when we lost her. Papa moved in to live with us. We lost him when Ary was fifteen. Papa often discussed you fondly though he had never seen you. We never tried to contact you. We thought it might disturb your world.

Wasn't just to love enough, the thought recurred to Maya. Did it have to be demonstrated and expressed afresh every now and then? She had ensured that there was never any room between the two of them. For none except Punya. Ah! There it is. As Punya grew up she needed more space. As that jostling for space in their circle of three continued, it developed cracks in the huddle and the woman slipped in. The warm huddle was now an all accommodating circle where each stood in silence in the dark. Maya stood holding her husband with one hand and the daughter with another. It was on the other side that the woman held Punya with one hand and her lover with another. Maya was too preoccupied to notice anything while her daughter struggled negotiating her growing years and meanwhile the two lovers leaned upon each other, holding the entire family together.

She tried to stitch for herself the semblance of how the story had perhaps been enacted in her life. It had to be completed. So what happened after the woman disappeared? Did the circle get back to normal? No. Did Punya and her father join hands? Well, only from time to time. On other times they handled with their free hands their own divergent destinies. While Punya searched her oncoming future, Manji indulged in his lost past. She remembered how at one time, which possibly coincided with this woman's disappearance, he began to drown himself drinking and at the same time burned his inner self in soft smoke. She remembered how everyone was worried by Manji's self annihilating behavior which lasted a few years till he had his first stroke before forty. It was at that time that Manji gave up his indulgence and the huddle was formed once again. Manji was over with his past, Punya had managed her future well and Maya became the present for them all.

Her eyes inevitably wandered back to the letter:

> *Forgive me Manji for doing it now or for doing it at all. I don't know whether I should have done it now. Ary is well settled into his world. It never bothered him*

much that he lost his father when he was two. Papa filled in a lot of gap. You must have reconciled with life. But why am I doing it now? Am I selfish? May be I am. As I told you Manji it makes it easier for me to die. I can seek that much help from you. There is none else to afford me that. You have no idea how soothing it is for me to be writing my heart out. It absorbs a lot of pain. I am writing a part of it everyday before I go to sleep. I don't want to take too long because I don't have much time. I don't want to write something incomplete and fall asleep. I may never wake up again. I am dying Manji. I was supposed to have died on Monday. It is a unique experience to live knowing that you are going to die very soon. It is certified by the doctors. I can almost see my death certificate in Ary's hands. The date keeps changing though. I have crossed a probable time period already. I was supposed to die last Monday. It gives me confidence. It makes me nervous. It makes me wonder whether I am a ghost and living in a dreamy other world. It was that Monday evening that I started writing to you. I write a few lines everyday hoping to wake up alive the next day so that I could converse with you once again. It makes me greedy to live. Two days ago I even thought I should contact your family on some pretext or the other just to be able to meet you. But that desire made living unbearable. Writing to you every evening is a reward enough. I look forward to it everyday. It is this greed to live that is probably keeping me alive so far. Imagine I was supposed to die that Monday. The doctors attribute my survival to something or the other which I am sure even they don't understand. Sometimes I feel I am a ghost. Today they changed the medicines. They hope I might live longer. Oh please forgive me I've got to go now. There are some visitors who have come to visit a ghost. So sorry I couldn't write to you yesterday. Even the day before that. I was very unwell. I didn't even have my meals. It was awful. I told you about some visitors who seemed to me to have come to see a ghost. One of them was a terrible female. An old friend. She made me feel so nervous. Ary was too upset with her. It was because she could not hide the shock upon seeing me. I don't blame her. You shouldn't too. It's not her fault. Yesterday I told you about how a woman made me feel sick when she was shocked to see my appearance. Let no one blame her. It is not fair to expect people to understand the pain that they have not experienced. Ary was too upset because he could not see his mother's condition shocking others. But that's the reality. It won't shock you. It is not because ... not because ... I don't know why but I know you will not be shocked. You won't be shocked by my condition at least. It doesn't shock me because I saw it happening to me step by step. It's like one doesn't get shocked to see one's children grown up. They grow in front of your eyes, an inch by an inch. Last night I slept early. It was because I wanted to. I saw you in my dreams. I was right. You were not shocked. I was so happy that I was right that you wouldn't be shocked. I was really happy that you weren't shocked. You just held my hands and touched it to your forehead. You kissed my hands till your tears fell on them. We didn't speak. We were too happy to see each other. I'll sleep early now but you have to promise me to visit me in my dreams. Good night. You broke your promise. But don't worry. I can understand you must be busy. Busy all day and then to visit someone in dreams. You have no idea how long I take to write these few lines. Almost two hours every night. I can barely manage to scribble a few of them before I am dead tired. I feel so privileged to be writing these lines since I was supposed to have died on some Monday. A Monday is separated from the other not by a week but by years. More than that, I feel sometimes. You broke your promise once again. Don't worry that one dream can last a little lifetime that I have. Before I sleep I imagine you meeting me in that same park where a few days ago you had touched my hands to your forehead and then kissed them till your tears fell on them. I imagine you in your favorite shirts and pullovers, sometimes with a bouquet and sometimes with something else. Do visit at least on Sunday night. You never know whether I'll ever get to sleep on Monday. You broke your promise once again but there is nothing to worry. Sometimes I wonder if I could live all my Mondays at once so that I shall have nothing to worry about. I want to live a little longer Manji. Now that you are with me it is so much easier to bear this pain, not of the ailment but of living this life. This is the pain that I have known for the last thirty years. It has been my most intimate companion. It has been dearer to me than many joys of life. Because I knew it is one thing that won't desert me till the last day of my life. This Monday thing has become a kind of a joke with me. Today I skipped one more. Ary wondered if I wanted to celebrate. I am sure the doctors know I am sort of looking more cheerful than I was a month ago. They might even be suspecting I am improving in a way but of course they won't admit it it will prove them wrong when I think of you it is the same man in the thirties the way I last saw you I might indeed be shocked to see you as an older man in sixties that day when you came in my dream and we met in the park and do you remember when you touched my hands to your forehead and then kissed them till your tears fell i remember i saw you as the same young man i don't remember whether i was the same or the old one that i now am no no i was old and in my present condition yes i remember i was happy to meet you and i was also happy that i was right that you wouldn't be shocked to see me do you remember yes i remember you keep breaking your promises but don't worry i imagine so much of you that you might spoil that by doing something silly in the dream don't worry i am fine you broke your promise once again but don't worry i am growing old you didn't keep your word last night i thought you would come but please don't worry manji you broke your promise again i am growing cold but please don't worry i am all right what makes you think i might be lying i am all right god you came last night we met in the park you kissed my hands your tears fell on my hands please ask maya and punya forgiveness for me say it in silence so that only god may hear

The letter was over. She closed her eyes, and pressed her eyelids tightly in order to keep away any shred of light that threatened to brighten the inside of her dark world. She collected the papers and walked into the house like a shadow. She closed the door behind her. She went upstairs to her bedroom with the letter in her hand. She drew in the curtains and sat on her bed. She did not move. She stared into one direction. That night she just lay upon her bed like a wounded animal. She spent her night away gazing at the carpet. The mixture of anger, disgust, sadness, anxiety, sorrow and to an extent, revenge, flooded within her from bosom to the head to the belly to the groin to the toes and to the fingers. She lay still like a stuffed beast, barely noticing her breathing. Towards the early hours of the morning, sleep overtook her and she was spared the tumultuous currents that had been raging inside her.

When she woke up late in the morning, she felt relieved of the burden of the night. She made a toast for herself and had it with tea. On her way back from the kitchen she noticed the family portraits on the wall but didn't look at them. She felt Manji might be embarrassed or nervous. She thought she had put the letter behind her. She sat on the kitchen table far longer than she normally used to. She knew it was unusual. She looked out at the garden trying to exorcize her soul. It was a little later when she saw Rattan enter the white gate that she was once again overcome with the raw emotion of disgust at the events of yesterday. She looked at the postman from the comfort of her kitchen verandah but did not answer his doorbell. The man left in a few minutes.

Mrs. Mehra did not leave her bedroom for three days and three nights, except for very occasional strays into the bathroom or the kitchen. At times she entered the kitchen but did not remember what to do there. She would stand there for a couple of hours and then return to lie on her bed. In the stillness of the nights and the silence of the days she would moan inwardly. Each time she opened her eyes after a prolonged nap she felt herself to be rising out of the debris that her life had been reduced to. As she moved out of the rubble, she clutched into her bosom a brick or two that was intact, and, with which she could now build a little structure anew; to lend her remaining life a meaning, if not a purpose; a resemblance of propriety, if not respect; a sense of belonging, if not home.

She asked many questions into the vacuum. She complained timidly. She sighed inwardly. There was no one to console her. There was no one to comfort. She knew she would never get the answers even if she screamed those questions into the sky. She held herself. She gradually decided she wouldn't behave querulously. She never did as a daughter and as a wife. And she wouldn't as a widow.

Mrs. Mehra, on the afternoon of the fourth day, holding the letter in her hands, having read it a few times since the morning, tired of being the nothing that she had been for those few days, realized that her tears too had fallen on her hands. The parting thoughts rang in her ears. *Please ask Maya and Punya forgiveness for me. Say it in silence, so that only God may hear.* It was late afternoon. Children could be heard returning from school. She was hungry. She was alone. She was dizzy. She was broken. But she was not angry. She would never be. It is one emotion she knew would consume her entirely. She had been angry with Manji long enough over some trifle or the other and she knew it never yielded anything. It only increased the heap of minutes, hours, days, weeks and months that were eaten away by this raw self-centered emotion. Those were moments wasted which could never be retrieved. That heap of wasted time was so steep that a little complete life could be built of it.

She was sad, indeed. She held the letter precariously. She was not angry. She did not even feel cheated. She felt deprived. It seemed to her that a huge chunk of her years had been stolen from her. She felt a large part of her life had indeed been lived by someone else. She needed consolation. She needed restoration. She was surprised when she felt that Manji and she could have consoled each other more effectively. She consoled herself. She began to miss him so much that she began to sob.

She walked into her bedroom. She kept the letter on the desk. She washed her face and combed her hair. She looked at herself in the mirror for the first time in those four days. For a moment she could not recognize herself. She stretched her cheeks into various forms to restore them to normalcy and rubbed the skin of her face till she felt assured that she looked somewhat normal. It made her feel that it would enable her to talk normally. Her forearm trembled as she lifted the receiver of the telephone. She dialed her daughter's number who lived in Delhi and with whom she had been ever since Mr. Mehra passed away. After the pleasantries she came to the point:

"Do you remember your teachers at school, baby?"

"Teachers at school?"

"Yes."

"Of course, I do, mother. Why?"

"Anyone, in particular?"

"I remember all of them…most of them."

"Was there some more fond of you than the others?"

"I was closer to some, of course. Why do you ask that maa?"

"Who were you closest to?"

"Well it was Mrs. Baatish."

"I remember her. Is there someone else you remember fondly?"

"Many of them mother. But…"

"Do you remember someone we met in a gift shop where you and I had gone to buy a birthday present for papa and she hugged you and wept because she had lost…"

"Oh, yes yes yes! I had almost forgotten her. Thank God, maa. You reminded me of her. She was very fond of me. But she left us all of a sudden. We were very upset. Is she back?"

"Well, child, I have a bad news. She is no more. I am so sorry."

"Oh, God! Sad. She was…she was really fond of me. Where did she live?"

"She went to Dehra Dun after she left your school. That is where she lived all her life till she expired some time back."

"Sad."

"Do you remember her name?"

"Yes. She was Aparna Singh."

"Aparna Singh."

"Yes maa."

There was a long pause.

"Maa? What happened?"

"No…nothing."

There was another long pause.

"Something else?"

"No. Nothing baby."

After yet another little pause she said.

"Baby…"

"Yes, maa…"

She said nothing for some time.

"Was she beautiful?"

Punya did not speak for a few moments. Then she replied.

"Yes, maa. She was."

Mrs. Mehra broke the silence that followed.

"Very beautiful?"

Punya took her time.

"I think so. Yes." She replied.

She made a call to the school office and spoke to the headmaster whom she did not know.

"My daughter was a student in your school from 1968 to 1980. One of her teachers was Aparna Singh, who left while my daughter was still in the school."

"I see. I joined this school much later. Forgive me for not finding any of this information too familiar."

"I've called to inform the school that Mrs. Aparna Singh is no more. She passed away in Dehradun. She is survived by her son."

"Oh, I am so sorry to hear that. We shall hold a prayer meeting for her tomorrow. So kind of you to have informed us madam. We are grateful to you. If you could kindly provide her son's address too."

"I shall. May I request you for some information from your office. I would like to know Mrs. Singh's tenure at your school."

"You'll get a call from our office over the next few minutes."

Mrs. Mehra sat upon the floor of her bedroom over which she had scattered hundreds of photographs of the family. Pictures of the perfect gentleman Manjiv Mehra, of the days during which he proposed to the young and beautiful Maya, of the days while they romanced all over the northern plains of India, their wedding, the honeymoon in the Himalayas, the birth of their only child Punya, her school, her growing years, of the days when Punya went to Delhi to study medicine, Punya's coming home from time to time, her wedding to her colleague in Delhi, the birth of her two children, their first birthday party, someone and somebody, the entire family on a holiday in Jaipur and on the beaches in Goa, years of now rolled into the years of then, moments of joy mixed with those of pleasure, the moments summoned from forgetfulness into remembrance. She arranged the pictures chronologically.

Other than a few older pictures of the family, hers began with the ones that related to the days of the proposal of the young Manjiv Mehra to the young, beautiful and inaccessible Maya Grewal; the photograph of the first lunch at the Darbar Hall, of their clandestine pre-marital visit to Delhi and the plains of northern India that lasted five days, pictures of hurriedly preened appearances of the moments immediately after the first intimate ones, smiled upon by Mrs. Mehra remembering they had remained in the closet for almost a decade as if the pictures would reveal their secrets; Mehra's first day in office and the lunch in the honour of his lady love to which no one else was invited; the wedding which lasted three days, attempted to be captured by many photographs showing many somebodies talking to as many nobodies surrounded by numerous whobodies; the honeymoon in Kashmir, Maya stretching all across the Dal lake in her husband's arms while the boatman measured the waters, then Pahalgam, Gulmarg and the rest; Maya setting up her office in the Lord's Lane, garments mostly for export, her parents-in-law merrily indulging in the garments factory with the workers, Maya's own parents joining the party; Punya's birth, family holiday in Ooty, Punya's tonsure at the Jwalaji temple in Kangra, the first birthday party, many kids adorning the guest list; the three of them with the four parents on a pilgrimage to Hardwar, Pushkar, Varanasi and Puri, all in a boat in Varanasi with majestic temples in the background, Punya on her grandfather's shoulders; Punya's first day at school, Punya toothless; the three of them on the tour to Europe, necessitated and sponsored by Maya's garments enterprise; Manji dozing on the kitchen verandah with a book in hand a moment before Punya threw water on her father; Punya's annual functions, parties, and annual class photographs, Punya and papa at the parents meet, Punya's numerous birthdays; her first day at the college in Delhi, the dateless picnics, parties, welcomes, get-togethers, farewells, weddings; house renovation, the lamps of Diwali, the colors of Holi, the little bonfires of Lohri, snows around Christmas and the new years, fancy dress competitions, Punya's favourite pup, Punya without her teeth, Punya in new dresses and with plaits, at the monuments and at the temples; Mehra's mother after the surgery and her jubilant husband garlanding her; Punya wrapped in a towel slung over her father's shoulder after a bath in the garden on a sunny day, Punya unable to climb down the plum tree in the garden with a bag full dangling down her neck, Mehra doing the laundry in the garden with the family applauding,

Punya showing off her toothless gums; at Hrishikesh with her mother- in- law's ashes; Punya's exchange program to Austria, her engagement at the Darbar Hall, Punya's first day at her clinic, her elaborate wedding in Delhi, Raj and she at the Nile; Mrs. and Mr. Mehra during the holiday in China, Punya's twins, Madurai and Bhaskar, the family with the senior Mehra's ashes in Hrishikesh, pictures of the couple's trip to Nepal following a change of place advice for Manji following a series of minor strokes, the couple at the Pashupati Ghats, photos with Punya, Raj and the children; Manji fragile, the last days in Delhi, with Punya, Raj, Madurai and Bhaskar.

And Maya. Only Maya. His Maya.

Was she beautiful? She asked herself.

Meanwhile she had gathered from the school office that the woman in question had been on the pay rolls from May 1974 to August 1976. That meant a sum total of twenty seven months; between Punya's tenth year to the twelfth, Manji's thirty sixth to the thirty eighth year, and the span of her own life that stretched from when she was thirty five to when she was thirty seven. Those were now settled to be the stolen years; the years during which her life had been lived by the woman whose name was Aparna Singh.

Was she caring?

She painstakingly separated all the pictures of her daughter, her husband and her own ones that belonged to the stolen years. They were twenty seven. It included two big size annual photographs of Punya's class. Aparna Singh's name was not to be found on either. She gathered all of the twenty seven pictures into a tight, fearful grip. She strung all the moments of those years, captured by the photographs, into a substantial whole. She wanted to enter those years once again to reclaim them. She wanted to impersonate the moments that had been lived by the other woman. It would have been much easier had they not been immortalized by the pictures that now seemed to burn her hands. She crushed the pictures as bitterly as she could. They were indomitable. For a moment she thought they should be consigned to the flames. But wouldn't fire immortalize them? She did to the pictures what her uncontainable frustration, supported meekly by her fragile frame, could do; she dug her nails into them and tore them haphazardly till she was overwhelmed by her own self and broke down in completeness; howling sobs into the pictures scattered on the carpet upon the floor. Streams of tears gushed down her cheeks and wet the tattered bits of the photographs. She felt herself shaking miserably and almost uncontrollably. She had never been so miserable, probably not even at the death of her husband. This she felt to be the real death, the hopelessness of her efforts at healing the wounds of the past. The loss of hope was not because the wounds couldn't be cured; it was just that there was only one way to do it: in order to be cured they had to be undone.

Was she more caring? Was she more beautiful?

Mrs. Mehra convulsed into violent sobs on the floor of the bedroom that she had lived in ever since her marriage almost forty years ago. She reached a point of frenzy where her sobs turned into fits that wrecked her body, which shuddered upon each sob into an uncontrollable and a powerful fit that made it difficult for her to move her limbs. By the time she began to be frightened by the destructive intensity of her sobs which drove her to near collapse, she was no longer in a position to gather herself. She shuddered from one such fit to another. She tried to grasp the thick carpet as hard as she could and held her violently steaming breath still for as long intervals as she could. She was struggling against herself and a long time passed before her sobs began to subside into prolonged sighs. By that time Mrs. Mehra was extremely nervous of her own situation. She looked around frightened and tried to lay still. She took deep breaths. She felt the cool air unstiffening her lungs. After many minutes of relief, she lay down on the floor, over the scattered photographs; now the twenty seven mixed inextricably with the rest. With her head on the pictures she settled into a soft sobbing nap that was irresistible. This was the calmest sleep she had experienced in months.

When she woke up a couple of hours later, it was no longer warm in the room. She lifted her head, acutely conscious that it rested firmly upon her shoulders. She leaned against the bed. The first thing that came to her mind was the dying woman's last words: *Please ask Maya and Punya forgiveness for me. Say it in silence, so that only God may hear.* She touched the photographs and some of them were wet with her tears and saliva. She smiled at them. She shuffled them with one hand, as if to mould them into one complete whole. *Please ask Maya and Punya forgiveness for me.* As she sat on the floor leaning against her bed of decades, the first tears appeared, swelled, stumbled upon the rugged but steep cheeks, without any discomforting contours on the face. *Please ask Maya and Punya forgiveness for me.* The tears that followed, slid smoothly down the wet lanes on her cheeks. The frozen rigid within was now melting into acceptance and forgiveness. *Say it in silence, so that only God may hear.* Behind her closed eyes was playing the perennial film of the life captured by the photographs, in a pleasantly prolonged motion. She too was in the film. Surprisingly, she looked happy and contended. The happy image of herself, along with those of the loved ones, seemed to whisper into her tender ears that it was not the lost years that she had to impersonate and reclaim but the memory of the joy of having lived a happy life that she had to allow to survive.

Next day in the morning she cooked breakfast for herself. While she drank coffee from Manji's mug, her mind wandered. How would Ary think of her? An illegitimate mother? She and Ary were two bystanders in a profound love story. They were the residue that existed on the periphery where the centre had demised. They were bound by a concealed past with which they would now have to frame their future.

While the taxi driver loaded her luggage, she pasted a note on the letter box: ***ALL WELL. GOING TO DEHRADUN.***

As the wheels rolled down the familiar road that had been her home for more than four decades, she remembered with fondness the last words of the dying woman, someone she now considered the most important woman in her life: *Say it in silence, so that only God may hear.*

3

The Tiger

Driving a few kilometers from Shimla, I am about to reach a little place called Kufri. On the way, one crosses the hill where the famous Oberoi Resort, The Wildflower Hall is. Kufri is very popular with the tourists for its snow, horse and yak rides, open valleys and lovely resorts. I left Shimla half an hour ago, driving up this road, in a hurry to get to my village which is a very long way.

It is the month of December. It has begun to snow. I know if I managed to get past the ridge till Theog, I'd be through. I struggle to cross the Kufri bazaar, as it is crowded with tourists; on their feet, in their cars, or even riding horses and yaks. The snow is increasing.

My car is moving on snow as a drunkard teeters meanderingly in a street. There are many other cars doing the same. As it continues to snow, I know I won't be able to get too far. There is no way I can stop here. Therefore, I carry on.

Within half an hour of a rickety drive, I've reached the town of Fagu, the foggy Fagu I have known since my childhood.

My drive has come to an end here. There are many cars stuck in various directions in the snow, like insects stuck to a liquid on a table. It is snowing heavily.

On this cold and dark afternoon as I sit in my car, in the warmth of the heater, I push my seat back and sit myself to rest. I see the local shopkeepers selling soups, beverages and snacks to the stranded travelers. I buy a cup of coffee, which I feel to be one of the finest I have ever had. It is a coffee as good as any but the occasion of its availability has made it special many times over.

As I sip coffee, I remember an incident of years ago, when I was in my early thirties. Sometime in the autumn of that year, in this very place, occurred an incident that changed the course of my life. Back then I was a big loader of fruits, vegetables and herbs, most of which I exported. Fagu was an important centre for procurement where growers from the surrounding villages and towns would bring their produce. It was the peak of the potato season. There were heaps of sacks of potatoes on both sides of the road. It used to be almost a festival season for the local growers who would sell their crop to many like me and go home with cash. Many of them would begin their celebrations in the little inns all over Fagu that offered varieties of non vegetarian food and liquor.

On one such evening in late October, having loaded my purchase into the Delhi-bound lorries, we gulped down quick tea and parted. I used to stay at a relative's house around this period of the year, since there were hardly any hotels or guest houses in Fagu those days. That house was in a village which was about half an hour of downhill walk. A path that led to the village bifurcated from the main road right from the market place in Fagu.

It was a full moon night, and I saw my shadow in front of me as if it were showing me the path. It was bitter cold.

I was rushing as fast as I could for I was afraid my shadow would leave me alone.

It was the third consecutive day I was going to that place to stay. It was my friend and his family's hospitality that made my business possible. I had been staying there previously; almost twenty five to thirty days during that part of the year, for as many as five years by then. I crossed a little stream which made me uneasy as I saw scattered shiny reflections of the yellow moon in it. It stretched unevenly across the water like scattered egg yolk. Till that point I had been oblivious to my walking or the path. My mind was too occupied in calculating the profits I had made that day. Having crossed the stream I had to be careful since it was a steep walk down the hill.

A few paces down, at the end of a pear orchard, I noticed a huge snake leap up in the air from below. Before I could comprehend the striped and the hairy snake, the huge beast strode up the way to the edge of the field. Upon seeing me, it slowed, and finally stopped. This was my death, I knew. I felt my spine go missing, and my body collapsed. I tried to hold myself together but I could not avoid falling thud on the ground on my hips while I supported my trembling body by clenching the dry grass with my feeble fists behind my back. I was gripped by a detestable shock. My body shuddered. I felt millions of sweating pores opening up all over my body. I happened to look at that grotesque beast in the eye and I found myself unable to look elsewhere as his two furnace eyes shot forward two long arrows of cold iron that pierced forth deep into my eyes and fixed them in that position. In the fire of his eyes I could see the flames rising from my pyre. It was the ugliest thing to have happened in my life. I hated myself for putting my life in such a position. My eyes were burning, and I felt as if iron rods were thrust deep inside my flesh, all over. I imagined his teeth digging into my throat. I felt blood dripping. It was sweat though, but it was hot. The monster sitting in front of me was the most dreadful thing I had ever experienced in life. With great calmness, as if mocking humankind, the beast settled upon his haunches, without allowing me to look away. I hated him. I would have liked a bolt of lightning to strike him and annihilate him right in front of my eyes. The more I hated him the more I began to pity myself. Before I had the time to judge that it was not a snake but the tail of a tiger, I saw the blazing eyes of the beast. The first thought that screamed in my mind was 'my daughter!' I thought of my two year old daughter playing next to her father's corpse, that is, if something was ever to be found of me. The thought of her being reduced to nearly an orphan pained my heart. It was her innocent smile, the remembrance of which made me hate the tiger so much that I would have liked to see him ashed there and then. His enormously powerful presence ridiculed my very existence. It was the sheer hopelessness of the moment that caused me to fall on to the ground. While I was gripped in his fiery glance, I mourned the aspirations that had occupied my consciousness all my adult life. I recalled with appalling sadness the truth, that in all her life of almost seven hundred days, I had never spent a single complete day with my daughter. It came as the greatest shock to me. I was shocked almost to death, not in merely knowing it but in realizing that I would forever be deprived of the joy of having spent an entire day with her while she was still a little child who spoke straight from her innocent heart. While he nailed me to the ground with his pitiless look, I could feel many arrows shot deep into my flesh. I felt I could no longer continue to look at him, as my neck stiffened to a point beyond toleration, but there was no way I could look away; I wasn't allowed to. While I looked into his eyes, I could see his enormous jaw half open. Was he allowing himself some rest before he would start? His white teeth would be the scribbling on my tombstone that was his body when I would be buried deep into his flesh. Within moments, all the drops of blood in my body, churned up by the life giving breath, rose up in a cyclone and I began to weep most profusely, but so fearful was I that I dared not open my lips. A stream of tears gushed down my throat despite two smaller ones flowing loudly down my cheeks. The remembrance of my daughter made me so vulnerable and bitter that I cursed God for having me lose my life in such a meaningless one sided encounter. In the span of a few seconds, I summed up the miseries of my life. With a meekly hateful, submissively conceding eye contact with the ferocious thing, I remembered with agonizing repentance that I had indefinitely postponed taking my ageing parents on a trip of the subcontinent, their only mutual desire apart from the happiness of their family, an endeavor they could have easily accomplished on their own in their long life despite a moderate earning, had the cause of their children not taken a precedence each time. First they sacrificed their choices for mine; and now I was doing the same with them, this time too for mine own. I remembered with piercing pain that I had not hugged my parents warmly in years, now that they were old, as they had hugged me as a child; old people do not choose their behavior independently as it might offend us young ones. I remembered how they wanted to do it at times, but I had conveniently ignored it since I just didn't feel like. Since my wedding five years ago, I had successfully stalled accompanying my wife on a belated honeymoon. We had been out only on a solitary lunch a year after we got married. Everything had been successfully procrastinated till happier days arrived. Needed I tell them all how much I loved them! What brought to me immense despair, and then accelerated my hysterical weeping, was the fact that I had involved an unreasonably huge amount of money in my business; only a fraction of which could be retrieved even if my enterprise was auctioned. Settling the rest would leave my aged parents, my wife and my only child, paupers. All these harrowing thoughts tumulted in my consciousness within seconds of my realization of the tiger's presence. In those few seconds, I remembered most of the important incidents and thoughts of my life in such an intensely entangled form that I can only mention the most significant of those. In those seconds following the onslaught of those flashy eyes, I re-lived my entire life with such an unbearable ache all over my body; my memories, my thoughts, my aspirations, my responsibilities, and my regrets had all been encapsulated into a pack of fractions; to be freshened up in my consciousness before I met my unfortunate end. Since the demon did not pounce upon me immediately, I had time; time to repent, time to sweat all over, time to feel my entire body crack up under a hundred aches under his beastly glare. By the time the fiend settled on his haunches, I was melting like a little snowman in front of a furnace.

As a couple of minutes passed, though I must confess my sense of timing may have been distorted to an extent, I knew I was still shedding tears of fear and repentance. The fiend looked amazingly calm. As time began to pass between my strife and his tranquility, my mind wandered into the possibilities of various alternatives. My mind tossed one or the other of them. I couldn't look away. I couldn't have walked away. I tried to imagine what the Death was thinking. Had he been walking long and now taking some rest before he would have a go at me? Had he just had a belly full and was now contemplating what best use he could put me to? And then entered a thought into my mind which to common sense might seem preposterous. Did he want to get rid of me as I wanted to? Were both of us afraid to lose eye contact? I don't know the answer to any of these questions, but I became aware of my eyes for the first time since the encounter. My eyelids were achingly heavy. I became aware of my breath. A passing belief that the tiger might be having second thoughts about me gave me hope. Even though I was petrified frozen cold under his imposing figure and fierce glance, I felt warm life-affording blood trickling down the veins through my icy arms that supported my upper body as they were shakingly planted on the ground beneath my hips. My fingers began to shake with life. This was the first voluntary movement of any of my body parts. That gave me a sense of ambition to overcome the catastrophe and a desire to live. I was overtaken with a strong emotion of setting everything all right. I wanted to spend an entire day with my child where I would look after her all by my own self. In my childish enthusiasm I decided to repeat it every fortnight. I wanted to go on a honeymoon, accompanying my wife to her favorite places. I would then like to take her to luncheons when we were not honeymooning. I would soon accompany my parents on a sub continental tour and repeat it every three to four years. I would take my entire family on outings to nearby places every six months. We would need to plan another child soon. Before I had the time to feel pleased with my new resolutions, I knew for sure that for all that to happen I had to get out of this situation alive. I could feel gathering deep within me, in the most nervous inner core, warm drops of determination, condensed from the vapors that had risen from the fire of the desire to live. The fingers of my right hand moved as if searching for something, even though my arms were shivering mildly. They moved out nervously, and to accommodate the search, my palm slid further by half an inch over a period of minutes, in a manner that no shift in my body as a whole was discernible; it was motion without movement. As my nails touched something that felt like a stone, my fingers struggled to acquire it. Such was my fear not to be seen moving that it took something like a few minutes of highly clandestine effort to approach the stone. Once I had it firmly in my grip I knew I would have something to fight him with. As my determination to fight him grew, I was surprised to see my hatred towards him turning into admiration. He could have mutilated me within seconds merely for play, even if he were not hungry at that moment. I was sure he had nothing to feel threatened by me for I had nothing at my disposal; things that people associate with scaring wild animals away, such as fire, noise or weapons, which too would have been of no use for I was taken by surprise and the distance between us was almost negligible. Even though I had been looking helplessly into his eyes, I could feel the aura around his figure. It was majestic. He sat upon his haunches with such authority that no human shape can ever match. My admiration was turned into awe the moment he brought his amazingly long tail around his front legs and laid it like a wreath. Was it a significant change in his mood? I had so often seen my cat do the same while taking rest. By now I had the stone in my firm grip. I held it so tightly that my palm began to hurt. I guessed it was enough to be stoked into his mouth if he chose to attack me. By now my determination to fight and vanquish my adversary had reached such gigantic proportion that I almost looked forward to it, for I knew it was inevitable. Thank God, it fell just short of taking an initiative! It was fuelled, no doubt, by the immeasurable fear of fear, and of losing all those promises of a fulfilling life that I had brought to my consciousness. It was the result of my determination to live.

Not knowing which way our encounter was going, I sat petrified in front of the mighty Prince of Darkness, waiting for my fate. I felt being consumed by that gaze of his. I even imagined myself being slowly eaten away by him; amongst the bushes, beside a pond of green water. That let me to grip the stone in my hand even more firmly. That stone was by now an important part of my body, in fact, the one that I was most conscious of. I knew if the stone were thrust into his attacking jaw at the right time, it would make him unable to act decisively. That was the end of my plan for him anyway, hoping that would allow me to run away, or even shout for help as I was sure the villagers in the vicinity were still awake. My painful romance with the various possibilities provided me a strange sense of relief. The pain had numbed my nerves to a point where they could not feel it any more. The fear had evaporated from my dried up flesh and cold bones. Since my tears had ceased long ago, I could feel my cool wet bosom; raised only from time to time by sighs from within. I felt like smiling voluntarily, but withheld, lest the movement on my face annoy him. Also, I found it difficult to move my lips in any way.

Time passed on. Thoughts, hopelessly incongruous with the situation, occurred to me. Strange though it may seem, a sense of pity for the devil arose within me. Despite all his power, ferocity and command, the Captain had no one for company. Was he consoling himself with my company? Was he offering me his protection from the forces of darkness? I sympathized with him for being so lonely; walking miles through night in search of food, with no family and no shelter; spending his days hiding away in caverns and deep wood, and wandering all night in the cold. The emotion of pity was so intense that I might have hugged him, had I been his equal in strength. Later, I often thought that pity arose in me partly, may be, because I wanted him to have pity on me. I have never been able to tell myself how true it was. Whether it was, at all.

Spent of my fear, tired of my determination to live and disillusioned with my sympathy for the Loner, I was beginning to see that encounter of ours as a profound joke, and I was growing desperate to get out of it as soon as possible. I was audacious enough to be prepared for a duel because to continue to endure the possibility of the looming disaster was the most unbearable ordeal. I wanted it to be concluded.

All my preparedness for an immediate end vanished the moment the tiger moved his tail away from his front and threw it straight behind him. The tail brushed away from right in front of my nose. I was already growing sick with the nauseating smell of his body, but this gush of wind that his tail threw into my near collapsing senses, made it unbearable for me to continue looking into the furnace that each of his eyes was. I began to think that he was readying for an assault. The fear that I had forgotten for a few minutes, now returned in multitudes. I could not believe fear could be so unnerving. I could hear myself shivering loudly. For the first time that night I remembered God. Fear had till then driven His memory out of my mind. Hope brought it back. I was acutely feverish. Both my nostrils were running cold down my lips. I recalled feverishly every form of God I had been brought up to pray. My prayers found it difficult to leave my wrecked structure. I had warm tears in my eyes. My grip on the stone in my right palm strengthened with every moment that passed. My palm was hurting, but that pain made this ordeal bearable.

A cloud passed over the full moon. It dimmed the appearance of the tiger to me though his blaze grew brighter. A still darker portion of the cloud passed over the moon. The skin of the tiger's face was less visible to me though his eyes began to burn more brightly in the semi darkness.

For the first time in that period of time that I later thought to be somewhat between four to five minutes, the tiger looked away. It looked away towards my left side, that is, the east, where little hills were glistering under the bright moonlight. I began to shiver almost uncontrollably. I lost my grip on the stone. I was prepared to be done in. Then, as if under the influence of an inexplicable divine intervention, the tiger slowly stood up on all four of his with great ease and strode away in a very graceful manner. The tail that I had taken for a snake in the beginning followed him, a few inches above the ground. That was all I saw in front of my eyes for I did not move them or my head. I continued to look at the same point. I did not notice the sound of his soft steps. Soon I began to imagine a pair of fiery eyes where there had been those that were his.

Also, possibly for the first time since I had got fixed into those balls of fire, I closed my eyes. Closing them after such a long time was painful, as if I had dragged my eyelids over sand and concrete. I kept them shut for a few moments. When I opened them, I slowly turned my head after the way he had taken. The Merciful Giant had disappeared. I continued to look in the same direction. Then, I think I saw him, for a few seconds, emerge from the third hillock on my left. He strode swiftly. Then he disappeared into the deep. I tried to get up. My body creaked as I attempted to stand. I found it difficult to hold my body on my shivering legs. Every joint of my body was cracking and every stretch of muscle was tearing apart. I do not remember how long I took to reach home. I do not remember what happened then.

I was told that I looked like a ghost when I appeared at the door of my friend's house. I fainted and regained consciousness only the next day. I remember I stayed in bed for three days, running high fever and unable to speak coherently.

Leaving my manager with some instructions I left for home which was miles away. I went home a different man.

I did not tell anyone about it. I hugged my wife. I embraced my parents and inhaled the smell of their old bodies after years of indifference. That night I slept, with my daughter in my lap, and tears in my eyes. I stayed at home for a week. I told them I was not too well. I gave myself up, to the four of them. It was such a treasure of joy that had always been at hand.

I have never disclosed this incident to any of them. Over the next four months, I not only did well in my business but also reinvented myself. My wife and I went on a honeymoon to Rajasthan. Next was a trip of the subcontinent that included my parents and daughter. Apart from the places we visited in India the tour included Pashupati Nath temple of Nepal and the Buddhist monasteries in Bhutan.

What came to me as a surprise was that not much had altered in my business despite having been absent from work for those few days following the incident. Not much had changed in the world either. When I went to the makeshift office in Fagu after recovering, I learnt that my manager had made sure that lorries had been loaded, sold in Delhi, and information over the telephone enabled the books to be maintained. At the same time not much would have added to my profits even if I had killed myself working. I realized, that with the right mix of delegation of responsibilities and power, I could run my enterprise efficiently, without letting life just pass by and coming home as a stranger each evening.

It is five in the afternoon now. It hasn't been snowing for a while. I had two cups of coffee while I was telling you the story. They tell me the road is going to be through in another ten minutes.

Sometimes I wonder, whether the tiger would have suffered from guilt, had he had a go at me. Kind hearted that he was, did he take pity on my tears? Did he feel touched by the state I had been reduced to? I shall never know. No one ever shall.

They tell me the road is through. I start driving. I have crossed this point beyond Fagu more than a thousand times but I have never failed to think of that benevolent beast. Whenever I am driving alone, I stop far above that hill where there was once a pear orchard, might still be there, and hope to catch a glimpse of that gentle soul who spared me momentary pain through annihilation, and my family, life long misery and sorrow. I am not sure if he would have felt remorseful but one thing is sure that my gentle savior couldn't have done anything to repair the loss.

I have three grown up children now. My parents are no more but we went on four more tours of the subcontinent while they lived. They had a fair share of their son's time and affection all their remaining years. My wife, I love her more than ever before, is content with life in every sense. No one at home is allowed to be cruel to animals, mice or even insects. They all think it's my virtue at play. No one has any idea that it is due to a single act of a large hearted lonely gentleman who lives in harsh conditions in the forests and caves and who, one cold night in October, gave up a nice meal.

4

The Consignment

The temple singer from Ujjain had spent many days at the largest government hospital in Delhi. He had brought his eighteen month old son who suffered from a disease that he could not comprehend. Nor could anyone else. He only knew that his child gained consciousness only for a few minutes, a couple of times each day. For the remaining moments of the twenty four hours of the day, the child would lie, as if lifeless.

They were spared the expenses of lodging and travel because of the temple singer's younger brother. He was a rickshaw puller and lived on the other side of the Yamuna, in an arrangement made of erected tin sheets under a flyover.

Each medical test that the doctors conducted to investigate the disorder, resulted in lightening him of a considerable part of the little money he had brought with him; only to be told in a way lacking any grief, pain, emotion and even concern, that it was something they thought was not curable.

In the sprawling lawns of the hospital, which to him appeared nothing less than a monument, he would read to himself and into the ears of his gradually invalidating child, the words of love that his mother and elder sisters wrote in broken sentences in a blue inland letter sheet. While the temple singer read those consoling words into his ears, the child would barely be lying still in the shade of his father's faded black umbrella. That umbrella was one of the very few things his father had brought with him from his home that was hundreds of miles away in central India.

Born after three daughters to a mother who sold flowers outside the Mahakal temple in Ujjain, the child dashed any hope of joy as he opened his eyes only for a few minutes a day. He showed a little movement when he was breastfed, only to relapse into lifelessness soon after. The child's condition brought immense grief to his mother, solely due to the pain that was his. On festivals, which were otherwise fortune making days, she would distribute flowers and garlands free to the devotees, secretly sending through them prayers for her child to the God inside the temple. The temple gate singer sang *bhajans* with devotion, the devotion aroused less by the inspiration of the deity and even lesser by the demand of the profession. It was devotion inspired by the suffering of the blameless child. Of the elder daughters, each helped the parents in their own ways; one sprinkling water on the flowers and weaving them into garlands, the other at the temple gate, collecting the coins that pilgrims threw into her father's vessel as he sang hymns to the lord. The youngest daughter played between the two.

By the end of his first week in Delhi, he had spent half the money. Medicines and medical investigation claimed a significant part of it. It was on the ninth day in the great city when the doctors told him that at least two more weeks were required for the detailed enquiry into the possibility of suggesting a cure, if any. The temple singer knew that he wouldn't be left with any resources to spend the remaining time in the capital city. On the tenth day, his rickshaw puller brother took them to a gurudwara on the banks of the Yamuna, where they were provided free food each evening.

The gurudwara spared them the ordeal of paying for food for both and milk for the child. The people who gathered there for food every evening were devotees, poor travelers and the homeless. The volunteers served them freshly cooked food with devotion. On the third day of the *langar*, when all had had their dinner, the temple singer, his rickshaw puller brother and the child stayed back along with the other homeless, most of whom were permitted to sleep in the premises. The elderly Sikh gentleman stepped out into the lawn with a harmonium. It was time for singing hymns. The others would join in. The old man's melodious voice made them lose the track of time. The temple singer from Ujjain sat pensively, holding his lifeless child in his lap, watching him constantly with hopeful eyes.

After a couple of days, the temple singer joined the elderly Sikh gentleman in singing the *keertan*. There were twenty listeners, all homeless. While the temple singer joined the white bearded gentleman in the lawn of the gurudwara, Yamuna glistened in the distance under the lights of the lofty bridge over it and the child lay lifelessly by his side.

The days passed, painfully. Most of the mornings were spent in the long queues outside the doctor's cabin with the child in his lap. The afternoons ended in the hospital lawn where the temple singer would read out the letter written to the boy by his mother and the three sisters.

Since you have gone away I can not see the color in the flowers
I do not think that the Mahakal is in the temple
I have more water in my eyes than Shipra in her bosom
Come home soon, your sisters and I are waiting to play with you
Noor says she wants to take you to pluck flowers on the banks
of Shipra
Parbati says she wants to take you to the temple stairs
Shipra says she wants to play with you and take you to see the
elephant that has come from Mysore.

Two elder sisters had written their names on the letter.

Then would follow another visit to the report room where he would submit yet another sample or collect another report which reiterated the incurability of the disorder. In the evening his brother would come and take them in his rickshaw to the gurudwara where they sat till the *langar.* Then they would assemble in the lawn and render hymns in the praise of the Lord. Later the elderly Sikh gentleman only played the instrument and the temple singer was the sole singer since it was his singing that the homeless identified with. The temple singer, in the midst of his sorrowful rendition, would look at the lifeless child and then melancholically away at the Yamuna. They formed a unison. He found a refuge in the overpowering flow of the river. It was the current of the river that drowned his sorrow as tears would sometimes flow down his cheeks.

After a couple of days he received another letter from home. He read it out into the indifferent ears of the child in the lawn of the hospital:

Baba come home soon
Delhi will make you all right and we know that you will walk
Shipra and you will run after each other
I see you in my dreams all nights my child
You are running all over and I can not even catch you
You should not run around so fast my son I want to hug you
Then one day your mother will be old
Will you still run like that?
Come home first and then you will see that your mother is not old
I can catch you quickly
I will never mind that I cannot catch you
As long as you run on your own.

That afternoon there was no need for them to be in the hospital but there was nowhere else to go. It was much better than spending the day under the flyover. After reading the letter he carried his son and travelled all the way to the gurudwara where the elderly Sikh gentleman offered him lunch. Taking his lunch he fed milk to his child and then carried him towards the river.

There, at the banks of the river, he sat with his feet in deep water and his child in his lap. He dipped his hand into the cold river and sprinkled a few drops of water on the child's face. The child did not show any movement. He then filled his palm with the holy water from the Yamuna and parting the lips of the baby put water into his mouth so that the power of the celestial river would cure him. The water was stuck in his mouth for some time and then had to be rinsed out with his finger. He washed the child's hanging arms. He dipped the child's loose legs into the river. He hummed hymns to the sacred rivers, the holy Ganga and the Yamuna. He wrapped the sleepy child in the large shawl and carried him some distance away on the bank where he stretched the child under the warm afternoon sunlight. The temple singer bent upon the feet of his ailing child, chanting those hymns that he sang at the Mahakal temple in Ujjain.

Later he whispered into the ears of the child how his mother and sisters were waiting for him at home. He took out the two letters from his pocket and read them out to him. The child did not exhibit any sign of life apart from the regular breathing. After shaking the child in all the ways he could, he broke down, clasping his angel's feet to his forehead. He had not opened his eyes all day, which he normally did about twice a day. He pressed him to his bosom and continued to look upon his shut eyes every now and then.

When he hadn't looked at his child for quite a while, he suddenly noticed his little arms shaking. He sprang to look at him. The child's eyes were open. His face bore a remote semblance of what could be called an expression. It was a sight that brought boundless pleasure to the man who had staked his everything to bring a smile on his child's face. He took him into his arms and spoke to him endlessly. He repeated to him what his mother and sisters had written to him. "Baba do not sleep now. Baba you have slept too long. We will soon go home Baba. Your mother and your sisters are waiting for you. They will go mad with joy when they see you walking Baba. Come, let's walk along Jamna jee, Baba. She is our mother and will bless us." He carried the child to the river and sprinkled some water on his forehead, eyes and mouth and wet his hair. He dipped his tiny feet into the river and then carried him away.

"Walk, Baba…walk," he screamed. He tried to put the baby on his feet but he collapsed on his toes. He tried to hold his hands and dragged him slowly on the soft warm sands.

He stopped, straightened him and attempted to walk him yet again.

The child's dragging tiny feet made a trace in the sand.

The father and the son struggled till some distance before the child began to relapse into his usual condition. The temple singer jolted his child to keep him in the state of consciousness. The child's relapse seemed irreversible. "Baba…Baba…O Baba…," the temple singer screamed. The child was lying motionless on the sand upon his stomach.

"Wake up Baba," he patted his cheeks.

He shook his chest and arms violently.

"Baba."

He lifted him and took him to the river where he sprinkled yet more water on the child's face and head.

"Baba."

He dipped his child's legs into the cold water.

"Maa Jamna…give life to my child."

He dipped him further into the water and pulled him out.

"Hey Jamna! Give life to him or take him away."

He plunged his child into water till his neck and pulled him out. The child did not exhibit any reaction to the cold water dips.

"Hey Jamna jee, give life to my child."

This time the temple singer plunged his child into water entirely, forcefully, screaming, "Hey maa Jamna."

He pulled his child out of water hurriedly to see if there was any symptom of life. The child's lips quivered for a while which soon subsided into stillness. The father, defeated, walked out of the waist deep water with his child in his lap, water dripping to the ground. He walked away along the bank of the mighty river till walking seemed monotonous and into no particular direction. The sad sun of the evening shone reluctantly in the western corner of the Delhi sky.

He stopped by a nearby rock, which seemed to him as purposeless as himself. He sat under it and saw that his son's body was not wet anymore. The child's face was as still as that of the deity in the temple; without life, beyond the reach of death.

He lay down along with his son and covered themselves under a low canopy of coarse sheet of printed cloth. The sunlight filtered in; dimmed by the fabric of the threads, colored and brightened by its lighter shades. Looking at the serene face of his child, the temple singer fell asleep.

When the temple singer woke, the earliest shades of darkness had covered the sky. So many people had gathered on the wide bank some distance away to breathe the evening air. He took his child in his arms, and walked away to the gurudwara.

At the end of three weeks in Delhi, the team of doctors, who had formed a special team to investigate the case, had drawn their conclusion. The temple singer had gone to the hospital that day as if it were a court of law where they would deliver the judgment of his life. He was accompanied by his rickshaw puller brother and the elderly Sikh gentleman from the gurudwara.

"It is the rarest of the rare cases," the head of the team of doctors said.

The three of them listened silently. The doctors named the disease but it sounded too incomprehensible to the three of them.

"This also means that it is not known to have been cured even minimally. Medical science, worldwide, has made a careful study of such cases as and when they have taken place."

"Would he have to stay back?" asked the old Sikh gentleman.

"It would not serve any purpose. We did not admit the child in the beginning because it would have been expensive. We knew it would not help the child's condition in any case. Of course, we gave him a choice."

"What should we do now?" asked the temple singer's brother.

"Nothing that I can recommend. All these days we have continued to inform him of the real cause behind the disorder. Even if a surgery was to be performed, it would cost a lot and it is a huge possibility that it does not yield any result. It could possibly result in coma or even death."

The temple singer did not utter a word. His child was in his lap.

"Your child's disorder is not within our reach but that does not mean his life is futile. His case could be studied more thoroughly over the years, even by experts from abroad. His life could be made useful by conducting studies into this disorder so that more expertise could be gathered in order to deal with such cases in the future. The child could be kept at the hospital. The government would take up the case. The child may also be shifted from one place to another as per the requirements of the research. Of course, there is no compulsion or hurry to oblige."

All three of them looked at each other. The temple singer looked at his son whose eyes were still shut.

"How long would that take?" asked the Sikh gentleman.

"It would definitely take years. May be all his life."

"And can you say anything about how long he might live?"

"Nothing. He could be no more in a few days and he could live as long as any other human being. And as far as current knowledge about this disorder permits, nothing can be said with any authority about when, if ever, the person could become normal. The greatest possibility is – never."

The elderly Sikh gentleman engaged in detailed discussions with the doctors. It all ended with the same conclusion.

The three of them sat in the sunny lawn. The rickshaw puller brother left. The temple singer did not speak for the rest of the day. He only responded to the warm gestures of the old Sikh gentleman who accompanied him all day. He tried to console him throughout. He narrated to him how one unfortunate incident snatched from him all his loved ones, and how since then, the gurudwara had been his only home.

The temple singer stared into the tearless eyes of the elderly Sikh gentleman, who said, "When God punishes you, it is with a purpose. Accept it. It is only when people ruin you for no crime, you find yourself cheated by humanity. They tied me to a rope, killed my two sons in front of my eyes, took my wife and daughter away, and left me to die in my burning house." As the elderly Sikh gentleman narrated his harrowing story, the temple singer was overwhelmed with emotion. His tears fell on the lifeless arms of his child.

That evening the temple singer did not have his food. He did not sing either. While the elderly Sikh gentleman was singing with his eyes closed, the temple singer lifted his child and walked away. At the corner of the lawn, he picked up the sandals of the elderly Sikh gentleman and touched them to his forehead.

He crossed the road, and walked briskly till he reached the familiar banks of the Yamuna. Before stepping into the river, he filled his shaking palms with its water, touching it to his forehead, he walked into the river as if it were an open field. He stopped when the water reached his waist.

His tears that fell into the Yamuna, did not warm its cold water. Beneath his trembling arms that had upon them his child lying Heavenward, the Yamuna continued to flow heartlessly. It had not learnt to stop for anyone, not even for itself. It could wash away your sorrow, but not stand still to console you. It can drown your tears, but not stop them. It can carry, not cure.

He was overwhelmed by his suffering which was too insignificant against the sorrowful might of the universe; too inconsequential amid the cosmic scheme of existence.

Indifferent traffic roared upon the Yamuna bridge. A train whistled in the distance. It could be the one coming from home. Or, the one to take him. He touched the child to his forehead and rendered his final prayer:

"Mother Perennial, my grief cannot be heavier than the burden that you carry eternally, but I fail to flow carrying it with me. Your burden is your body, the cause that sets you into motion, for me it's an impediment, an unannounced death. I thus consign my burden onto you. Let it be a debt upon me, that I may repay at the temple stairs and, what is yet left upon my soul, in hell. Be you his grave, his pyre, and, if you are merciful, his life."

With a stony expression on his face and legs trembling in deep water, he lowered his hands into the flowing water till the current of the water carried away from them the last shreds of the loose garment.

Trains whistled in the distance. He knew that one of them would take him home.

5

Gulmohar

Many ideas occur to many men at various moments in their lives. When some find them visiting too early, they treasure them till an appropriate time in the future; and those who find them their way rather late, bask in the joy of the possibility that could have been. It is from the labyrinth of numerous such could have beens that many derive the joyous consolation of life. Yet, there are some, who find those moments coming just at a time when they have the greatest possibility of being fulfilled, since their appearance from the outside and the desirability from within had never sought each other with such craving.

It was despite the joyous heaviness of such a thought, that walking up the winding road to the state hospital at the Snowdon, wasn't tiring for Madhu Sudan Tomar, though his bosom was anxious with expectations. He had been away from the place for hardly a fortnight, having been hospitalized there for almost ten days. Those ten days! Those ten days in October were like no other ten days of his life. In fact they were like no other ten months of his life, like no other ten years, nor twenty. The latter part of that period had faintly shown the promise of being the unsought answers for the unasked questions of most part of all his forty years. That destiny should have presented itself before him in such revealingly disguised form intrigued him but only after he had been discharged from the hospital. As the thought weighed upon him with increasing unbearability day after day, he had decided to allow it to ease and had left the town altogether for a change, only to return within a week with a multiplied desperation.

A few days earlier when he woke up that October evening, it had been three days since he was admitted to the hospital. His plastered left arm was heavier than usual. It gave him an irritation of a queer nature; not so much that it itched him and smelled but because it had him stay put at the hospital, which was more due to the aching back and a stiff neck which, they told him, would take another week to enable him to be free again. Displeased with himself for having woken up from sleepy forgetfulness that each evening offered, he only felt awake when he noticed a different nurse walking in through the door of his private ward. Not that he cared. For him they all belonged to a tribe of feminine shapes draped in green and white and he couldn't care less about not being able to distinguish them from each other. It's just that he would have to repeat to her all that had caused him the misery, the more testing part of which was to go through the necessary ordeal of being cured. He would have to repeat to her how he had met with an accident and how his jeep tumbled one hundred feet down the road before it was miraculously embraced by a pair of tall old deodar trees. He might even have to repeat to her how he was rescued from the jeep and brought to the hospital in time by a few kind men he didn't even know. He hoped that he wouldn't have to repeat the number and the types of medicines he had been taking since she had better look into his file that was placed by his side and find out on her own.

Meanwhile she had gone through the papers. She smiled and asked him how he was. The smile apparently failed as he answered irritably that all he wanted was to get out as soon as possible. She seemed unmoved by the plea and politely said, "Help yourself with the thermometer. I need to note down your temperature. I hope you've been sleeping well." He just nodded, happy to have the thermometer in his mouth. She readjusted the disarray of medicines and separated them from his scant personal belongings into two neat compartments while he looked at the ceiling. He then closed his eyes. He felt the thermometer being taken out and heard, "There's nothing to worry." He opened his eyes as she said, "I'll leave for now. Have your fermentation by eight and do not leave your bed too often. That's the only way you'll be able to leave in time and good health." Her dignified emphasis on 'leave' accompanied by a smile, thawed his shrunk face a little and as usual his eyes followed her as she began to walk away. She too had her skirt swirl in rhythm, her gait merrily suggestive of the shape within and he couldn't resist a cheerful feeling as this was the only blissful aberration he had treated himself to over the last three days at the Indira Gandhi Medical College and Associated Hospitals.

That night no one came to attend to him. He waited till ten and at the same time was relieved that he wouldn't have to go through the painful ritual of having the wounds on his left leg disturbed, washed and then dressed up all over. He lay in his bed with open eyes and slowly his eyelids felt heavier, and heavier, till they finally closed. The corridor outside the private wards was usually devoid of the general din of the hospital, and being so late into the night, there were all the reasons for it to be at its calmest. Much later that night he found himself stirring in the bed which woke him up slowly. As if in a trance, he sat up in his bed and found that the lights had been turned off and his beddings had been tucked in neatly from the sides. He also noticed a blanket on his quilt. It was probably for that reason that he had felt warmer. He had asked for one on the first night but due to certain delay in the laundry he was not to receive one for another five days. The streetlight that fell into his room became clearer and he found his eyes adjusting better to the otherwise dark room. He looked around and saw that the empty jar was filled with water and nearby on the stool were the two tablets that he was to have had after dinner. He looked at them all and then he turned to the blanket. He stared at the blanket and its pattern of design.

Under the light that was brighter, and with the vision that was clearer, he saw that the blanket was not one of the usual ones that they provided at the hospital. It was a very thick soft blanket with elaborate scenes in bright colors. The vines, the flowers, the leaves and the birds. The nest, the fledglings, the mother, the open beaks. His spread fingers ran all over the feathered blanket. He touched them; one by one he touched the bark of the tree and his fingers ran up the trunk, opened onto the branches, felt the smaller ones on which was the nest. He caressed the sparrow and her little ones. He spread his fingers over the little family in their nest and shuffled his fingers from left to right and in the reverse direction, quickly and repeatedly, so that through the spaces of the transient movements he could actually feel the mother and her fledglings move towards each other in a simple motion. He could almost hear the sharp chirping of the young ones, striving towards their mother.

He had not been touched that way in years. His mother had been dead for more than a decade, his father for more than two. He had not spoken to his sister for more than a month. He remembered them tonight, after such a long time, in the glowing darkness of a hospital ward. The worry in his mother's eyes as she lay dying years ago. The smell of her neck each time she hugged him. The emptiness of the promises he made to her to have a wife and many children; to fill the hollowness of the house with the cries of babies. He remembered his sister's wedding, the severing of the last connection he was left with of the only world he had known all his life. As his mind got crowded with memories, he felt he could not see clearly; the mother, the fledglings, the nest, and the vines around it. The vision got hazy and the mother and the babies began to sink into each other. They swam and wavered till he could see them no more and the vision melted into the warm drops that fell on the blanket. Suddenly realizing what was beginning to happen to him, he wiped his eyes with one end of the blanket and got down from the bed.

He looked out of the window. There was just one streetlight. The leaves were shining yellow golden. There was a solitary green bench right under the light. It must have been terribly cold out there. With his freshly wet and tear shiny eyes he gazed at the lonely bench. How many might have sat upon that bench all those years! How many might have broken good news to their loved ones. How many might have broken down on its shoulder. How many might have sat patiently to take home those that had been born or reborn. How many might have waited endlessly to carry home those that will no longer walk on their own. The bench does not mourn those that shall never be seen again. It does not rejoice with others. It sheds no tears. It does not smile. It comforts. It gathers all. It moves on, by staying right there. By being there for all, by sharing its cold nights with the lonely light, with golden leaves in its lap.

Through the window he watched the cold night pensively. The wet traces of tears were now cold. He went back to his bed and sat down. After some time he got up, put on his long coat and slippers, and walked out of his ward. He headed into the corridor. There was no one around. He was walking into the stillness of the night, the silent darkness sinking into him. He reached the end of the corridor. The idea of roaming around the place at night was tempting. He took the right direction but soon came back since it led to a stairway upwards. He opted for the stairway on the left which took him down. He could walk throughout the building and the other buildings, he thought. Through the streets of the hospitals and all over the roads of the town, upon the paved roads of the old Municipality house, along the Oak Over down to the Secretariat at the Ellerslie. Tonight, he wanted to see them all. All of them. The maid they said who could be seen mopping the floors of the general ward at night. The Alsatian of the British General at the Snowdon who haunted the streets of the hospital ever since it was buried under the heavy snow of 1892 when it was his master's residence. What a relief, he thought, that his master's staff members could not be seen digging around for him in the heavy winter snow. The ones people said had easy virtue, those helpless maids whom the merry making tourists saw off on the town roads in the early hours of the morning and had nowhere to go in the darkness. The old hand who sold delicious tea to the night staff of some government departments. The ones who slept under the eternal blanket in the sheds of municipality building. Tonight, he wanted to see them all.

Downstairs. He had merely gone down a couple of floors when he heard someone humming. He took a few steps and stopped at the door of the room wherefrom he heard the lullaby. He pushed open the door slightly and peeped into the rather small room. The bright light emanating from the incubator made it possible for him to see a woman holding an infant in her lap; attempting to sing it to sleep and visibly upset to see someone at the door. He could see through the clarity of the machine's light. He needed not ask to enter, he thought. He walked in slowly and stared at them. The baby was restless. "What happened?" he asked.

"What are you doing here?" she said, adding, "you should be taking rest".

Encouraged by the show of concern, he sat on a nearby stool and said "I am fine".

She kept the baby hugged close to her bosom, its face covered with a shawl and began to hum, conscious of the intrusion. He looked at the name embroidered on her jacket. It was Meera. It was she who had attended him on the first three days. He was familiar with her.

He sat there, on the stool, looking. At Meera, trying to sing the baby to sleep. At the incubator, throwing out light in abundance, appearing in that otherwise dark room like a fountain of white light issuing out of a cave. Then at Meera, singing swinging the infant across her lap. Then at the painting on the wall; mangoes grapes apples bananas papaya pomegranate three cherries peach pineapple, wondering whether all those fruits grew in the same season. Then at Meera and the infant. Then at the second picture on the wall, a couple of toothless toddlers smiling, lying on their tummies, their little shiny hips visible behind their bald heads. At Meera. At the third portrait on the wall, a pup and a kitten frolicking on green grass.

She looked at him. Meanwhile the infant shrieked. It threw the shawl covering its face away and he saw the pink face of the baby. Eyes shut tight. Mouth opened to its maximum. Shrieking. Shaking violently. The pink of skin was turning red. She raised the volume and the frequency of her lullaby. She held the child closer and began to swing at a quicker pace. The red of the skin turned deep red.

"Is there any problem?" he asked.

"No, not as such but she is hungry. I am not sure when she was fed. Could you please give me the milk bottle?"

He got up and walked straight to the trolley. "Where is the bottle?"

"In the drawer."

It was there but had no milk.

The shrieks continued and made him nervous.

"There is milk powder in the jar".

"Where is the jar?"

"In the rack".

"No. It's not there".

The piercing shrills were now unbearable.

"Check in the trolley".

He did just that.

"Not here".

He was afraid what she would say next.

"Look around the room somewhere. Everywhere".

Meanwhile the baby continued shrieking, making the both of them look around anxiously.

He rushed out of the room looking for a duty room where he could find someone who could provide milk or any other thing to calm the child. As he rushed further he heard the sound from the incubator cabin receding. He saw some duty rooms without attendants while some half-awake ones guided him around. He found his way back to the cabin by following the shrieks. The baby rocking in her arms was unforgiving.

"Is there a shop around here that sells milk?"

"Yes, there is one," she said, "but you won't find it."

He did not care to listen. He picked up the empty bottle and shot out.

He got out of the building without caring to see which one it was. It was the first time he had left it. He brisked past the next building, into the road that led to a security post which had someone inside. After a few minutes down there at the shop which sold many things all night, medical and others, he turned around in a hurry, with the bottle containing warm milk in his hands. But he did not know which way to go. He asked the shopkeeper the way to the security post. He had to come back twice to ask him the same question till the kind man sent his attendant to guide the man in a hurry. Once there, he still did not know which way to go. He went to the policeman in there. He did not know what to ask him. What he wanted to ask was – Where have I come from?

"Where are the private wards?"

"Why, it is the building right next to the shop you bought this milk from."

"Of course not. I remember having come a long way to the shop. There is a child and a mother there."

"How old is your child?"

This is one question he could not have answered in any way.

"Oh sorry! I got it. I mean the Pediatric ward."

"What exactly is that sir? I mean about heart, teeth, bones or something else?"

"It is an infant about a few days old."

"For those we have another hospital- Lady Reading's or Kamala Nehru Hospital- about two kilometers from here. God! I think you really need help."

The policeman stepped out of the post. After a brief discussion with him he found his way to the building. Thanking the policeman absentmindedly he entered knowing not once again which way to go.

He thought the infant's cries would lead him to the incubator cabin. He had not cared to count the floors he had jumped down in anxiety. Not the wooden staircases that he had descended as if in a flight. Nor the walls and the corridors which he had sped past lightningly, a brief reminder of which might now hint his retreat. The floors looked all alike, the elegant staircases with their mats the same and the walls and the corridors indifferent. D-14. Yes, that was the room. That was the number he had seen on all the papers and prescriptions on the table in his room. He read the room numbers till he reached his. From there he took the familiar path he had taken earlier that night. When he reached the corridor, he could not hear the baby's cries any more. After peeping in through the windows of all the rooms, he came across the one which shone with the light of the incubator.

He opened the door and walked in. She cautioned him with her eyes, putting her finger on her lips forbidding him to make any noise. He moved closer with the milk bottle in his hand. He stood speechless by what he saw. He watched in fullness that she was breast-feeding the baby. The baby's eyes were close, sleeping, yet suckling delicately. She put her hand forward for the milk bottle. Slowly she pulled out her nipple from the baby's mouth and inserted that of the bottle. Within minutes the child was fast asleep, no more sucking in any milk. She lifted the baby, blindfolded her and placed her on the bright screen of the incubator. After a few initial movements, the child settled into a sound sleep.

He sat glancing at the child. Under the heavy bright light from beneath and above, she must be having dreams of the plains of heavens, he thought. With trees of gold and lakes of silver. Rocks of diamonds and pebbles of pearls. Grass blades of emerald and leaves of ruby. Angels riding on low flying clouds singing to doves and fawns. Swans and fish of gold swimming in the rivers and ponds of silver in the valleys with sunflowers.

"Did you take your medicines?"

He thought the angel sang into his years.

"Have you taken your medicines?" she repeated, a little louder.

"Oh yes. No. I think I did…"

It was two in the morning.

"You should be taking rest."

With no more questions in his mind he got up to leave. He threw a parting glance at the baby, in the incubator, glittering like a gemstone in a pool of milk, and shut the door behind him. He had hardly taken a few steps when she opened the door and whispered, "I am required to say that you shouldn't have left your room at such an odd hour. Also, you are not expected to wander about the place at such a time. In fact, in your condition, at no time." Standing there for a few seconds, he moved on. She whispered something again. He could see her dark figure against the bright background. He gazed at the figure while she smiled and whispered, "I wouldn't have known what to do without you. Thank you so much."

He reached the main gate of the hospital. In that November drizzle he had begun to feel cold. He wrapped his overcoat around him more tightly and moved in under the huge arch of the gate. On his way he saw all the unfamiliar faces around him. How glad he was not to be recognized and disturbed by anyone. Just days before, while he was still admitted, Meera had once wondered whether no one knew him in the town since she saw no one coming to see him. He did not feel like telling her that only if he cared to let it be known around, he would never have been allowed to live peacefully on his own. He would have had no time for himself; answering questions all the time, some he knew how to answer, and others, he wouldn't. Aunts nagging why he had not married, depriving his mother's soul of peace; uncles regretting his choice of career that left his father's dream unfulfilled, friends wondering how he drove himself off the road and cousins bewildered what he had been doing up there all those years, which was something they did not care to understand. It had been a carefully protected solitude.

The fourth morning at the hospital had slowly drifted into the afternoon. Apart from brief wakeful intervals, when he felt some ghostly figures guided him about taking his tea, breakfast and medicines, there was nothing he could remember of it. He woke up at three in the afternoon. Ignoring the now cold lunch and coffee on his table, he swallowed his tablets and dissolved into his bed only to be woken up at seven. This time, she was there. It seemed to him that she had just had a bath; hair neatly braided and skin beaming. He sat up and they acknowledged each other. While she arranged things around, he arranged himself. He sat up and listened to the instructions. Then she took out small amounts from each little bottle and began to prepare an ointment.

"Who's looking after your daughter at the moment?"

No answer. He thought it was shaking the ointment solution vigourously that prevented her from hearing.

"How can you leave your daughter like that? When was she born?"

No answer again. The ointment was ready.

"Pull down your shirt." She started applying it on his left shoulder.

Meanwhile he thought of the possible answers to the unheard questions.

"Does it hurt?"

"Yes… sometimes it …could," he drawled.

Realizing immediately what he had said, he attempted to mend, "No. It doesn't. Not at all. Just feels a bit itchy.

It's perfectly all right. I am sure it's going to be greatly beneficial."

Not knowing what to say in order to sustain the conversation, he added, "How kind of you to be doing that."

She smiled. "You don't want to know when you're likely to be discharged?"

"Yeess…indeed. Of course. Is it going to be any time soon?"

His lack of eagerness about his release didn't go unnoticed by either. He tried to make himself sound more convincing in the latter part but didn't want to do any more mending this time. He just let it go and sat back with a blush. "When is it by the way?" he asked.

"Well. Not now. Not any time soon. Sorry. But take care."

Pleased with her prank she quietly left the room.

By eight that evening he had had his dinner. Hours later, he went out in the little garden behind the building and sat upon the lonely bench. He kept the cigarette case beside him and smoked one after another under the bright night. He remembered how his mother had told him about his birth. That was in Hamirpur many years ago. It was a similar building and a children ward, ninety miles from Shimla. For his mother it was the birth of her second child. The wife of a senior revenue officer had her three year old daughter playing around all day. They would watch squirrels running all over the majestic gulmohar tree that was outside their window. In the spring of that year, like any other, it was in full blossom. Every evening, Sabby would gather the fallen flowers and arrange them in the flower vase next to her mother's bed. Mr. Tomar would arrive in the evening. Sometime in May that year he was born.

His fingers gathered another cigarette and placed it between his lips. As another mist of smoke rose above his eyes he tried to remember all that his mother had told him about that memorable month in the hospital in Hamirpur. During the pre-monsoon showers of June the gulmohar was washed afresh. Its branches and leaves were drenched, and so were the squirrels. She told him how she would cheer upon seeing the gulmohar from her bed. The tree with its arms raised towards the heavens, offering flowers, yet allowing some to shed for the ones on the ground beneath. Years later she told him she wanted to name him just that, Gulmohar.

At something past eleven he got up. He walked up to his room. He washed his face, put on his long coat and left his room. With quiet and forgetful steps he walked all the way to the little room with light beaming out through the fluorescent panes. He stood at the door, his fingers on the knob. He couldn't push it in. He stood there, thinking. He kept standing. Slowly pushing in the door he could see the darkness of the room lightened by the light of the machine. Meera was there. She was singing her child to sleep. He entered, avoiding looking at her as if he were getting into a common waiting room with strangers. The child was fast asleep. She smiled faintly as she put her daughter into the incubator. She sat on the little bed while he sank into the armchair, though consciously.

Meera…Meera…is this your child…he asked…or he thought he did…are you the mother of …he asked …or he thought he wanted to.

"She is not my daughter."

He thought he did not hear her. He looked at her blankly. She sat nonchalantly.

"What?" slowly rising in his chair.

"I am not her mother."

He sat up in his chair.

"How …? You mean… but are you…..?"

"No. I am not. Haven't thought about it yet."

"But then…." he dragged, looking at the child illuminating in the machine.

He sank back into the chair peacefully, as if receiving an assurance of some sort.

Things became clearer. He could see the paintings on the wall clearly. She continued to sit in front of the machine, looking at him.

"She is eleven days old. Has been diagnosed with jaundice."

He nodded in acknowledgement. He did not know where to start asking. There were still the three of them in the room but the equations had changed. The stillness of the little room just hummed with the sound of the machine. What was it that had brought the three of them together in this room even when none of them had any relation with each other? Was it just a coincidence? Like meeting on a terminal? In a market place or somewhere driving past each other or just waiting to cross each other?

"Her mother is no more."

He was sure he had heard it.

Was it like the friends of childhood? Together for a few years and then never to meet. The leaves and flowers of one spring, to be strewn in autumn and not to be seen beyond the winter. The winter snow, all over now, untraceable then.

The love songs of adolescence, sung then as if never to be forgotten but irretrievable later.

"Her father is not known."

He heard that too.

Or like the mother he knew for just twenty years but remembered his every living day. The father he knew even lesser but whose blood he carried in his veins. The only sister he now sees once in a while but without whom he can no longer imagine his world. The limbs he is not aware of he has but which perform their tasks and make things possible.

The gaze at the infant on the incubator screen grew hazy. The vision blurred under the strain of the gaze. He saw two hands lifting the baby out of the machine.

"What happened?"

"She has wetted her diaper." She took off the cotton diaper and threw it into a plastic basket, which, he saw had many such wet ones. The child was still asleep while she folded a new one around the baby's bottom. She sprinkled a liquid on the screen and wiped it clean. After placing the baby back on the screen she took the plastic basket and before leaving said to him, "Just see she doesn't hurt herself."

Gazing at the child on the incubator screen he remembered the windows of the Hamirpur hospital. The baby was fast asleep. He shut his eyes. Through the glass pane he, as if through his mother's eyes, could see the splendid gulmohar peeping into the room, at the mother, at him the infant, and Sabby the sister. He could hear the whispers of the tree: *Those flowers that are in the vase are mine. Those that are hanging on the string, on the window, strewn on the bed and on the floor are mine. Those in little Sabby's hair are mine too.*

He could see he grew up under the tree, beneath its all encompassing arms. His parents sat on the parapet while Sabby and he ran around it. Sometimes they climbed the branches and chased squirrels. They fed birds millet and corn on the parapet and gathered flowers on the ground. Flowers came on gulmohar each spring. Father passed away. Gulmohar had the same flowers next spring. Mother passed away. Sabby grew up and went away somewhere. Gulmohar had the same flowers each spring. He grew old under the same tree. Children came and played under the tree and he watched them all with a grey beard.

When Meera entered with the washed cotton diapers, she was relieved to see the child sleeping peacefully on the screen and the caretaker dozing over the edge of it. She did not disturb them. She put the clothes into the drier and sat on the bed, watching the both of them. She allowed her head to rest against the back of the chair that he was sitting in. Soon she was asleep.

Everything in the room sounded still except the drumming of the incubator. The infant slept on the shiny screen, he over the machine, and she sat asleep above them both. Everything seemed to have sunk into a blissful stillness, as if the entire universe had lulled itself to a dreamy sleep and were in a trance. The numerous angels sang themselves to dreams, lying lifelessly on the golden stars in heaven, their long hair and shiny drapes hanging loosely into mid heaven. The golden yellow moon dozed upon its folded arm, the other hanging down helplessly, holding in it a flute of silver. In the paintings on the wall; the fruits, in their bed the bowl, had their heads hanging in slumber, the pup and the kitten lay drowsily on the ground entwined and the toothless toddlers had long closed their eyes.

It was sometime after midnight that the infant shrieked and everyone stirred to life in a reluctant motion. It was a call for milk.

"She wants milk. Could you get the bottle out of the cabin?"

He brought the bottle while she took the child into her lap. The baby calmed down as Meera began to feed her. He could not adjust himself to the wakefulness, and pulling away his coat, walked straight towards the door. As he closed the door behind him, he heard, "Why do you want to leave?" He stood outside the door, not knowing how to answer. He responded by walking in, closing the door behind him and sitting back into the arm chair. She was looking at him while his eyes were closed.

"She was an invalid, her mother. She died a few hours after giving birth. God knows whether she had been raped or ever had a husband. She had been abandoned at the hospital nearly a week before the child's birth. A few of us in the nursing department decided to take care of the child. Now I seem to be the only one."

He looked at her with confusion and bewilderment. She knew it.

"But how do you manage it? Don't you go home?"

"It's been three days now. It has become a routine. I am on duty around here in the daytime and I sleep here at night."

"Who all are at your place? What do they say about… all this?"

"My mother, brother and his wife. They don't mind," she said, and added, almost abruptly, "A few months ago I lost my father in an accident. He was rushed to the hospital but died on the way."

"Sad," was all he could say with his dry throat while he continued to look at her. She looked at the baby sucking milk or at his chair or at the door.

"We could not nurse him in his last moments. It seems to be a loss that can never be overcome."

The child had taken milk. She removed the bib. The child was not in a mood to sleep any time soon. With her half open eyes she looked around.

"Want to hold her?"

"Yes, I do." His arms shook forward. She placed the baby on his palms delicately.

"Is this the first time you are holding a child?" she asked.

"Yes. In fact I never thought I would ever be holding one." The infant moved her tiny legs and arms as if cycling. The child looked up towards him. He did not know how to respond to that queer glance. She was frightened and at the same time, bore a curious look, as if asking questions. The child smiled. She did smile. Indeed. The smile lasted almost a second. It vanished as soon as it had appeared.

"I have been a nurse for almost five years. Since my father's accident and death I have volunteered for the emergency ward to look after accidental cases. In the beginning it was difficult. Now it seems to be rewarding because it is so satisfying. It makes me feel my father's wounds are healing. I hope it adds up to something and makes a difference to someone, somewhere." She began to sob.

"Anyone. Anywhere," she continued.

"The loss seems recuperating. It was only after her birth that I shifted here. But when I heard about you I thought I could serve the same purpose here as well. How did you feel at the Emergency?"

"Terrible," he said. She wiped her eyes.

"Thank God, it was only for a few hours," he completed.

"I know."

"How?"

"Mentioned in your report. That's how."

They both smiled, looking at each other. Meanwhile the child had gone to sleep in his lap. Both her thumbs were in her mouth.

Later that night, without trying to find out what time it was, he walked up to his room and buried himself into his quilt. He could not sleep. After some time he got up and sat back on his bed. He got down and looked for his cigarettes. There was none. He looked everywhere but couldn't find any till he looked out of the window at the bench. There it was. He gave up the idea and lay back in his bed. Then with a sudden jerk he got out of his bed and walked out of his room. He walked all the way to the back of the building and sat on the bench. He picked up the case and found two cigarettes in it. He sat on the bench, smoking. He shut his eyes. He felt he could see that the gulmohar still bore flowers in spring. He sat under it. He had white beard. He sat on the parapet but had no children playing around. He did not know where they had gone or why they did not come any more. He imagined he sat alone on the parapet. There was no one to gather flowers to put them in the vase. There was no one to put those flowers in her hair. He could feel himself fall asleep under the gulmohar tree.

He entered the nurses duty room. The one who sat there was familiar with him.

"Hello, Mr. Tomar. Are you all right now?"

"Absolutely."

"Any problem?"

"No. I am fine."

"Yours was a shoulder dislocation, wasn't it?"

"True but it was a minor one."

"Some bills to be verified? I mean for insurance."

"No. Not that at all. Oh yes. In fact, why not? Yes that too. Indeed."

"Don't be so confused. Come I'll tell you where to go. Get it done fast. It's about to be five. There is a change of duty at six."

He walked to the duty chart and read the one for that week, the first week of November. Meera was to arrive at six that evening. He walked up the familiar corridors and straight to the little room with the door with the fluorescent glasses. He opened the door familiarly. The machine was on. The little child was lying on the screen. His steps towards the armchair suddenly stopped when he saw an old woman sitting in it already. A younger one sat on the bed. She was eating something. Probably jelly. Both of them looked at him blankly. The smile on his face disappeared.

"Oh, I am sorry," was all he managed.

"Come in," said the elderly woman. "Please sit down."

"I was looking for someone else. There used to be a girl child here… she was…"

"How long back was that?" asked the older woman.

"Because the one before us was a baby boy," said the one who had been eating jelly, probably the child's mother.

"How long does one normally stay here?" he asked.

"About three to four days. A week at the most," replied the elder woman.

"I see."

For a while he sat on the cold chair outside the little room.

Fifth day had passed like the fourth day and the night had passed like that of the fourth. During all this he had almost forgotten his pain. He had forgotten why he had been admitted. He had also lost track of the number of days he had spent at the hospital. The discomfort he had had with the shoulder, his leg, the back and the forearm had assuaged over the period. He knew he was getting better but didn't particularly look forward to being discharged. Though he did want to, of course, but he did not want to imagine it. At least not now.

Each night he walked down to the little room. The two of them sat looking after the baby all night and parted in the morning. Lately, he had begun to change her nappies. He felt great pleasure in washing the cotton ones. Initially, Meera didn't allow him but he had his way. He took the infant in his arms and fed her milk. He felt charmed by the movements of the little fingers, the occasional smile, and the way she contorted her facial muscles before she wept. They spoke to each other while she slept on the incubator screen and remained busy with her when she was out of it.

He told her about a small organization he ran in the Trans-Giri regions of the Sirmour hills, the fine education he had had, the life in the country and the enormous inheritance he had not put to much use till then.

"How long has she been here, in this room?"

"The day you first visited. We had found out her jaundice a day before."

"And before that?"

"In another hospital, about two kilometers away. She was sent here due to her mother's other complications. She had to undergo an emergency surgery but she died before that."

"The jaundice seems to be getting better now."

"Yes."

The child was lulled to sleep meanwhile.

Then came the last night. He was to be discharged the next day. He walked in just before midnight. She could smell cigarettes. He sank into the arm chair.

"I am leaving tomorrow," he said evenly.

She smiled.

"Meera!"

"Yes?"

He remained silent for some time.

"I had never thought I would feel this way leaving this place."

"Like what?"

"Like leaving something behind. Someone."

"Who?"

"May be just a part of myself." There was silence for some time.

"Have you ever been admitted to a hospital before?" she asked.

"Never. May be sometimes in childhood but I don't remember."

He wondered why she changed the course of the conversation. Not that he had intended to channel it in any particular direction. He didn't mind it either.

"So that's not why you feel that way," she said.

"What?"

"The fact that this is your first stay at a hospital."

He couldn't fathom which way it was going. He wanted to tell her something. But he did not know what it was. He really did not know.

"Meera, I am forty. I have never felt so stranded in life. Or, so static. For the first time in my life I feel like staying for a while. *Staying.* I mean, staying with myself. One gets tired of running away. Especially, from one's own self. It will all be over one day."

"What?"

"All this. Everything. Forty. Then fifty, and sixty. Fine. Nothing to regret I think."

He looked at the floor. She was looking at him.

"How old are you, Meera?" he asked, looking up suddenly at her, and into her eyes.

"Twenty three."

"And she is less than two weeks."

He smiled at her. She smiled faintly.

There was so much to say, he felt. He did not, quite obviously, want to tell her they had dancing peacocks cross their paths as often as they encountered bears and leopards in the forests there. It was also not the time to tell her that they once escaped a cloudburst in a matter of a few minutes, nor even that his efforts helped country women earn a decent sum by making brooms of pine needles which local people bought for cleaning their fireplace and the kitchen, while tourists took home as souvenir.

"What do you intend to do with your life, Meera?"

She looked up at him in surprise.

"I think it will go on as such. There is not much else I can do with it."

"Sometimes life throws questions at you Meera. It expects you to answer them at once. Or even over a period of time. Then it stops asking at all. That is when you should begin to worry. Then comes a stage like mine. Life provides you answers. And that is not when you should go about searching questions to mesh those answers with. That is the time to embrace them and start life anew."

'Do you see those answers?' he expected her to ask.

"I see them now. I had never sought them. I never got them. But now out of nowhere I see them everywhere."

He looked at the floor. Then, at the ceiling. At the pup and the kitten, smiling; at the fruits, keening; and, at the ever smiling toddlers, hearing.

"I see those answers now. In her," he said, looking at the sleeping angel on the incubator screen.

He looked around nervously.

"In you, Meera."

He was discharged the next morning.

He waited in the cold chair till a few minutes after six. He got up to walk to her office. Instead, he suddenly started walking upstairs, to D 14. To the room that till a few days ago, for a few days in October, had been his. He stood outside the door. There was no one in the corridor. He leaned his forehead against the closed door. He touched the knob with his fingers. Then he let it go and walked away.

He walked downstairs and went straight to the duty room. He opened the door. Meera was there. Her eyes opened wide. She got up from her seat and asked him to sit. He sat quietly. "How have you been?" he said.

"Fine," she said, with her spreading lips.

"What a surprise though! I didn't think you would come back," said she.

"You didn't?"

"Well! Not so soon."

"You don't have to be so polite, Meera."

They sat without speaking to each other for some time. The heat pillar was turning around in compliance. It hummed its own tune as it merry-went-round on its single foot.

"I had gone to the little room. But there were some…"

"Oh yes. I have issued a private ward for her. Upstairs."

"Who is looking after her?"

"My mother."

"Mother?"

"Yes. She'll be discharged tomorrow. We are taking her home."

"Home?"

"Yes. Home."

He leaned closer. She was not looking at him. He was not looking at her. He put his hands into his pockets.

"Meera."

She didn't respond.

"Can you marry me?"

She said nothing.

She turned to look away from him, at the window and through it into the cold dark.

"Do you want to see her? She is upstairs."

"Which room?"

"D-14. Your room."

He rushed out and charged up the stairs. He stormed through the corridor and stopped just before the door. He gathered his trailing heartbeats and slowly pushed himself in. Careful not to forgo acknowledging the gentle lady's presence he went to the bed and took the wakeful child in his arms.

"How are you?" the old lady said.

"I am fine. Thank you so much."

The telephone rang. The elderly woman answered it. After exchanging a few sentences with someone on the other side she indicated to him, "It's for you."

With the child in his arms he took the telephone receiver close to his ear.

"What shall we name our daughter?" asked the voice on the other side.

"Pardon?"

The telephone disconnected. He limped to the bed. The gentle looking elderly woman was smiling. After some time the door opened.

She was there. Meera.

She closed the door behind her and softly walked to the bed.

"What shall we name our daughter?" she said.

He; pleased, perplexed, replied: "Gulmohar."

6

The Table

I - The Aftermath

It was that curious time of the duration when the day had ceased and the night had not yet begun. Common folk were retreating after another daylong toil, and those who derived their existence from the night were preparing to grope into it.

Ren was alone in her kitchen. The dinner was ready for the three of them which included her husband and her child. But she was restless, for it was an unusual thing; it was late and her child, though grown up, was yet not home. She walked into the yard and looked through the gate but there was no one in the distance. She returned to the kitchen.

That afternoon Ren had gone to call on Dew in the neighborhood. She had entered Dew's yard with hasty steps and found her sitting all alone in the sun.

"Ren, dear! How do you do?"

"Fine, Dew. Just a little tired."

"Doing what?"

"Oh! Just helping Bru get ready."

"Where to?"

"God! You really have no idea, do you?"

"Not a bit unless you tell me."

"Bru's been invited to the Master's. His son's birthday party. It was early. Must be lunch."

"Oh, I see. Lucky really."

"You don't have children yet, Dew. Have them soon. You're not much younger than me. You don't know what joy it is to have your own ones and then to see them being so lucky. There're many here otherwise. But Bru's special. You know he is."

"I may be having mine soon. By next season I hope."

"Dew, you know Bru's been a good friend of our Master's son. When Bru was still an infant, the Master's son used to come home everyday and play with Bru. He used to carry him away and play with him all over the place. He wouldn't miss a day. In fact, I believe they grew up together. Though, Bru's grown much faster. Master's son seems to be more or less the same. Of course, they take long."

"But I haven't seen him since long."

"Yes. The Master sent him away to a school in the town. He returned just a week ago I guess."

"Did Bru miss him?"

"I am sure he did. Master's son missed him much more. He had come with his father our Master just yesterday. You won't believe he almost didn't recognize Bru. All he said to his father was 'it's grown so much.' He was quite right. Bru's grown amazingly. Why wouldn't he? He's been accompanying his father hunting down the stream, of late. He prefers meat now. He used to be too scared when he was young. Moreover, we only have one child to look after. Master is kind indeed."

"Master is always kind."

After a brief silence Ren continued, with caution, "Dew, don't let that out, but I think, Den is really jealous of my Bru."

"Really? How can you say so?"

"You see her Ben is as old as my Bru but half his size. Also, Bru won the races and the fights this season. Now, if she learns that he's been invited to the Master's for his son's birthday celebrations she might just jump into the well I'm afraid," they burst into a laughter.

Having thus spent a great deal of time Ren rose to leave, saying, "I must be going now. Bru could be home anytime. He'll have plenty to share with his mother. I'll let you know tomorrow."

II - The Chase

It was getting dark and Ren was worried. She strolled nervously in the yard. She sprang to open the little gate when she heard some footsteps, and screamed, "Broooo." It was Den who spoke in a somber tone, "Sorry to disappoint you Ren. It's me."

"What brings you here?"

"Just came to see you."

"At this hour?"

"Yes. Where's Bru?"

"I knew you would ask that. I could imagine you couldn't wait till tomorrow."

"Is he home?"

"Well, he's away at the Master's. I'm sure you knew that. He's gone to attend the Master's son's birthday lunch. I am sorry if that disappointed you."

"Are you sure, Ren?"

"So, you think I'm lying?"

"Not at all. It's just that I have a very different news."

"You are bound to have one."

"I am sorry you have such an opinion."

"What exactly is it?"

"My son, before noon, was passing by the Master's when he heard someone shrieking. He hid behind the bush and all he could see was someone struggling, beating up dust, both his legs tied. Before my son could see any further, a man carried him away."

"So? What shall I make of it?"

"Whatever," Den replied, looking stern and suspicious.

"This is malicious," Ren complained fearfully, "It is unfair to the Master and undermines his special treatment of our family. People like you can think of nothing else."

"I am not thinking, Ren. It is what my son told me he saw. I thought I should inform you," she turned away to leave but added, "Remember, Ren, it's been too long since lunch."

Den hadn't gone too far when Ren screamed after her, "Do you believe all that, Den?"

"Yes."

Ren continued to stare after her.

"I hate to say yes, though," Den said loudly, from the other side of darkness.

That intrigued her. She was now afraid to be alone there in the dark courtyard. She sat pensively in a corner. Could Den be true or simply jealous? She entered her house calmly and walked straight to her husband who had been lying injured on his bed. He was recovering from a bad accident he had recently had. He could no longer hunt for himself. It was the Master who provided the rations. Ren thought it very kind of the Master. For his share of meat he depended on Bru who had lately become an accomplished hunter.

Ren sat next to him and nearly complained, "Bru isn't home yet."

"Calm down, dear," said he patiently.

"Calm down? How do you mean?" she yelled, "Your child isn't home and you preach calm. What kind of a father are you?"

"Sit down dear. There is something you must know."

"There's nothing I want to know. There's nothing I want to hear. Anyway why should you be worried? You've had so many sons and daughters in the past. Just one more won't matter to you. Why should you worry about a fifth wife's child. But for me he is the first of my children and I am worried about him," she thundered. She stormed out of the room and leapt towards the little gate. She stood at the gate. She was afraid to go out but pushing it slowly she strayed out into the dark.

She walked towards the Master's house. On the way, she thought of the times when the Master had been more than kind. He had sent the other two siblings of Bru away to His own sister's place because she also must have been very fond of them. Had it not been for the sake of the Master's loving sister, neither she, nor the kind Master, would've parted with those lovely offspring of hers. And, of late, when a wolf chased her husband Kuk, it was the Master who shot him dead. That's how Bru still had a father.

She reached the Master's orchard. She was tempted to suspect that even Kuk was jealous of Bru. Just yesterday, she remembered, when the Master's son invited Bru to his birthday party, Kuk had come up limping, shamelessly insisting that he be chosen instead. 'Choose' was the word he had used. God! Ren was more embarrassed than angry. How unbecoming of an old father to be jealous of his son! Thank God, the Master still preferred Bru, she thought. She remembered how the Master had ridiculed Kuk, saying, "This one can hardly walk straight. Let it recover first." Thinking about it she smiled a little as she walked further towards her Master's house. 'Of course, the Master wouldn't like a limping sick old fool as a guest at his son's birthday. They would be proud to have the young Bru there among the other distinguished guests and relatives,' she thought.

III – *The Funeral and the Feast*

She could see a well-lit window of the Master's house. She couldn't see anyone though. She climbed up a tree and was able to see the inside of the room. She could see people sitting on a round table, probably eating. She climbed a little higher. Yes, eating. She could see the Master, His wife and a few others. She stretched a little further and was able to see the Master's son. She stretched much further to see who sat next to him, for, that is where Bru must be. But, before she could see any further, she slipped and fell on the ground with a shriek. It was loud enough to alarm a wolf in the bushes. The thought of a wolf in the dark provoked her trembling feet to run homeward. She closed the yard gate behind her, shut the house door, and went straight to Kuk who was still awake.

"Where have you been?"

"Oh, just around here."

"You've been running."

"I saw through the window. The dinner is on. We mistook it for lunch. Let's get over with our dinner as well. He could be home anytime now," she said joyfully.

Kuk's face hanged in despair.

"Ren, dear, I have known these dinners much better than you can imagine."

"God! Have you been to many of these?"

"Ren, it's time you learnt the truth about life. I know it's too early for you to be thinking about all this. You are a kid yourself."

"Tell me, then. How does it feel to be at these dinner tables? You must feel honored."

"One doesn't feel anything there. We go to The Table but once. There's no second time."

She stared at him blankly while he looked out of the window. The long silence led Kuk to believe that she had understood the truth that he couldn't tell bluntly.

"I can understand. It can't happen many times. Look at me. I have never been invited. But Kuk, I have a strong feeling Bru's life won't be like that. You know he is so special."

"Precisely. That's why he went to The Table so early."

"It's because they love him so much."

"They don't love him," Kuk thundered, shaking violently and suddenly.

"They do. And not just Bru but even us to some extent. Didn't the Master shoot the wolf just to save your life? Wasn't that out of affection for you and for us?" she screamed back.

"They don't love anyone," he was still loud, spitting through the corners of his lips, "They save their crops from fire Ren not because they love the crops but simply because they need them. They have spent money on us not because they love us or care for us but simply because they need us for their pleasure."

"You mean the Master saved you from the wolf because He needs you. What use does an old useless thing like you have for anyone?" She stormed out of the room.

IV - A Silent Prayer

She sat outside, behind the closed gate of the yard. Her eyes were fixed on the rickety gate. She would open it as she saw Bru. It was very cold. It was very dark. The night around her was dead. The air, the leaves and branches did not move. Ren was feeling the weight on her eyelids. Pushing them up from time to time she was trying to fix them on the gate. She did not want to miss the sight when Bru would appear at the gate.

She kept herself awake by raking up old memories. The gate had been the same ever since she had been brought there to live with Kuk. For months, she had opened the gate each morning to let Bru out with the first rays of the sun. For days before that she would not let Bru and the two other siblings venture out as they were too young and vulnerable.

She remembered the Master and His son had come the previous day. Bru, Kuk and she were out in the sun. She tried to remember what they had been talking.

"I am going to expand this portion of the farm," the Master had said.

"We already have more than a dozen couples, don't we daddy?"

"Quite. We need more. Many more. The market is expanding amazingly."

"This pair had three of them. Where are the other two?"

"I have gifted the couple to my sister. She wants to start a farm of her own."

"Soon aunt will have as many as us, isn't it daddy?"

"Now, which one do you want for your birthday tomorrow?"

"This one. He's really grown papa. How small he was. He spent most of his time in my palms or on my pillow."

"That's right my boy. I haven't fed them for nothing."

"What about this one daddy?"

"Hurt. The wolf had nearly seized it. I wouldn't have allowed that rascal to get away with it. He had to pay with his life. It hasn't recovered yet. Moreover it's quite a stud. We'll need it for much longer."

Throwing his arms around his son the Master had said, "What do they generally give you at school?"

"It's mostly fish. It's readily available there. I am dying to have some country chicken now."

A powerful gust of wind threw the gate open. Ren woke up. She had been dozing by the gate. She was shivering. Is it Bru? She thought she almost asked it aloud. The wind was blowing. She saw the gate swinging. Is it a wolf? Leaves were falling on the yard. It was dark. It was cold. The night, for her, was dead. At her door, closing her eyes, she shivered, "O Lord! Bless…..all…..that you have created." The gate was swinging in the dark air.

7

Cashmere House

It is eleven in the morning. Mrs. Khan is walking home. She didn't want to stay in the bazaar too long. She must walk home alone though. Of the well nurtured family of five, she is left alone. Two have been claimed by this world and two by the Other.

It was a short visit to the town. At ten it was a reception by the new Lieutenant General of the Northern Command at the Gaiety Theatre on the Mall Road. She had been invited. Mr. Salve, her late husband's private secretary who still owed allegiance to Cashmere House, ensured that she continued to be engaged in the higher circles. Then she walked up to the Trishool Bakers and left a list of things to be sent home. She looked at the new arrivals at the Asia Book House. Then she walked down to the Minerva Book House. Her late husband considered both of them to be as important institutions in the cultural life of Shimla as the Gaiety Theatre or the Mall Road itself. She walked down the Mall Road with conscious grace. Some familiar faces nodded from the either side. Shops. Stores. Showrooms. She walked down Hotel Combermere, watching its sunlit terrace restaurant beginning to crowd with tourists. Children swaying away from their mothers, swinging to one side of the road, or the other. Down the famous photo studios;

Latawa, and then, Bindra; through the huge glass show windows of which were lurking the portraits of erstwhile royals pompously attired, and the eminent townspersons of Shimla of the decades gone by, who were elegantly dressed, peeping out helplessly at the changing times. She offered a *salaam* to the old Mr. Grover, who sat inside one of the studios like the caretaker of a pictorial graveyard. Shelley waved at her from inside the other part of the studio. Behind the dazzling glass wall of the left side of the studio, glittered huge pictures of well preened local politicians in power. They displayed fixed smiles, with haloed backgrounds. Further away from the main window, were the politicians out of power but not out of use, faded from the earlier five years in the sun. It also displayed huge portraits of elaborately dressed men and women. One of the portraits was theirs; Anjumman and her husband, many years ago. She peeped further in, to see if her family portrait was still there. It was. Her husband, her three children and she; all five inside a single frame inside the Bindra Studio. She had a sad smile on her lips; of all the places on earth, this was the only place where her entire family still lived under the same roof.

She walked past the hotel Oberoi Clarke's, through the glass door of which she saw the suave official smiling charmingly. She walked beneath the windows of the Lefroy Chambers, once a favourite place for elegant parties, now often blaring with the melodious noise of film songs. She tottered past the mighty gates of the High Court, Chalet Day School, and the Simla Club.

A few meters short of the Marina Hotel gate, at the centre of a horse-shoe bend, she sat down on a bench, facing the fountains and the waterfall. It was a pool of water with a marble woman in the middle who clung a pot on her out swinging hip, through which poured a stream of white water. She sat facing the pool and the woman with the swing on the hip. She felt anxiously relaxed. Quaasim and she would always sit on the same bench on their short walk back from the school. Leela and Murtaza were in High school and returned home later. She had never sent servants to bring Quaasim home. With the youngest one going to school she had little work at home in his absence.

She always sat here on her walk back from the Mall Road. She remembered Quaasim hiding behind the woman's hips, whom he fondly called white aunt, and then calling out to his mother from behind the white pot. A reluctant smile spread across her lips as she vividly remembered her little boy winking at her from behind the white lady before naughtily jumping into the pool. He had to be taken home with his clothes soaked in water.

Behind the bench on which she sat, that is on the lower side of the road, could be seen the majestic Cashmere House. Remembering Quaasim while sitting on the bench, as she often did, she rested her head on her stretched arm on the shoulder of the bench and looked fondly at her house. Built in the sprawling field below the imposing Oak Over, the chief minister's official residence, Cashmere House was built by her famous and celebrated lawyer husband. The Cashmere House of Intiqab Alam Chaudhry and Anjumman Khannum. Of Leela and Murtaza, the two elder children. Of Quaasim, the much younger and the last of their three children. She saw the red roof of the house. It had been red only for the last three months. It pleased her that people noticed the change. She received a few complementary calls. When the roof had been green for thirty years, people said it matched well with the green color of the roof of Oak Over and the green deodar forest. Now they say it contrasts well with it. The House had a tennis court at the back and a lawn in front. On the west side was a subsequently built two storey attachment which Alam used as his office. Five people sat in the rooms on the ground floor and Alam and his secretaries on the top. This attachment was fondly and famously known as The Edge. Alam has been dead for more than ten years now. She maintained both the floors as such for almost three years before finally donating all the contents.

When a wisp of cold breeze touched her cheek, she realized she had had a little nap. Saliva had reached the end of her lips. She pressed her eyes against her cold arm and adjusted herself on the bench. She smiled at the snacks seller standing nearby and pressed a currency note into his palm. She would often do it. He offered her tea. She said she would have some other day. The man had been very fond of Quaasim and used to offer him something or the other to eat.

She walked along the nicely trimmed hedgerows to the gate of the Cashmere House. She went up to her bedroom. She sat on the sofa. The Edge was an extension into the corner of the front lawn and was entirely visible from her bedroom. It was in The Edge that Alam worked himself to death. Sometimes he slept in the office; living on little food and coffee, and drink and smoke all night.

She sat down, allowing her perspiration to dry up. She could check her mail meanwhile. Husna brought her tea.

"Where is Munna?" she asked with visible irritability.

"*Korat mein.*"

She meant the tennis court. Husna's three year old grandson Mubarak was forbidden to enter the top floor of the house. The unruly Mubarak's frequent ins and outs irked Mrs. Khan enormously. Since his mother was away all day on odd jobs, Husna was allowed to bring him into the compound but he had to stay with Kamal, the gardener, in the outhouse in the tennis court.

The doors of the five bedrooms on the floor were opened each morning and closed in the evening, though they were now no more than ghost chambers as it had been years since anybody slept in them. The largest room, which had been the children's bedroom for years, was swept and cleaned every day. Their crockery was placed in a glass shelf. Various garments of her three children; flannels, coats, raincoats, scarves, shoes, picnic bags, sports uniforms, gloves, handkerchiefs, knickers, wrist bands, writing gloves, caps, frocks, frills, school bags, vests, shoe-laces, travel kits, mufflers, pullovers, cardigans, shawls, sweatshirts, socks, shirts and head bands; were routinely washed, dried, mended – buttoned, zipped, stitched- then ironed and shelved till they are taken out again, week after week, by their own turn. In another rack were football bladders, tennis balls, cricket bats of various sizes, as if the same bat grew from being little to the big one, guitar, shoe laces, skating board, various masks, radio sets, cassettes, flutes and posters of sportspersons, movie stars and that of George Harrison pasted on the wall. She had kept them fondly all these years, not necessarily for this lonely day, not really for this monotonous purpose. Also kept were school report cards, old letters, class test papers and annual photographs. The only thing she had destroyed was Quaasim's medical reports from Dr. Matharoo's clinic. Destroyed along with it was his death certificate because to her he had never died. For her he was always in her lap. She wouldn't allow him to grow more than that. She could always feel him by simply embracing herself with both her lonesome arms. Slowly, she would forgive him.

Adjacent to it was their own, and now out of use, bedroom. The four-poster bed, with its maroon silk canopy, had continued to be slept in for decades till Alam became an indispensable memory. After the two elder children found their own ways in the world outside home, she discontinued to sleep in any of the bedrooms. She slept in the corner of the glazed verandah where she had had a little cot erected for herself. It was in the same corner on the carpeted verandah where Quaasim had spent his last night at the Cashmere House. It was going to be the same verandah where, a few years later, Alam would be kept for the final rest, the night before his burial. Into his closed fist she had rolled a small piece of paper on which were written a few tearful lines for Quaasim, ending with a lovely note for Alam, with whose passing had ended the only life she had known since she last played amid the strewn leaves of the Chinar in Kashmir. Married to Alam at nineteen, the third daughter of the affluent merchant from Pahalgam had left her everything and walked into what was then named Cashmere House. Quaasim had shattered her inner world, Alam wrecked the outer. Leela and Murtaza would then be her eyes to see the world through, her ears to listen the world speak, her crutches of joy. With their going away far from her, she was left alone to converse with shadows; two of spirits and two of humans.

Over the last two years, the Shimla town *wallahs* were quietly given to believe, through very selected channels, that The Edge was to be rented for family residential purpose. Many worthy citizens had politely let Mrs Khan know that they were interested to move in. It had not been allotted to anyone so far: It was not going to be.

Husna brought her a letter. It was from one Mr. Singha, from Keleston. It read: *Thanks for the invitation. I shall feel privileged to be a tenant of The Edge. My wife and I look forward to seeing you anytime soon. Our daughters are particularly excited.*

Mr. Singha was to join an elite club that already had about nine families, the suitors who could afford to pay the yet undisclosed rent of The Edge. Mrs. Khan enjoyed the new social circle she had prepared for herself.

Renovation on. Meanwhile you could come over for lunch with your family next Sunday and have a look.

She would write such letters to them by turn. Some began to be weary of the procrastination but had started to enjoy Mrs. Khan's indulgence. Each of the families was sent sweets on Diwali, delicacies on Eid and greetings on the New Year. Each would also be sent notes such as: *It would be a great help if you could bring your family along next Saturday to suggest minor internal modifications to suit your requirements. You would not be able to leave without dinner though.* Some would be asked about their choice of paints on the walls of the lobby, kitchen or the bedrooms. Weeks later that combination of paints would be changed to accommodate someone else's choice. This was a little galaxy of friends she had nurtured outside the crumbling social citadel of the glorious years of the Alam era, the remnants of which were now reduced to being kind in answering an occasional call and only a few obliged with visits. She took all pains to nurture her new society as a safeguard against her loneliness.

Having had her tea, she sat in front of her computer. She went through her mail. Leela has been in Amsterdam for all the five of her married years. She has had a son. Mrs. Khan receives videos through the internet every week. The child seems to be growing well and rather quickly. She played the video. She watched Leela giving him a bath. It lasted a few minutes. She played the video once again. Mrs. Khan touched the screen. She smeared it with the perspiration of her palm. She played the video yet again. And again. She took her lips to the screen. She kissed him. She pecked the child's tiny hips. She kissed his feet. His cheeks. Leela talked to her son. Leela talked to her mother across the screen, showing her something or the other. Mrs. Khan grabbed the screen with both her hands and hugged the computer, pressing the screen against her cheek. It had been years since she had hugged someone her own. She longed to press a child or a grandchild to her bosom. The computer screen deprived her of that pleasure. It seemed to be a wall that separated her from her loved ones, instead of what it indeed was, a facilitator of their meetings; despite devoid of smell and touch. Slowly, she pushed the computer away, and stretched her arm to catch the phone.

She dialed Leela's number. Oceans away, in another continent, her daughter was woken up.

"Leela!"

"Mamma?"

She spoke nothing for a while.

"Leela!"

"Yes, mamma. Good morning."

She said nothing.

"Mamma, can you hear me? Why don't you say something, mamma?"

"Can I smell him?"

"Mamma?"

"When can I touch him?"

"Oh, mamma!"

"When can I see you, Leela?"

"Mamma, are you………are you crying mamma?"

"Where have you all gone, Leela? Where have you just disappeared?"

"Mamma. Please, don't cry mamma. I love you so much mamma……listen, mamma. Are you there, mamma? Mamma…"

Disappointed she was that her daughter could not give her any assurance of her visit. Disillusioned she was that her life could not afford her any lasting hope of being part of a family, a family that lived together. Murtaza and Anjali could now not be expected to have the sensitivity to measure the bounds of her loneliness. She thought of Alam. She thought of Quaasim. They were closer.

She switched off her phone. She switched off her computer. Switched off her mind. She rested her head upon the desk. She allowed her mind to wander till it began to get solace from remembrance of the years she had left behind.

When she woke up minutes later, she called Husna to let her know that she would have lunch in half an hour. She went downstairs to write a note to one Mrs. Kapoor about the garden work of The Edge to be completed by the end of the season. Her eyes inevitably fell on the envelope she had decided not to open for well over two weeks. It was from Murtaza to his mother:

Mrs. Anjumman Khannum
Cashmere House
Shimla-1

She finally opened it. It read:

Dear mamma, Anjali and I send you a million wishes on your birthday. We promise to be there before Diwali. Full ten days, mamma. Love you.

She couldn't resist a wry smile on reading the *full ten days*, which she thought betrayed condescension. She kept it away. She completed the note to Mrs. Kapoor, and left it in the basket to be taken away by Husna to be posted. She took a small walk in the lawn. She inspected the flower beds and walked on the soft grass. She went in and began to walk upstairs. Halfway up the mahogany staircase, she felt an excruciating pain in her right knee. She couldn't walk further and bent over, pressing her right knee with her fingers. She waited and hoped that the pain would subside. She grabbed the handrail with her other palm to draw support. She sat down on the steps and leaned her head against the banisters.

After a few minutes, when she opened her eyes due to reduced pain, she found her eyes looking at a picture that had become too obvious over the years to be noticed. It was the day Quaasim took seventy six steps across the width of the front lawn for the first time. He was fourteen months and eight days old. More than fifty of the main guests had been invited. Of course, it was Anjumman's birthday as well. Murtaza and Leela led him at the porch. Quaasim walked the entire breadth on his own. He fell down thrice. He even attempted to return after one such fall. But once he had crossed the halfway, he did not look back and walked straight to Alam and Anjumman on the other side. All the guests clapped and cheered him. His springing into his mother's arms was followed by a deafening applause.

Mrs. Khan sat on the steps. She could still hear the applause. She could see the line of guests in the background applauding the first public walk of Intiqab Alam's third and the last child. In the huge picture on the wall, she could see Quasim just three steps away from reaching her. In the background were most of those who counted in town: Aslam Khokhar, Jamail Osman, Dr. Shiva Armani, Shailja Shikhar, Urmila Singh, Som Bannerjee, Anmol Sharma, Devi Dayal Chauhan, Shyama Bhaskar, Yashodhar Samta, Rao Umed, Bernard Hames, Jaya Pardhan, Umesh Dewan, Dr. Gian Chand and many more. Mr. Salve was standing next to the both of them. Quaasim was a second away from leaping into his mother's arms. The photograph, in a four feet by three frame, had been here for the last twenty years.

She got up slowly. How they had celebrated their children's first steps. Now she was left all to herself to mourn and nurse her first tottering ones. She threw another glance at the two other pictures on the wall as if to mock herself. Leela's first day at the kindergarten, sulking away from her mother towards the classroom. Murtaza riding his first cycle at three.

For almost thirty years the roof of the Cashmere House had remained green. Curtains remained hung for years together. Alam's career was meteoric. Children were growing up. Many of these household things were never changed for they were held as paraphernalia of permanence that stubbornly resisted the maddening pace of change and the flight of time. The outside of the entire building remained yellow. She regretted how quickly time was fleeing. Alam, graying and balding, drowned in work; children, growing by inches month after month and, with time, less dependent on her. The abundant space in her life that Alam had encompassed wholly and whole-heartedly, was ceded to the children. She was filled with sadness when Leela's nappies didn't have to be changed. Leaving her at the Kindergarten on the first day was mourned by Anjumman as the first clear signs of separation from the growing up child. The birth of Murtaza filled that longing with hope of lasting happiness. The boy was as darling to her as Leela and grew up with a joyful mixture of scolds, cycle and school. The children would leave at eight in the morning. The morning tennis games of Alam and Anjumman which had stopped around the time of Leela's birth, resumed. Alam used to leave at ten. As the children went to higher classes they returned at four in the afternoon, and Alam at seven. Then was born her last child. The birth of Quaasim was her last effort at arresting time. It was Anjumman's greatest secret wish to stop time there and then, and, forever. Alam, two lovely children and an angel in her lap. As that angel began to crawl, and as the years began to slip by alarmingly under her feet, Anjumman's desperation began to push the boundaries of expectation towards insane realms. In all desperation, she prayed frantically that the wheels of the chariot of this heartless deity would cease to move, to build a little temple for this deity of Time at the porch of her magnificent Cashmere House and chant into His ears her greatest prayer- stay! Stay here. I shall worship you forever!

But now were different times. Anything that stood for permanence of any sort only threatened with the dreadful monotony of existence; it magnified the sickening loneliness of Cashmere House and its sole occupant. Shades of that loneliness had appeared from time to time; when Leela began to wear her clothes herself, when Murtaza no longer needed her help in mounting his bicycle, and when Quaasim became grown up enough to no longer ask questions like why he didn't have a tail like a monkey, why a cauliflower was not called a tree or when he ceased to be surprised that his mother was once a child and had parents too. Darker shades of loneliness cast themselves upon her cheerful skies when Quaasim was a boy enough not to throw himself flat on the trafficless Mall Road near the Chalet Day school demanding the airplane that flew miles above them under the clear blue Shimla sky, the plane she had pointed out in order to amuse him. Perennial loneliness began the day they brought Quaasim home from school with high fever. All the family nursed him. That night, he slept in the glazed verandah. She wet his feet, thighs, palms and forehead with cotton dipped in cold water, throughout that long merciless night. In the morning they took him to Dr. Matharoo's clinic. He showed little signs of recovery. She sat by him for three days and three nights at Dr. Matharoo's. Leela and Murtaza would come from school every afternoon and play with him. Alam came late from office and stayed till the early hours of the next day. On the last of the three nights, Quaasim slept in his mother's lap. He never opened his eyes again. He never came home. Staring at the portraits with an open mouth and open eyes she moaned, "Quaasim........ Quaa..aassim." She didn't want to burden Quaasim with the question but still looked at the pictures and asked, almost scornfully - where have you all gone?

Husna quietly walked down the large staircase and helped Mrs. Khan walk up to the living room, quietly informing her that the lunch was ready. She instructed Husna to wait, and after thinking for a while said, "I want to eat in the dining room, Husna."

Husna had to make the necessary arrangements. Now that Mrs. Khan was all alone it was only when there were guests in the house that the dining room was used, though plates and cutlery would be laid out each morning ceremonially. It would be wound up each evening after dinner. Amid the noisy sounds of clanking dishes on the table, Mrs. Khan felt herself to be with her family. Husna had got perfectly used to carrying out the detailed empty rituals. The silver dining sets and the cutlery of the first two days of the week had to be replaced by the magnificent china with motifs of yellow flowers. Towards the weekend it was supposed to be steel. It provided the desolate empress of Cashmere House a sense of normalcy and a busy routine. Of course that did not enable her to breathe life into the now somber dining room. She could not fill the other four seats on the table nor could she bring back the kids who had marked their own plates distinctly and continued to eat in them till they needed them no more.

For her solitary meals, she had placed a little table in the corner of the large kitchen. Different colored cups were used each day; from the morning tea to the evening juice, accompanied by an appropriate and a rapidly changing combination of plates, saucers and sets of spoons, knives and forks. Curtains too. If it were yellow cotton with red motifs this week, it has to be blue velvet drapes the next.

Today, she wanted to have lunch in the dining room, even though all by herself. Lunch was laid out. The table was for six. She sat where she always did, with Quaasim beside her. She sipped some water and Husna went to the kitchen. Before touching any food she got up and walked to the wall of the room. There were five photographs. Alam and Anjumman. Beneath, Leela Murtaza Quaasim. She touched them all, one by one. She put her cheek on Quasim. Her cheek cooled against the glass of the portrait. She walked back to the table. She could not sit down. She stood at the chair, gazing at the floor. She caught the table cloth. It absorbed the moisture of her palms. She held the cloth firmly. She looked at the floor with sharper eyes. She wanted to see Alam at the head of the table. Murtaza and Leela in front. Then Quasim and she. She did not want to eat alone. Why should she? She's been through years of dining alone. She continued gazing at the floor. She pulled the cloth slightly. The crockery tittered, and so did the candle stand. Her view of the floor blurred. She felt she could hear her children at the table. They were chirping and, with their spoons, beating their plates. She opened her eyes and looked at the table and saw no one. She smirked. She saw the rumples on the tablecloth. She had space. She wanted to people it. Her wishes assumed gigantic proportions.

Grasping the table cloth tightly in her weakening fists she felt she would have liked to spread out and fill that entire space. She shut her eyes tightly and took a sharp loud breath. With those tight fists of hers she thought she could uproot the trees and dig a fountain there, dismantle the garden walls and scratching with her nails spread it by digging it into acres of forests, with her anxious palms, powered by the madness of her monotonous existence and loneliness she would have liked to push all the walls of the dining hall into one corner and frenzily hug her loved ones far and further while shattering the walls of the temple of the deity of Time at her porch and scream into his indifferent ears - go away… go away - hoping that the next round of time might have the possibilities of some joy, she, with a sudden jolt, pulled the entire tablecloth away with such lightning insanity that the china flew up in the air and crashed, splashing the contents on the floor and before she buried her sobbing face into a huge bundle of the white table cloth clutched tightly into her unforgiving fists she shrieked: "Where have you all gone?" and flung herself helplessly on the floor while Husna came rushing and stood frozen by the door.

Mr. Salve came at three. He walked in with the familiarity of years. He still had the habit of knocking at the door before entering the room. She would not say 'come in' and he would walk in and sit on the sofa. She looked at him, barely acknowledging his presence. He continued to sit.

"Not well, ma'am?"

She just shook her head and meeked, "all right."

Mr. Salve sat patiently. He looked at her but her eyes were closed. It was the first time that he had seen her depressed. There had been worse times, he knew. He knew all. He knew her. He began to get conscious of his presence. Her eyes were shut.

"Are you tired?"

She did not answer. He looked at her constantly and her eyes were closed.

"It's nothing, Alok."

She did not open her eyes.

He sat for the next fifteen minutes without moving. The initial confusion turned to sympathy. The sympathy then turned to embarrassment. After almost half an hour in the chair he got up. He went near her. Their minds had a thin haze between them. It helped. It made life simpler and bearable. He did not want to clear it. He knew she too wanted to protect the haze through which they could not see each other more clearly, across which it became easier to walk away. On the other side of the haze it was easier to be yourself. Salve could feel her sleeping tenderly, even though he sensed the heaviness of her eyes. He left the room quietly.

She woke up at five. She called out for Husna who had been waiting outside the door. She was asked into the room.

"Sit."

Husna felt very awkward. Though she had greatly benefitted from Mrs. Khan's generosity but it had mostly been devoid of any personal touch. She saw her ruffled hair. She noticed the haunted gaze in her eyes. She sat timidly in front of her.

"Will you comb my hair?"

Husna smiled. She knew that her mistress had never asked her such a service. She collected the beautiful large comb but was not sure where to sit. Mrs. Khan invited her to sit behind her and she began to comb *begum saheba's* beautiful long hair with visible care and fondness.

"Where is Munna?"

"At home with his mother. She came at four."

"Is he mischievous at home?"

"Very much. It's difficult to keep things safe from him."

"From tomorrow let him play in the lawn. He need not be in the tennis court at the back all day."

"But he can be very destructive. Once you allow him, it will be difficult to keep him away from there. He will pluck all the leaves from some plants and all the petals from the others."

"Let him."

"*Begum Saheba?*"

"Yes. I have been too unkind to the little child. I'll instruct him how to keep a good garden. I am sure he will learn."

"As you wish *Begum Saheba*. I would still warn you."

"Don't worry. Please bring me some tea and something to eat."

Husna Biwi got up. Before she left, she looked at Mrs. Khan and said, "Are you really fine?"

"I am perfectly all right. Don't worry at all."

As Husna reached the door, Mrs. Khan said, "From tomorrow feed Munna in the kitchen. He will not eat in the tennis court."

Husna stared at Mrs. Khan in surprise and slowly closed the door behind her.

She sat in her bed waiting for her tea. It had been drizzling while she was asleep. The garden below her window was wet. Flowers were soaked in rain water and leaves were dripping. Mist was beginning to rise through the thick forest. She switched on the phone. There was a recorded message. She played it. It was Leela's voice.

"Hello, maa! Are you fine? Why is your phone off, maa? There is a surprise. We are coming home next week. Hussein is taking a month off. Murtaza and Anjali are joining us from Pune. They will start a new office in Shimla. Within two years they will shift it there entirely. His office will be housed in The Edge, maa. Anjali and the kids will give you company. They have had this plan for quite some time. Wanted to give you a surprise. Don't tell them I have disclosed it to you. Love you, maa."

She smiled. She smiled at the curtains. At the garden, and the flowers. At the forest and the stars, most of which were yet to come out. She dialed a familiar number, "Mr. Salve, could you kindly join me for lunch on Sunday."

"Pleasure would be mine."

"Some important discussions regarding The Edge. Very important."

"Okay, ma'am."

"Your family too. All are invited."

"Thanks very much."

8

Maidens of Trafford House

"This is the backside of Birdwood," showed to the two young women, Debon Roy, a large canvas which had been completed recently.

"You mean this is how the school building looks from the other side," said one of them, smiling.

"Yes. Precisely. That's what I mean. Yes."

"That is indeed marvelous, Mr. Roy."

"My name is Debon Roy….Oh…yes…I just realize you know that. I am the art teacher here."

"Don't you realize we might know that as well," said one the two women as she continued, "Mr. Roy, I am Jacqueline." She shook hands with him.

"My name is Rosalind," said the other one.

"I am so glad to meet you in person, Rosalind and Jacqueline. I remember the Headmaster announcing your names yesterday, but till now I couldn't tell one from the other. Rosalind and Jacqueline. Nice," Debon Roy couldn't hide his pleasure that the two should have shown so much interest in him within two days of joining the new school.

"You might take longer still to be able to tell us from each other," said one of them.

"Mr. Roy, we've been visiting the departments to know our colleagues," said the other, who seemed more charitable.

"I see. How many have you been to so far?"

"Almost all by now, including the school press. Though we are yet to go to the department of electrical and engineering works."

"That may not be necessary," said Roy, as they all laughed.

"Could we take a round of the gallery, Mr. Roy?"

"Most certainly. My pleasure. May I escort you?"

"That would be so nice of you."

As they went from one painting to the next, they ceased to be a single group. Rosalind and Jacqueline stopped at paintings that differed from each other in their very nature and Roy didn't know where to stand. He went from one to the other, uttering something to each. He was happy that it would take long and placed an order at the Master's Common Room for tea. By the time they got over with the tour of the art department gallery, the tea had reached his office.

"How many years have you been at Sanawar, Mr. Roy?"

"I joined this school five years ago. That was as soon as I got over with graduation in Dhaka."

"Mr. Roy, do you teach art as a mere profession or is there some other reason? I mean is it a mere job or a passion?"

"It is the latter. Please forgive me but you are…"

"Jacqueline."

"Yes Jacqueline, it is a passion."

"The passionate Mr. Roy," remarked the other.

Roy, embarrassed, continued, "I busy myself doing just that. There's not much else I can do other than paint."

"We can see that. Art teachers normally don't paint to that extent."

"The hall next to the main gallery had been lying unused when I joined. It had housed the ceramics department. They moved into a new building many years ago and the hall remained locked up. It's as big as the main gallery where you saw students' paintings displayed. The headmaster obliged by allowing me to use it for my own purpose."

"And this is your office."

"Yes, but I don't usually spend time sitting here. I could easily be found in the other hall when there is no class to engage."

The tea continued.

"Many classes to engage?"

"Only two to three during the class hours, that is from morning to lunch. Then there are hobby classes after lunch."

"Mr. Roy I see that most of your paintings follow a rather regular pattern. They are more conventional in nature. You follow nature, or reality if I may say, more or less as it is. You don't really break the pattern."

"Yeeeess…and…"

"Jacqueline."

"Yes Jacqueline. I convey things without necessarily meddling them up with my own views on the subject. Whatever little I may have in my mind regarding my subject, I normally allot it to the background or the surroundings, without distorting the theme."

"You don't believe much in what a modern artist may find interesting," said the other one who would inevitably be Rosalind.

"Modern art shocks me. It may suit some as a form of expression but to me is not very satisfying."

Tea continued.

"It violates harmony that nature bestows upon its creation. It is like watching a corpse whose skin has been ripped off. What we then see is reality, yes, but what to do with the reality that serves no purpose. Not only is it not aesthetic, it also gives an undue advantage to the artist to be interpreted into varying meanings, depending on the order or even the disorder in the mind of the beholder."

The tea continued, and so did he.

"It also makes it easier for anyone to qualify as an artist even if one knows just about enough to splash colors along lines, circles or even haphazardly. Shades of paint, if not woven into a meaningful whole, is something like mud slung on the canvas. A piece of art need not necessarily qualify as great simply because it is complex, or even vague, because that complexity or the vagueness may not add up to anything desirable."

"It would be both naïve and audacious to counter your views on the subject Mr. Roy but many pieces of modern art are truly expressive even though they might seem to be complex at first, especially to the uninitiated. I can tell from my own experiences, after a lot of exposure to art." It was Rosalind.

"I do not intend to say that all are such. What I mean is to warn the least suspecting of admirers against artistic debauchery. After all there should be a discernible difference between a riddle and art. Of course, on rare occasions of genius, what appear to be curious may touch the high pinnacle of art. Rare, indeed, but true. But only a few achieve that sublimity, while most of the other imitators drag that rarity into everydayness and trivialize the stroke of genius, which, I must reiterate, is rare, especially in modern art. It is similar in music I might say."

The tea was over.

"There are two processes at work simultaneously, Mr. Roy. In our age arts have become accessible to larger sections of the society. These arts have undergone vast changes in order to cater to the ever growing patronage from myriad sections of the society, to the majority of whom they had been inaccessible for long. Also, for similar reasons, the practice of most arts has gone out of the hands of a selected few, into the hands of many of those who would never have had such opportunity in an earlier age. Many of them have proven to be truly gifted. As a result of both these processes, arts have undergone unprecedented upheavals, improvisations, silent revolutions and enhancement of capacity for tumultuous interpretations," said Jacqueline.

"True, and at the same time it has had to undergo a reasonable amount of trivialization as well. I do not wish to risk being taken to be pedantic but I do feel that complexity in art should only be encouraged or indulged into, if, and I must emphasize, only if, it promises to involve more faculties of the human sensitivity and serve a larger purpose, aesthetics may be one of them, if not the only one. What I detest is a piece of art that resembles something and is nothing, a figure without a soul. Most of what claims to be art, which is indeed taken to be modern art, is nothing but a snaggled ensemble of attitudes. It inflicts upon ordinary minds a forced intelligibility that they pretend to possess from within and not, what it, in reality is, a helplessly acquired trait, to express which they secretly wait for the other people to give their expressions first. This compelled cultivation of cultural understanding is so painfully internalized, lest they be taken to be brutes, less culturally sensitive or less discerning," Roy said.

It had been a while since the tea got over.

"Quite agreeable views, Mr. Roy, but…," Rosalind said.

"That's not all though. I must admit, the modern art has provided a much needed break from the linear symmetry of normalcy that much of art has followed for most of its history," Roy said.

Roy paused, and noticed how well and quickly he could express the thoughts that entered his mind just then for not many had been pondered over but did reflect what his mind as an artist had been fundamentally made of. He continued:

"The problem with conventional art, however, is that it follows life or reality meekly. Conventional art conceals the incongruence and variation of human emotions beneath the even layering of their skin by masterfully taming the senses into compliance. Modern art, thankfully, rips that snobbery apart and tears away the inner self of the portrayed, into a proportional projection."

The discussion continued till it had been long since the tea was over.

"We should be leaving now or we would be late for dinner," said one of them. Roy had lost track of which name belonged to whom.

"Indeed. Thank you, Mr. Roy for your hospitality and for sharing with us your views on art. I'll be thinking about it."

"There's something you wanted to say," he said, pointing to Rosalind.

"Oh, yes. But…I've forgotten I'm afraid," she replied. They laughed loudly.

He was pleased to let them go as he was at loss of things to talk about. He saw them off at the gate. It was getting dark. He knew they were going for dinner. He knew he would be going for dinner too. He knew, all too well, that all of them were late. He still spared for himself a few minutes at his desk, and his opening remark to the two new piano teachers from London. *This is the backside of Birdwood.* Nothing could have matched that in lack of elegance, and that in the opening of the first conversation with new acquaintances, made it worse.

He locked his office in a haste and paced towards the Master's Common Room for dinner. On his way to the MCR, as the common room was called, he thought of them. Two young women from London joined as piano teachers every year in February. They would stay on till December till the school closed for winter vacation. In his last five years at Sanawar, Roy had seen ten of them, but he had not had any walk up to him and be known. He had not known any of them, not beyond polite familiarity. Rosalind and Jacqueline were exceptional in going about all the departments to know their colleagues.

When he entered the dining hall, the bearer wasn't pleased to see a new visitor at eight. In a corner of the hall he saw the two Englishwomen dining quietly. But for the three of them the hall was filled with the noise of the attendants collecting the dishes from the tables.

He was nervous while choosing a table to sit. Should he be sitting with them? Would that amount to intrusion? He knew he wanted to sit all by himself but was afraid lest it look snobbish. In the turmoil of the confusion he planted himself firmly on a chair in another corner. As the bearer brought him his dinner, one of them called out, "Mr. Roy, why not join us here." He was obliged to acknowledge their presence in the hall by "Oh, I see, thanks, sure," and found his way to their table.

"This is a wonderful place. Really," said one of them.

"It is," said he.

The two of them reshuffled and all three rearranged themselves into a circular triangle around the wooden table. Mr. Roy treated himself to geometrical naivety, assuming himself at the centre, while the two Englishwomen flanked him, equi-distantly.

As they were dining, Debon Roy saw that it would make a beautiful painting. He tossed in his mind the various ways in which it could be made to look like a classic. A gentleman dining with two women in a hall that has no one else. He imagined to give it a Victorian touch. He dressed them up in evening gowns made of soft colorful silk, one wearing blue and the other purple. He did their hair appropriately. The one he thought to be the quieter one was given an elegant swept back with a centre parting and a low bun. The other's hair was done with a classic Victorian bun with side-swept bangs and curly fringes. A chandelier loomed over them and eleven candles were lit on a crystal Italian candle holder and placed on the table. He had them look at him endearingly while he bestowed upon them his enchanting blush. He was painting a necklace around the low neckline of one of them while the other said, "Where do you live, Mr. Roy?"

Roy blushed, after the indulgence of the painting, but soon pulled himself out of the spell.

"Oh, me? I see. Well, Garden City."

"Garden City. Fascinating! How far is it?"

"It's a fifteen minute walk from where we are."

"How's the place?"

"Lovely. I don't know why it's called Garden City. If I may warn you there is neither a garden nor a city. A lovely place nonetheless. It's a huge beautiful structure which has eight spacious flats. I occupy one of them."

He immediately realized the folly of *I occupy one of them*. It was too obvious.

"Isn't that far?"

"Not really, if one takes into account how much walking one needs to do in this place. Most places where one needs to be are usually very far from where one is."

"That's interesting."

"You must be staying at the Trafford Courts."

"Yes. How could you be so sure?"

"That's where the new piano teachers stay."

"Interesting, isn't it?" said one of them, looking at the other.

"Rosalind and Jacqueline," he continued, noticing that his growing familiarity with them was assisting his eloquence, "the allotment of residences at this place has a certain scheme to them. When you join as a bachelor... male, you are allotted a two room flat at the Stone View, which is below the school hospital and has four flats in all. I spent three years there. I am still a bachelor but they have new ones to occupy the Stone View. The Trafford Courts is the female equivalent of the Stone View except that you have to walk much longer to the Stone View while it takes just a minute to the Trafford Courts."

After they had had their dinner the three of them walked down the stoney stairway under a covered passage to The Ledge. In his immense joy of being with the two of them, Roy announced, nearly patronizingly, "Do you know, Jacqueline and Rosalind, this lovely place, lovely for no particular reason though, is called The Ledge."

"Nice. Lovely for no reason?"

"None in particular, I think," said the other one.

"It's lovely because it is lovely," Roy said, "need there be any reason?"

"That's lovely."

"What?"

"That remark of yours."

The three sat at the Ledge.

"Want to come over to the Trafford House Mr. Roy?"

"Some other day. Thanks. I would love to."

Within minutes the two had reached the Trafford House and Roy was on his way to the Garden City.

When Roy tried to sleep that night, he couldn't quite get over the raw taste that emanated from his-Trafford Courts being the female equivalent of the Stone View-observation. He felt it was utterly unnecessary. He was glad on the whole. He slept well that night. He saw in his dreams that the two, in Victorian gowns and decent jewellery, went to sound sleep too.

Another week passed by. They met occasionally, but did not dine together. By the second week of March, the school schedule had settled well into a hectic activity. One day Roy found on his table a hand written card that requested his company at a little party that was to be hosted by Rosalind and Jacqueline at six that evening at the Trafford House. He did not know whether to discuss it with any of his colleagues as he wasn't sure who else had been invited. Being in the art block, he was mostly away from the classroom teaching staff.

At six that Saturday evening, he was happy to see himself going down the MCR staircase to The Ledge from where he took left, walked a few steps to the lower entrance to the Central Dining Hall, the CDH, and then walked down more than a century old stairs of stone that led to the Trafford Courts. In his more than five years at the more than a century and a half old Lawrence School at Sanawar, Mr. Debendra Nath Roy arrived for the first time at the Trafford House, in front of which was a tennis court. There may have been two in the past. He walked up the wooden staircase to the wide verandah on the first floor and was greeted by Rosalind and Jacqueline. Already sitting there was an elder couple whom one of the girls introduced as some Robinsons from the British High Commission in New Delhi who had driven up to Sanawar just to meet the two of them. He noticed that the girls called the gentleman uncle.

After exchanging pleasantries with the Robinsons, he felt absorbed into the surroundings. The wooden pillars supporting the roof of the wide verandah were covered by the creepers that grew out of huge golden metal pots. The three broad wooden arches had baskets hanging down them, with flowers and long branches with leaves that spread around extensively, forming a penetrable wall of leaves and flowers, leaving ample spaces for sunlight to filter in. As

Mr. Robinson busied himself wiping his spectacles clean, Mrs. Robinson said to Roy, "How long have you been here, Mr. Roy?"

"Five years, ma'am."

"Reasonably long for one of your generation to be staying at a place," remarked Mr. Robinson.

"There are many around here who've stayed longer. Of course, most of them are married and have children."

"And what is more important," Roy continued, "this place gives you the chance to be alone if you choose to."

"Why should you choose to be alone dear," said Mrs. Robinson sympathetically, "and at this age?" Just then came out from the room one of the two girls, carrying a tray of snacks. She sat down opposite Roy and said to her visitors "Oh, did I tell you, Mr. Roy is a fine painter."

"I see," replied Mrs. Robinson with a smile.

"I am glad to know that, Mr. Roy. I am fond of artists," said her husband.

"Are you, uncle?"

"Yes, Rosalind. I should have thought you knew that."

What got Roy immediately interested was that there was an opportunity to know the girls; to be able to tell one from the other.

"Thank you, sir. That's truly encouraging," said Roy.

"In fact, I had wanted to be a musician and not a file pushing bureaucrat that I ended up as. But to be able to do what you want to, takes some bold steps at the right time…. Now, at this stage of my life, even if I take a thousand steps back in time, I won't be able to find the spot where I willingly lost my way."

"Oh, that is so poetic darling," said his wife with a patronizing smile.

"And, if I somehow succeeded in finding it, I may not be able to recognize myself."

"Coffee," and one of the shees placed the tray bearing five mugs on the table.

"And the greatest tragedy - even if I did, there would be nothing I could do about it."

"Painful," said his wife.

"Isn't it?"

The coffee mugs were on the table.

"Are you girls serious about your music?"

"Yes, uncle," said one or the other of the two girls. Roy would glance at each one of them as their names were called from time to time to see each respond to her name.

"That's right," said the other, "that's why we opted for this assignment at Sanawar as we thought this trip to India would enrich our learning."

"How long do you intend staying here darling?" asked Mrs. Robinson.

"Our term ends in December."

"And then?" asked Mr. Robinson.

"Back."

"I would rather you considered spending some more time here in India," he said. "Travel all over the north. Go south, and the great West. Don't forget the east and the north-east. Add as much to your senses as you are capable of. Breathe in this air and extract music out of it," Mr. Robinson continued.

Both Rosalind and Jacqueline nodded in agreement and appreciation.

Roy meanwhile acquainted himself with the sight of both the women that he had learnt to distinguish from one another during the conversation. As it grew dark, several little bulbs of yellow light began to shimmer in as many baskets of flowers that hung from the wooden arches of the wooden verandah. It looked like a little paradise in which sat a few people who had begun to sip their drinks.

Dinner started at nine. By then they had talked about a whole lot of things.

"So, Mr. Roy, how many paintings have you done so far?"

"Around forty, Mr. Robinson."

"Ready?"

"Yes, for an exhibition in Delhi next year."

"Splendid."

"Thanks."

"Was the one you showed us that day one of them?" asked Jacqueline with a smile.

"No, no," Roy brushed it away with his hand, "That's been done for the junior school show next month."

He couldn't help bring to his mind the disastrous *backside of Birdwood* remark.

"I don't do that sort of stuff. Not that I don't approve of it."

"Did you have to fight your way to follow your heart?" asked Mr. Robinson, as he sat up and then leaned forward towards Roy, "I mean did you have to go against your folks in your choice of career?"

"In case you did, Mr. Roy, you are a hero in my husband's eyes."

"I did. Thanks, ma'am." He went on as the others listened.

"I went to a boarding school in Darjeeling. My family had huge stakes in the tea gardens there, along with an ever expanding real estate enterprise in Calcutta where we lived. By the time I left school I knew I had to be a painter. When I announced it to my parents they were heartbroken. My father suggested that I could be a painter in the tea gardens once I joined as a manager but that was only after completing my business studies. I was sent to a business school in Bombay. I was given a car by my father to give me a feel of how comfortable things would be in later life if I followed his path. Within two months I sold the car and joined an art college in Dhaka. The Bangladesh capital offered me a new life; friends, teachers and a promise of a great career. I used to live in a hostel. Only my mother knew about it. It was going on well till I ran into my father one day and he has never spoken to me since."

"So sorry," said Mrs. Robinson.

"Wow! That's like a man. Sorry about how your father may have felt but I'm really happy for you. How did you end up here?" asked Mr. Robinson, who seemed to be impressed with the story.

"My teacher at the college in Dhaka had taught at Sanawar in the 1960s. He recommended the school to me. I could work here for a few years before I establish myself as a professional painter."

Conversation jumped from one topic to another, including some war anecdotes from Mr. Robinson, who remembered them from time to time, absentmindedly.

"Don't you go home, or speak to your folks sometimes?" asked Jacqueline, looking straight at Roy.

"I go home and meet my mother. I meet my father though he doesn't speak to me. I can understand that. My elder brother and he look after the business. I haven't been home for three years now. I speak to my mother on the phone."

"Do you think you'll patch up with your father?" asked Rosalind.

"We're going to invite him to inaugurate the exhibition in Delhi next year. I am sure he will be glad to see my hard work of years. Also, he will realize that I would've been no use to him in business."

The remark was followed by a mild laughter. Mr. Robinson laughed out rather loudly.

"When I was in your position Mr. Roy, I had nearly joined a musical group in Leicester. Those were different days. My father wanted me to enroll in the army and defend the Realm, mostly away from the shores. He himself had been a war veteran. I could not refuse for I thought it was the will of England that my father had voiced. I thought a few years commission in the military would help me gain some experience. But a war later, I had been completely de-sensitized. By the time I left the service I had little of that musical sensibility left in me. It is not to suggest that it happens to all or many in the armed services. But it did happen to me. I joined the High Commission thereafter." Then Mr. Robinson fell into a silence.

"Let me tell you all," remarked Mrs. Robinson, "he's doing exceptionally well there. This is his last posting. He retires in two years. He's going to join a band of musicians called *The Surreals* in Kenya. By the way he plays the saxophone really well."

That cheered Mr. Robinson to some extent.

It was ten thirty and the hosts had cleared the table. Robinson lit a smoke and it was followed by everyone. The tiny bulbs, in their baskets, shimmered ever brightly, as if responding to the cool breeze of the hills that had begun to blow.

"Could I have coffee, Rosalind, before I leave," said Roy, surprised at his growing familiarity with them.

"Sure," she said, and left for the kitchen.

Before they had finished their smoke, she was back with coffee for everyone. Conversation, lazy and animated, lasted till Mr. Robinson declared, "We shall call it a day, folks. Come on darling, time to leave," he said looking at his wife.

"Whereto, sir?" asked Roy, who had no intention of leaving or let anyone else.

"To Kasauli. We have a hotel room there."

As Mr. Robinson stood on top of the wooden staircase, he looked back and spoke in a loud voice, "Look folks, there are innumerable particles of human experience that are floating in the air, most of which get lost to eternity. It is the ones with a finer sensibility who extract them out of – thin air - if I may say. It is the artist who simplifies and enriches them. A musician gives them a voice, an artist gives them a shape and a poet gives them expression. God bless you kids."

The car could be heard speeding away in the dark. Roy lit a smoke and resting his head on the chair, blew circles of smoke above him. Rosalind and Jacqueline joined him. No one spoke for those few minutes during which it seemed each one was pondering over what had happened and all that had been said.

Jacqueline looked at Roy and asked, "Mr. Roy…"

"Yes…Jacqueline," he smiled at her, possibly for he knew their names now.

"I want to ask you something," she said, looking away and narrowing her eyes.

"Yes…," he said, inviting the possible question.

"Mr. Roy…, what are the genuine concerns of art?"

He nearly blushed, "Genuine concerns of art! Concerns of art…That's interesting Jacqueline." He continued to focus on his smoke.

"For me…it is to…to depict the beauty and the sublimity of a human being and the human nature. I focus on the aesthetic part of art. I care little about reality, if it does not appeal to me aesthetically."

"Is it the indifferent artist, then?" said Rosalind.

"Indifferent may be, but in a limited sense of the word. I'm stubbornly indifferent to many cares of the world, even if they are starkly real or compellingly appealing to humanity. They would appeal to me only aesthetically, if they will at all."

"Would you then ignore many attributes of human nature?"

"Let me put it plainly. Beauty of human nature or form appeals to me in a way that no magnitude of pain or intensity of human sorrow can."

"What about the aesthetics of pain or sorrow?" asked Jacqueline.

"I would find it difficult or even irrelevant to trace beauty in either sorrow or bliss. I might respond to such emotions out of sheer duty if I were the only one of my species left on this earth. But there are many, most of them much more gifted than I am, in order to render service to humankind. Therefore, I feel free to follow my heart."

"I admire that conviction, Mr. Roy," remarked Jacqueline.

"Thanks. I have pulled this concept a little lower, that is, towards myself. I don't burden it with too much obligation where poet philosophers make it sublime and put it at par with the truth. For me it is simple. Beauty is in being. Beauty is in longing. Beauty is merely in being beautiful. Beauty is in itself sublime. It is the manifestation of the sublime."

"Mr. Roy I gather this place, tucked away in these beautiful hills, has given you a great opportunity to accomplish your task," said Jacqueline.

"That's true."

"But doesn't it sometimes make you lonely? Or you have quite a society here?"

"There is a vibrant society here that sees to it that each member has a great time but as you may have noticed by now that I am not really a part of it. It is the result of a deliberate effort on my part though."

"Thanks for making concessions for us," said Rosalind.

"You took pains. Also, you are artists like me."

"Otherwise, this place is full of trees, scattered old and lovely buildings, endlessly connected roads, covered passages and pavements," Jacqueline said.

"And ghosts," said he.

"Ghosts? Are there really?" exclaimed Rosalind.

"Mr. Roy?" screamed Jacqueline.

"You'll scare me. Don't worry. There are just a handful of buildings and roads at Sanawar that do not have ghosts associated with them. You are fortunate. The Trafford House is…"

"The Trafford House is…?"

"Is one of them. That is…without ghosts."

"Are you saying it out of some obligation to us?"

"Not at all. By the way isn't it quite natural for a place which has been inhabited for more than a century and a half, to have its share of lost souls? Almost all of them are related to the school. It has as many as three graveyards to start with."

"Are you going to tell us some of the stories?"

"Not now. It's getting late and I have to go. All the way to the Garden City."

"What about staying here, if you don't mind?" said Rosalind. He couldn't help blushing, "I don't mind but it would be tragic to lose my job on account of some scandal."

"It won't get to any scandal Mr. Roy," Jacqueline said, smiling.

"We could only hope so. How I wish I had brought my car up here. I didn't know it would be so late."

"You don't use it often?"

"I prefer to walk. Most people here do."

He teetered down the wooden staircase, "Thank you Jacqueline. Thank you Rosalind. Goodnight Rosalind. Goodnight Jacqueline. Goodnight."

Early next morning Debon Roy's door was knocked hard. He ignored it. The pounding on his door wouldn't stop. He woke up very reluctantly, opened the door and saw his neighbor Raunaq Singh, the Soccer coach, at the door.

"Morning, Chatterjee. Sleeping? Still?"

"I was, till you hammered the door. Not now, of course."

"I see. That means I haven't disturbed you. Good. I am back from my walk. I didn't see you doing your butterfly exercises in your lawn you see. I thought you were ill or something."

"I am fine. Nothing wrong really. Thanks."

"O mention not oye. Get ready quickly. Time for breakfast now."

He locked his door at half past seven and pushed the keys under a flower pot. He used to carry his residence keys to his office till he forgot them there many times and had to walk back to the art department in order to fetch them. He was joined by Raunaq Singh and his equally muscular wife Priya, the girls' basketball team coach who were waiting for him at the gate of the Garden City compound.

"Come quickly oye Chatterjee, we are late."

"Coming."

"He's not Chatterjee. How many times I have told you. You don't change your bad habits," his wife said sharply.

"Oye Guddy, all bangaaleez are Chatterjee Bannerjee or something. I did my training in Guwahati you see. I know all bangaaleez. And also, calling a bangaali bhai Chatterjee is not a bad habit."

"There's no point arguing with you."

"Ha ha. I thought you had realized that by now you see," he said, winking at Roy.

They walked up the steep road that wound up the hill.

"Slept late last night Dwinder?" said Raunaq Singh.

"Yeah. Quite late."

"Painting?"

"Yes. Painting."

"Good time pass. But quite boring actually. I listen to music or play cards. Anyway, it's your choice. No one can challenge that, you see."

"He's not Dwinder even," shot his wife, throwing angry glances at her husband.

"O, how does it matter yaar? A friend is a friend," he said, hugging the lean Roy rather enthusiastically. What was a cheerful outburst for Raunaq was almost violence for Roy.

"A friend is a friend and even a name is a name," she wouldn't give up.

"Oye Guddy yaar, you don't know these young people. What is Debunn by the way? He has made Debunder into a shortcut Debunn. What is that yaar Dwinder?"

"It is his name," she stressed loudly.

"Of course, I know. It is not mine. My name is Raunnaq," he thundered with laughter.

"Then who are you to decide what it should be," she stared at him as they continued to walk up the tiring slope.

Raunaq hardly heard his wife's last bit and put his arm around Roy's shoulder.

"Where?" said Raunaq softly.

"Pardon?"

"Pardon? What?"

"You asked- where?"

"Yes, yes. Where were you painting?"

"At home."

"No, before you reached home?"

"At the gallery."

"What time did you leave?"

"Quite late. Around nine."

"And you reached home at one?"

Roy felt that he was out of breath. He didn't look Raunaq in the eye. He didn't know what to say.

"Didn't I tell you darling," said Raunaq to his wife, "that look Dwinder is coming home so late. It was one o'clock, don't you remember?"

She didn't show much interest, and said, "I don't remember the time."

They had come half way from the Garden City. Just then, Roy found out that he didn't have his office keys.

"Oh, excuse me, Mr. Singh. I have forgotten my keys at home, I'm afraid. I'll have to go home and find them."

"Don't worry. We'll wait for you here," said Raunaq Singh.

"Oh, no. No. You must carry on. I might take a little longer," said Roy as he rushed back to the Garden City.

He returned twenty minutes later, ensuring that he wouldn't run into Mr. and Mrs. Singh. He reached on time for breakfast. He entered the CDH where the staff members dined with the students. He occupied his seat at the head of the table of the class nine students of his House. He appeared to be pre-occupied and nervous.

As soon as breakfast was over, he found Raunaq at his side.

"Got the key, Dwinder?"

"Yeah. I've got it," even though he looked confused.

"Let's go then."

"Yes. Please."

As they were walking down the slope of the dining hall, Raunaq observed, "Lucky man. You didn't lose it on the way last night. It must have been dark."

"Yeah, lucky."

"One o'clock at night yaar Dwinder. Dark obviously. Where were you till one? You left the Art department at nine."

Before he could answer, Roy was shocked to see Rosalind coming up to him. She wished them both and handing a key to Roy said, "Mr. Roy you forgot your key at the Trafford House last night. Haven't you been looking for it?"

"Thanks, Rosalind. I didn't quite realize I had lost it."

Raunaq Singh cleared his throat loudly while Roy asked his leave and walked down with Rosalind.

For three days he didn't happen to meet Rosalind or Jacqueline or Raunaq Singh or his wife. On the morning of the fourth day, at eleven, Roy had an unusual visitor at his department. It was Raunaq Singh. He walked in pompously when Roy had just finished his class.

"So, Dwinder. How's life? Difficult to find you these days."

"Yeah, just a little busy, painting," he gestured nervously towards the many hanging on the walls, most of which had been there for years and were not his.

"I was just going down to the Peacestead. I thought I should say hello to you."

"So nice of you, sir," said he nervously.

"When I was in school, Dwinder, and later in the college, I used to have a very colourful life, you see. Of course, don't tell Guddy all this."

"No, I won't, of course," replied Roy, meekly.

"But, there's a time for everything. You should get married man. You'll stop coming home late."

"It's not the…"

"And these girls, you see, different ones will join each year. They'll have fun you know. But you've got to focus on more serious things now. Family and all you see."

"These are nice people. You can't just…"

"Of course, they are nice. Had I not been married, you see, I may not have come home at all."

"You're getting it all wrong. It's…"

"O, Dwinder, you don't see you see! You might end up wasting your life you see. Not just these two, there are many around here."

Raunaq Singh was walking towards the door and Roy had no intention of engaging him in any conversation lest it delay his departure.

"I was just going down to the Peacestead. I thought, why not see Dwinder and have a little chat, just like that, you see."

"It was so kind of you."

"Don't come home late. Come over for dinner sometime. It's your home also."

"Thanks, sir. I paint till late you see." He immediately felt he wanted to chew the last two words he had spoken and spit them out.

"O, you'll keep painting all your life. Good time pass actually. You've already got a job. Now you can take it easy on your painting and focus on life. Get it right by getting married. That will get real color in your life you see. Then you keep painting," Raunaq winked at Roy.

"I will think seriously about that soon."

Raunaq crossed the door. Putting his hands in his pocket he looked at Roy and said, "You are a nice man, Dwinder. In case you don't mind marrying someone from outside your culture I could be of great help. Guddy knows a lot of good girls in our circle. Qualified girls you see. You have a job already. Caste is a problem when you live in the village. You don't. It becomes worse when you're without a job. And you are not."

"Quite true. I'll let you know."

"I am going now. I was just going down to the Peacestead you see. I thought I should speak to Dwinder. Think man. Don't get late."

"Yes. Thanks. Come again sometimes."

"I will. Think about it. It's time, you see."

That evening, Debon Roy went to the MCR late, which means eight. He wanted to eat all by himself. He had a quiet dinner. He then sat outside on a sofa and lit a fag. He looked at the stars. It was the last week of March. It was getting warmer. He walked down the staircase of paved stones. He knew it had been there for more than a hundred years. At the bottom of it he stood at The Ledge, from where branched off nine different paths. One of them would lead to the Garden City. He had known it for six months. The middle one led to the Birdwood, where most of the classrooms were. He had known it for five years. The one to his left led to the Trafford House. He had known it for years but seen it only recently. He took that path. And he didn't believe it.

He sucked on his cigarette slowly. As he reached another old stone stairway that led down to the Trafford House, he put his hands into his pockets, with his cigarette stuck loosely in his mouth. It was dark but he could measure his steps one by one. More than half the steps down, he ceased to walk. Standing above the high retaining wall behind the Trafford House, he came face to face with an upper floor bathroom window, a few meters in front of him. For no reason that he could have explained to himself, of decent behavior, he stopped, and breathing through his cigarette, gazed at the window with partly drawn curtains. He found his eyes fixed on a spot beneath which must have been a bath tub. Someone emerged from the bathtub. The yellow light, through the parted curtains, helped him see a woman, from whom were dripping strings of hundreds of tiny droplets of water. She ran her fingers through her long hair and his eyes ran down her perfect back. Roy was stilled by what he witnessed. He measured the perfect back up to its culmination. He did not miss to notice a jet black mole on her left back. He held the cigarette in his mouth. She turned around. He couldn't believe it. She had indeed turned around, facing him. He celebrated the perfection of the spectacle in absolute awe. He could see up to her collarbone. The view further up, was concealed by an elaborate frill of the curtain. Her arms suggested she was wiping her face with her palms. His eyes of an artist trod downwards. Her bare breasts charmed his view. The light in his eyes illuminated merrily. His sight slid down, reluctantly, till the navel, the view below which was blocked by the wall. He chewed the butt of the cigarette which was now wet, with sweet fragrant smoke emanating from it.

Both her palms rested around her chin and she stood there. While his eyes feasted on the view, her stillness suggested to him that she suspected being watched. He saw that her palms moved down and covered her breasts. She turned, and walked away till the light was turned out. Roy could not see her anymore. With absolute calmness he took out another fag and putting it firmly between his lips, struck his lighter and prolonged it in front of his face. He had a strong feeling she was watching. He was glad he had probably been recognized. He looked up, in the direction of the window, and took a long puff which shone the tip of the cigarette brightly. It gleamed upon his face. He wanted his face to be clearly visible.

He took one puff after another, leaning back against the wall. He knew she was standing at the window, with her palms still on her breasts. With each puff a part of his face shone under the gleam of the cigarette tip. He stared into the little window in front of him, across the huge retaining stonewall. No switching off of any lights could eliminate from his dreamy eyes the strings of droplets dripping from the bosom, the hair falling over the back, the innocent breasts walking towards him, the pink buds that he kissed with his eyes before they were covered with her palms. Such was a poet's dream, he knew. He multiplied the charm of what he had seen with his eyes awake, into countless replicas to fill every corner of the realm that formed the blissful sight of the waking moments of his dreamful eyes.

Once his eyesight had settled into the semi darkness, he could see a dark white figure standing behind the window glass. When he had finished his cigarette, he lit another; even this time the flame of his lighter glowing his fair face amid the darkness that enveloped him, to the one behind the window panes, the one who had her palms on her bare breasts. He looked into the window, precisely where her eyes would be. He continued to stare dreamily. He took a deep puff and stood up. Dragging away slowly the cool blaze of his glare, he turned back. He walked up, slowly, each of his steps overwhelmed by the heaviness of reluctance. He did not look back but he knew he was being followed by a pair of eyes that might accuse him of abandonment, of indifference, of snobbery, and even of arrogance. But he knew in his heart that all he carried within him was longing. He dragged himself away and reached The Ledge. The distance back from the Trafford House to The Ledge was many times that of The Ledge to the Trafford House. He remembered, after such a long time, that this place was called The Ledge. He was pleased to remember that it was called The Ledge. He liked it. The Ledge. He sat down at its parapet with his head hanging loosely upon his shoulders, and a cigarette dangling from his lips.

He overcame with an agonizing rationale, the overwhelming impulse to walk down once again to the Trafford House. He didn't even know who it was. Was she Rosalind? Or Jacqueline? What would he do even if he did? He got up, and walked away resolutely. Not to the Trafford House. Not to the Garden City. Yes. Not to the Garden City. He walked to Birdwood. His steps were stern so that they couldn't be persuaded to retreat to the Trafford House. He wanted to drain his heart off the melancholy that was beginning to spread inside him like fragrance. While he walked across the front yard of the elegant structure, he couldn't help attempting to find answer to the question that arose from within, with a sting in his breath. Was it Jacqueline? Or Rosalind? He did not know. He would not either. He knew the shape. He fell for the moments that marked the figure emerging from the pool, throwing back her hair, walking towards him wiping her face, covering her own self with her palms, and then conversing with him in darkness and silence. He sat down under one of the many arches of stone along the corridors of Birdwood. How long would he revel under the trance of ignorance! He lit another cigarette. He sat there under the warm clouds that emerged from his fag. He was crushed by the longing that engulfed him, not of Rosalind or Jacqueline, but of the figure that covered herself with her palms and stood for him by the window, and of the moments that canopied the passage of that time in a sequence of images that were not disjointed into fragments but merged with one another to flow like a clear stream of various colors into a coherent vision. He lit another cigarette and abandoned himself under the arch and the quiet darkness.

The idea of going home occurred to him the moment he knew he had no fags left.

The next morning he woke up late but made it to breakfast just in time. He saw from a reasonable distance both Rosalind and Jacqueline and a whole lot of those he did not care to see. Breakfast was followed by the morning assembly, where the students and the teachers gathered formally for prayers. He was glad to know that it was not his duty that day. He sat drowsily in one of the rows at the back. As the staff member on the assembly duty walked down the aisle, he rose from his seat along with the more than four hundred students and the teachers. It was Mr. Gill, whose tall figure walked elegantly up to the podium. Roy noticed Jacqueline sitting two rows in front of him, on the left side, along with the girl students. He looked at her fondly. The series of images of the previous night floated around her. Imagining them to be related to her endeared her to him.

Just then Mr. Gill announced *Sunshine* to be sung. Rosalind struck the first key on the piano. He had not noticed her on the piano. They began to sing the hymn in a great chorus while Roy savored the near perfect female shape that ran her fingers on the grand old piano. His eyes ran up her back, till he entangled pleasantly into the long hair coiling himself along the golden locks. He recalled those images again and imposed them on her as she played the piano. The singing continued. Mr. Gill's polite sermons, Mr. Malvia's Sanskrit prayers and the students' chorus went on like voices from beyond the distant mountains while Roy lurked in the beautiful garden of his mind, where Rosalind and Jacqueline, and then, Jacqueline and Rosalind, appeared in variant shades of the same images of the night gone by.

Roy went to his department after the assembly. He could not help submerge into the recurring thoughts of the night, now involving the two, after the way he had just seen them. His trance was altered by the classes that walked into the main hall from time to time. Three classes a day was too much for him to bear that day. And then there would be hobby classes in the afternoon. He just couldn't have enough of the moments of the previous night. He re-lived them as many times as he could summon the exact scene with the assistance of his imagination.

He skipped his lunch. He laid stretched back in his soft chair, lost in thoughts that were both pleasant and made him afraid at the same time. While in his chair during the period that numbed him with its solitude, he fell asleep. His siesta was interrupted at three when the first lot of students screamed in to attend their hobby classes. When he woke up he felt as if he had been sleeping for years. He felt soothened by the effect of the sleep. The heaviness exerted on him by the last night's moments was gone. And gone was the fear that had lately crept into his mind along with the pleasure of those moments.

At half past four, he walked to the MCR and sat down for tea and snacks. He was the only one in the huge hall. He was disappointed that Rosalind and Jacqueline were not there, though he realized immediately, the folly of his expectation. They had not arranged to meet there. He just hoped to see them. He smiled to himself that he should continue seeing them as Rosalind and Jacqueline. Wouldn't he like to see just Rosalind? Or Jacqueline? He thought of them as one or the other since he had always met them together. He had always thought of the usual piano girls as one; because by the time many like him had been able to identify them individually, they were gone and replaced by another pair.

Having had his tea, when he thought the world was too busy or sleepy to notice his steps, he walked into the Tin Roof Huts, the rooms that housed the piano cells. His heart beat violently. He did not know which one of them he would run into. He had taken the most unusual step of walking into the piano cells. He was desperate to see Jacqueline. Or Rosalind. His unusual heartbeat came to rest when he knew that it would be neither of them. Boys and girls practicing their piano lessons told him that they had gone to the Quarter Master's on some business and would be back very soon. Roy disappeared as soon as he heard that and gulped two cups of steaming coffee at the MCR before vanishing into the familiar galleries of the Art department.

In the evening he went as late for dinner as he thought would enable him to dine alone. He did not want to meet anyone nor did he want to miss it altogether. It was the first week of April. He had come to fall in love with this part of the year at this lovely hilltop. More than five years of his stay had made him sensitive enough to things that his earlier life had not offered him. April in Sanawar is like it is nowhere else. Evenings become longer. Nights are warm. Thereupon emerge through the months of dormancy not just the plants, soil, the air, birds and animals but also human beings and their desires. The MCR had little tables placed outside so that dinners could be planned till as late as nine, under the clear skies.

He arrived a few minutes before nine. He knew he wasn't going away immediately after dinner. He had planned to sit on one of those tables till late. Since they kept them out April onwards, he could put his legs on the table and sit away beyond midnight. When he sat down to eat, the bearer brought him a note that was written in neat hand. It read : *You had stories to tell us.* It was signed by Rosalind. The bearer went in. Roy couldn't resist. He picked up the note and brought it close to his nose. It smelled nice.

He smiled helplessly, without knowing that he was smiling. Where was the need for her to sign it? The note would have been understood by him, even if it weren't singed by any of them. Wouldn't it have been clear enough, anyway? Well, he understood the desired implication of the signature. Wasn't it clear to him now? He got up resolutely, the note held tightly between his trembling fingers. He read it as many times as he could as he walked out of the MCR, almost directionlessly. Now there would be no more ambling through the lane strewn with that image and the conflicting options of reality. There was just one reality, and, he knew it.

Once outside the MCR, he remembered he had dinner to take. He walked back. He sat down at the same table the three of them had occupied that evening for dinner. He tried to remember the chair that Rosalind had sat in. He couldn't quite figure out. He tried to remember them individually as they had dined together that evening. He found it hard to figure them apart. To almost that day they had been to him the two components of the same embodiment. He gave up and sat back in his chair impatiently, waiting for his dinner to arrive.

He thought of the previous night. His figure now had a face. It was that of Rosalind. He wiped out from his consciousness the sad truth that he had not seen the face of his enchantress. She had it now. That of Rosalind. He knew it. Now he dreamed of it. It was Rosalind who had emerged from the pool, with tiny droplets of water dripping off her breasts. It was Rosalind who had walked away as she threw back her hair. It was Rosalind who had walked towards him and then covered herself with her palms. He did not want to demean that intimacy any more by venting it in words, even to himself. It was a speechless conversation between them. It was an intimate feeling since he had been seen too. It was Rosalind who had walked back and switched off the yellow light. It was Rosalind who then walked back to the window and looked out at him, into the dark, as he gazed upon the lightless window, his face revealed by the fire of the lighter and shining under the gleam of the cigar.

The dinner, the contents of which he could not register in the memory of his dying appetite, did not take long and within as long as a few desperate minutes he was gliding down the old stone staircase to the Trafford House. He stood there trying to look into the same window. It was dark and there was no one at the window. He smiled and walked down. He knocked at the door which he knew was open. He could hear soft piano playing upstairs. He could also hear violin. He walked up to the verandah. It was well lit, lights illuminating through the earthen pots and leaves, as it was on his first visit to the Trafford House.

"Hi. Thanks for coming, Mr. Roy," said Rosalind, turning towards him from her piano.

"My pleasure, entirely."

Jacqueline stopped playing the violin. They received him with warmth and excitement that took him by surprise.

"We didn't expect you to oblige immediately. I hope it was no trouble."

"Oh no, Rosalind," said he, taken aback by the self-consciousness that gripped him as he took her name, "I had been looking forward to it for some time. I knew I had to tell you those stories. Coming to the Trafford House is never a trouble."

"Are there many of them? Ghosts, I mean," asked Rosalind.

It was difficult for him to believe that Rosalind should like to start with some godforsaken ghost, even though it was story telling that had paved his way to the Trafford House. He liked to believe, though, that Rosalind had some other purpose too, as he did; the purpose that neither of them could have put into some tangible expression but understood too well.

"It is quite natural for a place, that has been inhabited for almost a century and a half, to have its population of those who can be seen no more, but only talked about."

"That's poetic," said Jacqueline.

He would have liked the compliment to come from Rosalind, though Jacqueline looked pretty as she said it.

"Is it?" The compliment had come from Jacqueline, but he chose to smile at Rosalind instead. His mind wandered all over her face and eyes as he said it, in his mind, 'poetic was when I saw you emerge from your bath,' even as he took out his cigarette case, and looking at her, intended to say, 'poetic was when you held your breasts in your palms and stood for me by the window, knowing that I was watching you, and knowing that we were aware of each other's presence.'

He offered a cigarette to both of them. Lighting his own, he continued, "There are many, you see." He couldn't help believing that Raunaq had got into his skin, as thoughts about him had unfortunately become inseparable from those of Rosalind. And Jacqueline.

"Let me tell you a love story," said he looking at Rosalind.

"Love story of a ghost?" It was Jacqueline.

"Not quite," he said looking at her. Then turning to Rosalind he completed, "Ghost story of love."

He shuffled and then settling into his chair comfortably, said, "It was during the first World War when Sanawar was a military school, and boys and girls had separate classrooms. They were not allowed to meet unless they were brothers and sisters, or if someone had something worth meeting about, and no one could have thought of any pretexts for which they expected to have got approval."

Debon Roy took a deep puff.

"As you can imagine," he said looking at Rosalind, "it must have been the worst of times to fall in love."

"Surely," said Jacqueline, as Rosalind nodded.

"And, see the irony! It is the oldest co-educational residential school, surviving anywhere in the world today!" Roy added, as he had a mild laugh.

"Henry Haynes, the greatest all rounder of his time at Sanawar, was in love," he said, looking at Rosalind. "He was in love with Christine, a girl two years his junior. During those days one had to endure one's melancholy for much too long till it was nursed once in a while, not by a rendezvous but by a mere occasional glance at the beloved," said he, throwing a prolonged glance at Rosalind till Jacqueline asked, "How did they fall in love then, without seeing each other so often?"

"That is what love is all about. Just one good meeting would triumph over a life-long denial of the beloved's sight," he said, looking at Rosalind, who, Roy thought, seemed to miss the meaning in his eyes. During the conversation he threw occasional glances at Jacqueline.

He was beginning to feel irked by Jacqueline's demonstration of attention towards him, and that not due to itself but by Rosalind's lack of it. He could not, however, avoid feeling the superficiality of his 'triumph over a life-long denial of the beloved's sight' expression.

"Henry was an excellent military man in the making. Those were the days of the preparations for the First Great War. Men like him were going to defend the Empire, and Henry, being an asset of the Royal Military School that Sanawar then was, knew his future, like many of his peers. The one good meeting that I was talking about happened to them when one Sunday all the boys had gone to their dormitory after a long day at The Range, that is the shooting range. He was cleaning his rifle for another round of practice on his own. Sergeant Calphoy had allowed him to be there till the evening. This bunch of girls from the Observatory Club walked up the hill from the main playground that subsequently came to be known as Barne's field. The girls were part of a science club that not only went butterfly catching on Sundays, but studied the flora and fauna of the hills of Sanawar and Kasauli on weekends. It was there that Henry happened to see his girl. He was smitten as he sat there, with his rifle between his legs. It is not possible that Henry had any conversation with Christine that day."

He dragged in the last bit of his cigarette. Looking pleasantly at Jacqueline he said, "Wouldn't it be nice to have some coffee? Or tea? I would prefer any."

Before he realized the folly of his 'I would prefer any' which he had said in a hurry to be alone with Rosalind, it was Rosalind who volunteered, "I'll get some quickly. You'll talk to Jacky of anything but the story." She stormed into the kitchen leaving him alone with the one he was obliged not to call Jacky.

Roy could not resist a genuinely felt admiration of Rosalind. His earlier sense of disappointment gave way to appreciation and helpless sympathy. He knew she was determined not to betray their chance rendezvous of the previous night. She had kept it not just from Jacqueline but was anxious to keep it from the both of them too. He marveled at this fine theatricality of pretension that made her look so sinfully innocent. He knew she and he would unravel the mystery one day. He knew she would choose the day.

Sitting face to face with Jacqueline he did not know what to say to her. He felt awkward in initiating a conversation with her as he was not prepared for it and felt he had been left alone with a stranger.

"How far does one good meeting last, Mr. Roy?"

She said it with such a smile that he thought she was mocking his assertion.

"Well…," said he, without looking at her.

"Would it survive a life-long of denial?"

As she continued Roy grew nervous.

"How is one to know that *this* is that one good meeting? Does the encounter indicate its goodness?" she asked.

Their conversation was marked by long pauses on both sides. For Roy, Rosalind was present between them; invisible, inaudible, inexplicable.

He was intrigued by the seriousness with which Jacqueline sought her answers and his inability and reluctance to answer were overtaken by the pleasure he felt as a result of being chosen to be the target of her queries. He might have felt at ease to answer the questions had Rosalind asked them for he knew how to get her to understand the answers without being told what was so obvious.

"One has to experience what I was talking about, Jacqueline. One knows when one goes through it. It doesn't have to be told."

Rosalind came out with a tray bearing three mugs of tea.

Roy was relieved, and had no intention of going back to what Jacqueline was talking about. He thanked Rosalind for tea and sat comfortably into his caned chair.

"As the war progressed, Empire's forces demanded more reinforcements. Please ignore my lack of knowledge of the exact circumstances. The result was that Sanawar was required to send troops, that is, its students, who were all

British, straight to the front. That is what earned this school unprecedented honors after the war. Great tea, by the way, Rosalind," said he as if not mentioning Rosalind might have led Jacqueline walk away with the credit for the good tea.

"A week before the first troops were to leave Sanawar, a ball was organized for the departing soldiers at the Headmaster's Lodge. Some girls had been selected for the ball. Christine was one of them. Henry danced all evening with her. During the dance, he whispered something into her ears. Once everyone had gone back to their dormitories, Henry and Christine did what no one had dared before them. They met. What made it worse, was that they chose a time that is considered inappropriate even today. As they pledged their undying commitment to each other, Henry was startled to see another man's reflection over their heads in the clear shining water of the open air swimming pool."

"Was is it that of a ghost?"

"It was that of Manohar, the night watchman of the main school building which came to be known as Birdwood much later, and the area that includes this Trafford House. The swimming pool was where the present Central Dining Hall is. Right above where we now are."

"'Get back to your dormitories. I am going to report in any case' said the guard, 'You are not doing that and you know it. I am going to the front in a week,' Henry replied in desperation and anger. While the men argued, Christine broke down since she knew too well the repercussions of this to her future. Henry cursed himself for getting caught. He embraced Christine as he pleaded with the watchman to give him a few minutes to escort her to the Girls Department and not to report the incident as that could lead to his suspension from not just the school but also from the troop."

He sipped his tea.

"It resulted in an argument. Later Henry saw Christine off to her dormitory in what was a real feat, that is, without getting noticed. No one knows the details of what happened after that except the result of that quarrel. The guard was murdered behind the chapel. He was beheaded with his own sword. Henry was found guilty after the police measured the footsteps that led to the muddy backyard of the chapel and returned. The unusually large sized shoes had gone to the site and walked back while the one bearing the smaller foot size never returned. Henry had the largest feet in the school. It was easy to trace their prints on soft wet soil as it had rained that day."

Both Rosalind and Jacqueline were spellbound and still, as if about to ask what happened next.

"Nothing disastrous happened to Henry. He went to war to save the Empire. Every Friday students back home would huddle at the Ledge to hear the news from the war. Also announced were the names of those who had laid down their lives. Special prayer meetings were held every Sunday. Those huddles, with a bonfire at the center, became the place where fellow Britons were acquainted with the necessity of the war. Sermons were given on the importance of defending Britain and the empire against all odds. During one of these Friday huddles Christine heard it announced among the names of those who had fallen in the war, the name of Henry Jonathan Haynes."

Dreadful silence prevailed in the verandah of the Trafford House, where Debendra Nath Roy was narrating the tale of Henry Haynes, Christine Mayer, and of the slain guard, who would later be known as the Headless Gateman of Birdwood.

"Manohar was cremated in his village near Bareilly but a tombstone was erected in his name where he had been slain, in a little graveyard at the back of the chapel. It was an act of appeasement as no Indian could have dreamed of such an honor in an area that existed only for the Europeans. It is believed that his restless soul still does the rounds of the corridors of Birdwood. Many recall him as the 'headless *chowkidaar*'. Some amongst the older staff claim to have known those before them who are believed to have seen a figure around Birdwood that walked about after midnight without a head on his shoulders."

"Who told you the story?"

"Everyone here knows it. But I know it better than everyone else. Henry's younger brother Thomas was a student in the school. Many years after Henry died in the war, Thomas and Christine got married in Kent. Their son Christian Henry Haynes was sent to Sanawar. He was schooled here for nine years. It was during his years at Sanawar that he lost his mother. Christian's son James provided me with some of the pictures of Christine while she was at Sanawar and a few belonging to her later years. She was stunning. I have painted a portrait of her youth with the title 'The Belle of the Ball' which shall be displayed at the exhibition next year in Delhi."

Roy noted that both Rosalind and Jacqueline heard with rapt attention. Not till the next round of fags did anyone speak. He loved to watch the two women who were lost in their own thoughts even as they looked at him and smiled.

"How sad, that all three of them died within a short period of time." It was Jacqueline who said that.

"We could go to the grave of the gateman someday," Rosalind said.

"I don't expect his grave to be marked specifically, may be too difficult to locate," said he.

The cigarettes were smoked in silence. He wondered what each one was thinking. Within minutes Roy found himself walking to the Garden City. He did not care to look at his watch but he knew it was very late. In fact it was quite early. He knew it would be morning in a few hours.

For several evenings over the next few weeks, Debon Roy played the story teller to the young women. He enjoyed every moment of it. He summoned all the tales of love, frustration, heroism, and ghosts, that he could from his reservoir of years. He enjoyed the attention with which the two listened to him and the spellbinding effect that he had on them. Sometimes he wondered why they took so much interest in stories about a place they knew they would be leaving in a short while. The truth then ascended upon him. You stay in Sanawar for a year, it stays with you for life.

One Friday evening in May, after the school had had its dinner, amid a mild drizzle, Roy could think of nothing but to walk down the old stone stairway that led to the Trafford House. His earlier visits to the Trafford House were planned, in a sense that all three of them knew that they were going to meet. Today's visit of his was not. He reached the main gate on the ground floor, walked up the wooden staircase and reached the closed door which he would shortly knock gently. He spent a while facing the closed, wooden, old green door, listening to the violin being played within.

When Jacqueline opened the door he could not hide his slight disappointment as she could not hide her excitement. He had expected to be surprising Rosalind first whereas Jacqueline had not prepared herself for such an occasion at all. He was quick to adapt himself.

"You surprised me, Mr. Roy."

"I like surprising people," he said and immediately realized the utter stupidity of saying something so foolish merely because he could think of nothing better since he was more disappointed than surprised.

He was relieved she did not pay much attention to his remark as she continued, adjusting the cane chairs, lifting her violin, "I have been learning to play the violin."

"You play so well… Jacqueline. I had been standing at the gate before I knocked…In fact…Oh, where is Rosalind by the way?"

"She is away. She's gone for the House Show rehearsals. It is next Saturday."

For the first time since dinner, he became aware of the noises coming from the Barne Hall and the other rooms of the Birdwood school building which was on top of the ridge above the Trafford House.

"I see," was all he could say.

Birdwood was where all the students of a particular House and the staff members attached to it rehearsed for their annual House Shows, spread across April and May of each year. He knew the practices would go on up to nearly eleven.

"Rehearsals would go on till late I guess."

"Yes."

He felt a little embarrassed for he realized that he should have heard the din issuing out of Birdwood. Why didn't he? He could not answer. He had been too occupied with himself.

"Jacqueline…may be, I should be leaving," said he, not knowing what else he should be saying, because he had never met any of them alone at the Trafford House, or anywhere.

"Without coffee?"

He blushed.

"No. Not without coffee."

He could see that Jacqueline too lacked the ease with which she presented herself on his earlier visits to the Trafford House.

"Rightaway?" asked she.

"No. We can….a little later."

They sat down facing each other, as they normally would. Rosalind was present in the midst of the two in the form of mutual unease.

"Have you played the violin for long?"

"Yes. Fairly long. I have always enjoyed it. I feel if there is an instrument, the sound of which can communicate directly with the soul, it is the violin."

"That's true. While I stood at the door listening, I found it difficult to resist the desire to not to knock at all. I stood at the door long enough before I realized I was getting wet in the drizzle. I regret having given up, else you would be playing and I would be standing by the door listening."

"Thank you very much, Mr. Roy. I feel truly flattered. And I like it. It satisfies to know that while I was playing it only for myself, there was someone else, enjoying secretly."

In the verandah that was shimmering in dim light as usual; shadowy beams of yellow light filtering through the leaves and flowers of the earthen flower pots hanging from the wooden arches; softly could be heard the drumming of raindrops on the old tin sheets of the roof, and coldly could be felt the fresh gusts of wet breeze of drizzling May, which gushed in through the wall of leaves and flowers, and the shimmering little bulbs in the flower pots hanging from the wooden arches of the verandah. Jacqueline had her violin in her lap which she slowly positioned in order to play. Against the background of sounds and voices rising and subsiding from Birdwood, she began to play her violin. She submerged into her music and he sank into his chair, looking at her. He lit his fag. As Jacqueline progressed on her violin, he sank deeper in his chair and closed his eyes. The sounds and voices from Birdwood seemed to fade from the background as the violin claimed increasingly larger spaces amid the humming of raindrops on the roof. Warm smoke from his fag was freshened by mingling with the fresh wet breezes that ushered into the verandah from all sides. In the stream of that soothing music, images of that night hovered around Jacqueline and made her more endearing to him. He opened his eyes. Jacqueline had her eyes closed as she played her violin. She looked beautiful. Debon Roy walked to the switches and turned off the lights.

He pulled a caned chair and placed it very close to Jacqueline. He lit another fag as he sat in the chair. Now there was no yellow light beaming through the leaves and flowers of the earthen flower pots that hung from the wooden arches of the verandah. The sounds from Birdwood had subsided further in their consciousness. Now, it was the rain, the violin and the fag. And in the centre of the charm were she and he. He sat close to her. He, looking at her playing the violin, took a deep puff, the faint glow illuminating her face, and she, playing her violin, looked at him. He took a deep puff again. He took the cigarette butt to her lips. She took a puff. The soft sound of the violin filled every pore around them. He took another puff of his cigarette, got up, pressed another butt into the ash tray in the dark, and with his fingers, gently pushed her knees to one side of the cane chair and sat in it alongside her. While she sat playing the violin, he sat laying, stretched lazily like a tired traveler and placing his right cheek on her left shoulder, beneath the violin, yearned: "Jacqueline!"

The sound of her name spread throughout, seeping into that of the violin and the humming roof.

"Go on," said she, very softly.

She eased out the violin and placed it slowly on her lap.

"I wish I were not so enchanted!" said he breathing deeply.

The soft rain hummed all over them. Fresh cool vapors of wet winds flushed in from all the three open arches of the verandah.

"After that, I had a dream," she said, running her fingers through her hair.

He did not respond. It seemed he had not heard her say anything.

"How I wish, I weren't so enchanted," said he.

Fag over and the violin silent; now it were just the two of them, with the rain playing guard. "I had a dream," she said. He did not hear. He did not listen. He did not, of course, respond. He was lost to the world.

Jacqueline turned silent, like the darkness that let nothing be revealed.

"Mr. Roy, do you want to sleep? You seem tired."

"No, Jacqueline, not tired. I am happily bewitched, though I wish I were not so."

"Then let me give you a cup of tea. It may help you come off it."

She parted gently and walked into the kitchen. Before the tea was ready, she had him walk in and stand next to her.

"Jacqueline, what if, Rosalind were to know of it?"

She thought for a while, looked at his face and said, "Know of what?"

They did not speak any more before they walked into the verandah which was still dark. She pressed a switch which let only two tiny bulbs in the flower pots be on, offering dim light, enough for them to look at each other.

"Mr. Roy, what is it that Rosalind may not know of?"

"Of course, nothing in particular Jacqueline."

"Fine, she won't know that you had visited. But, is it just that you want to keep it between the two of us or you don't want it to be known to *her*?"

"It's nothing, really."

"Or, are you afraid, she might be offended if she knew you and I spent some time alone?"

"How should that matter to her?"

"It might bother you, I thought," said she.

They sipped their tea in silence.

"Mr. Roy, all these days that you've been at the Trafford House, I see you weaving a web around yourself and Rosalind, while I stand outside it. It hurts me to be there at all. I cannot even disappear. And then to be conscious of being outside of the woven part."

He sat silently. He did not look at her.

"I see that there is a very fine glass film growing around Rosalind and you. I cannot blame you entirely for having created it. I mean you both are clearly visible to me, yet out of reach. The film is impenetrable. It grows thicker by the day. I speak from the outside but cannot be heard inside."

He lay in his chair like a dead snake. He would have liked to move and say something. In that dim light she could see he wanted to vent some expression. And then the desire to take in another sip of tea enabled him to lift the cup up to his lips. That helped him stir.

"But I must assure you, Mr. Roy, there is nothing for you to worry on this account. Please forgive me if I made you anxious. I did not want to. Yet I had a great urge to share it with you. I thought you owed me at least such a favor where I could burden you with a bit of my concerns."

Roy, with great difficulty, got up from his chair and bent upon his knees right in front of her.

"Jacqueline, why do you feel so?"

They both understood it was neither a denial nor an apology. It was yet a question for Jacqueline. Why did she feel so? He might have felt the ambiguity of his remark and the nature of an answer that he knew she would not provide, nor did he expect. He knew she could have asked him more appropriately: *Why do you do so?*

"I feel the hurt I may have inflicted upon you these many days Jacqueline. I apologize if I ever made you uneasy."

"Please don't be apologetic. It's not why you do it, or why anyone does it that way. It's about why things turn out that way."

It was the rain still. The noises from Birdwood were beginning to subside. The rehearsing students would be going back to their dormitories. He knew it well. Which also meant that Rosalind could be back soon.

"I must go now. It's late."

"You will be wet. It is drizzling rather heavily. It's cold. Wait."

She went into her room. He looked into the darkness and tried to find out the extent of the rain. He could sense it was not too much of a rain. It was as Jacqueline had said, a heavy drizzle. Turning away from it he came and stood by the table. There he happened to look into the ash tray. It had two cigarette butts and he knew both were his. He took them out and put them into his pocket. He placed the ash tray where it had been. She came out of her room with something which she spread around his shoulders.

"Thanks, Jacqueline, but I could very well do without it. It's not necessary."

"Come on. This shawl will save you from the rain and keep you warm. You have a long way to go."

He knew it was too late for any further conversation. He knew Rosalind would be home any moment. He walked towards the gate, Jacqueline following him. He opened the door. She switched on the light. They stood at the door. He stretched out his arm in the rain, and said to her, "Nothing to worry."

Somewhere near The Ledge could be heard some people talking loudly and approaching the Trafford House. They both knew it was Rosalind being seen home. Without looking at her, he said, "Switch off the light Jacqueline."

She obliged without asking why.

Without wishing her goodnight, he hurried down the old wooden stairway, and taking his left, went under it.

On top of the stone stairway, the group of students bade goodbye to Rosalind and he could hear her walk down. Jacqueline switched on the light that fell all over the wooden stairway and the ground around it. Within a minute Rosalind was at the gate.

"Jacqueline!" she exclaimed with joy.

"I heard you coming," Jacqueline replied.

"So nice of you. Thanks."

As she ran up the wooden stairway she almost screamed, "Let's get in Jacky. It's very cold."

He heard the door closed. He saw the light turned off.

He waited for a few minutes before he left the shelter beneath the staircase. He moved out of it and walked up the stone stairway. He saw the lights in the bedroom, kitchen and the bathroom not switched on yet. He sped up in darkness and drizzle, though he was oblivious to both. At The Ledge he halted to ease his breath. He did not stop there. He walked leisurely, as he usually did. Under the heavy street lights at The Ledge he took off the shawl and spread it in front of his eyes. It was lovely maroon. He slung it around his shoulders and folded its ends across his breast.

He walked below the Golden Staircase, on the lower side of Birdwood, the same way that eventually led to the War Memorial and the Chapel. He looked towards the dark heavens. The drops of the drizzle fell upon his forehead, eyes, lips, chin and the throat. It was the first respite of May.

He allowed his lips to be washed by the rain. He opened his mouth and allowed some tiny drops in. The fragrance from the shawl mingled with the cool air of the drizzle. He stretched out his palms and welcomed tiny drops onto it.

He walked past the War Memorial. At the gate of the chapel he lit his fag. Puffing impatiently, he walked down to the Boys Department Quadrangle, from where he took right, on to the long path down to the Garden City. Before he went to sleep that night, among other things that he thought about, he could not decide whether he should have said 'he had found it difficult to resist the desire not to knock at all.' He wondered whether he should have said 'the desire to knock at all.' He knew what he wanted to say, or, what he should have meant, but wasn't quiet sure how he could have put that into words. He was also not sure whether she had noted how it could mean opposite things. He forgot about it. He missed Jacqueline, her violin and the drizzle. Under the blissful burden of these thoughts among many, he fell into a sound sleep.

In the morning he was woken when Raunaq Singh thundered on the door.

"Oye, Dwinder?"

He didn't answer, hoping, he would go away discouraged.

"Oye, Dwinder! Sleeping? O common, yaar."

He opened the door finally.

"Good morning."

"O, very good morning yaar. Are you sleeping?"

"Not now, of course."

"O, good yaar. It's no time to sleep anyway."

"Yeah," Roy smiled, "please sit down."

Raunaq was sweating in his tracksuit.

"I am back from a long run and you are still in bed. You younger lot are so lazy. Almost good for nothing, yaar," he said, having a hearty laugh.

"Tea?"

"O no, Chatterjee. You know I'll drink a jug of water and then milk. No tea."

Roy drank the glass of water that was near his bed.

"You were late again last night."

"That's true."

"Painting?"

"Yes sir," he said as nervously as a school boy.

"I have got you something," he said, zipping open his tracksuit top. He took out a photo album and threw it into Roy's lap.

"Take it seriously Chatterjee and then you'll do all your painting at home," Raunaq Singh winked at him.

Roy opened the album, the covers of which had Raunaq's sweat all over it. It had many pictures of a woman in various outfits, in as many locations. The first few were shot in a studio, in as many poses as there are possible.

"What is it?"

"Don't say what yaar, say - who is she."

"OK. Who is she?"

"O, Dolly yaar. Guddy's sister. My sister-in-law, you see."

"Oh, I see."

"She is two years younger to you. A qualified teacher. Teaching in Delhi. It will suit you the best to marry a teacher you see. That is one way you could both live together for the rest of your life, wherever you go."

"Very true, sir."

"So what do you think Chatterjee? It's time to decide."

"I might need some time to think it over. After all, it's about all my life."

"Yes, yes. Of course. These decisions are not taken in a day, you see. So should I expect a decision?"

"Yes."

"By when?"

"By breakfast."

"By breakfast? Oye, that's like a man Chatterjee. Fine, see you then."

He knocked the door again, as soon as Roy had bolted it.

"Don't let Guddy know about it. I haven't told her as yet. She might have some reservations about her sister marrying a bangalli, you see. Ladies you know yaar. But don't worry. I'll make sure everything is OK."

Before leaving the room Raunaq noticed the maroon shawl on the chair and said, "Whose is it?"

"Um…my mother's," said Roy with ease.

"Fine see you after breakfast then."

After breakfast that morning, as students were marching down to the chapel for the Saturday morning prayers, Roy met Jacqueline at The Ledge. Most of the teachers were already away, walking down, along the marching squads.

"Good morning, Mr. Roy."

"Hi, Jacqueline. Getting late I guess."

"You forgot your keys last night."

"God," said he biting his lip.

"Don't worry…," she said, trying hard to look away from him, "she didn't notice them."

Roy, said nothing.

"She's on the piano duty today for the morning assembly," she said, looking away at the red roof of the chapel. She placed the keys on his open palm.

He felt the warm moistness of the keys, knowing that she had held them in her palm for too long.

"Huh...huh, excuse me." It was Raunaq Singh.

"Good morning, Mr. Singh," said Jacqueline.

"Hello, madum," he responded rather abruptly.

Roy put his hand into his pocket hurriedly but not without Raunaq Singh indicating that he had seen the transaction.

"I didn't notice you," she said.

"Don't worry I did," Raunaq laughed.

Roy looked away.

"May I take your leave? Getting late for the prayers," she said.

"Oh yes, please," Raunaq was quick to oblige.

Jacqueline hurried ahead of them and they followed; the distance between them increasing steadily.

"So, you haven't had your breakfast, it seems," said Raunaq, rather sternly.

"This breakfast will take long, I'm afraid," said Roy almost in defiance, looking away, knowing that Raunaq was looking at him without blinking.

"It's an insult to Dolly."

"Who?"

"Dolly yaar. My sister-in-law. You've already forgotten the name. It shows how little serious you are."

"It's not about her at all. She's not in the picture."

"I know there are other people in the painting."

"I wish they were."

"O they are Roy. They are. There are two of them in the picture. But in this way you shouldn't insult others."

"How on earth do you feel I insulted anybody? In fact, you just insulted Jacqueline."

They walked quietly till they stopped at the chapel gate.

"Don't worry, sir. The breakfast is still on."

"Oh Dwinder, you are like my younger brother yaar. This breakfast must not last too long. You can't eat porridge and oats all your life you see."

Raunaq was satisfied to have said that. Roy smiled. Just before entering the chapel, Raunaq held him by the arm and whispered into his ear, "A good breakfast, and in time, is the only way you'll have an appetite for lunch."

Inside, Roy saw that the assembly was yet to start. He immersed into the silence that had sunk into every corner of the chapel. Before he closed his eyes he admired how more than four hundred students and teachers could observe a silence as still as that.

He opened his eyes minutes later when the assembly stood up for prayers. It was Rosalind at the piano. She had her back towards them. He could not see her face but he knew she was beautiful.

Then came the last week of May. An entire week had passed since Roy's last visit to the Trafford House. He had seen Rosalind and Jacqueline occasionally during the meals. He parried any advances from Raunaq Singh saying that the breakfast was still on. The last of the four House shows was staged on Saturday. The next two weeks would be spent quickly to wind up the entire academic term. The school was to break up for summer vacation in mid-June.

The show ended at eight on Saturday. Students and teachers associated with the House were leaving for their dormitories and homes respectively to get ready for the dance and dinner. The rest of the school had had their dinner. As Rosalind was crossing The Ledge she heard someone whisper her name. She looked in that direction and saw Roy.

"Good evening, Mr. Roy. What a surprise!"

"Congratulations! It was a great performance."

"Thanks very much. I hope you liked it."

"I did. Everyone did, I am sure."

"Come along. I am going home to get dressed up for the party."

"No, I must leave. I was waiting to congratulate you. The girls and the boys did well too. Very well rehearsed. And you were outstanding."

"Thank you so much. The students would be proud too. Please come home. You could come back with me in half an hour. I'll give you a cup of tea."

"All right. I'll come back with you."

They walked down to the Trafford House. It was a usual walk. Rosalind unlocked the door and they walked up to the verandah.

"Please sit. I will set tea for you and get ready meanwhile."

She went in and he lit a fag. In ten minutes she was back; dressed elegantly and with two mugs of tea.

"You've hardly taken any time."

"Yes. Tea doesn't take that long. In fact I took longer. I was busy and it kept boiling."

"No, not the tea. You got ready so quickly. My neighbour Raunaq Singh keeps screaming from the lawn while Mrs. Singh is getting ready for any such occasion."

"I've hardly got anything to do."

"You look pretty."

"Thank you so much."

He puffed his cigarette, sipped his tea and without looking away from her eyes repeated, staringly, "You look pretty."

"Thanks," she blushed.

He sipped his tea with concentration.

It was only much later that he remembered to ask something so important.

"Where is Jacqueline?"

"She's left for Delhi."

"Delhi?" he wasn't prepared for such an answer.

"Yes."

"When?"

"Immediately after the show."

"How?"

"She had arranged a taxi."

"Why?"

"I have little idea. She said she had some work at the High Commission."

"Did she discuss it with you earlier?"

"Yes. This morning."

Rosalind sipped her tea as Roy looked at her.

"She hadn't been keeping well for a week. May have gone for a change."

"Anything in particular, Rosalind?"

"Not something that I know."

"Did you care to know?"

"She was all right physically at least. Just seemed to be a bit occupied mentally. I tried to inquire but I soon realized she would rather she kept it to herself. Nothing in particular and nothing to worry I guess. She seemed to be just about OK."

"You were busy with this House Show thing, weren't you?"

"That's right."

He sipped his tea.

"That means you will be alone tonight…I mean now on…for a few days may be." He corrected himself hoping one expression might be less explicit than the other.

"Yeah."

"Not afraid?"

"Of What?"

"Anything."

"Nothing."

They looked at flowers that grew in the little pots that hung from the wooden arches.

"Could I have a fag," said Rosalind.

"Lovely. I wanted a company for a fag."

"You'll never be too far from one."

They lit their cigarettes.

"Life is strange, Mr. Roy. If I hadn't come to India, I would've been in Tanzania."

"Tanzania?"

"Yes. Or, may be, in Yemen, Madagascar, Taiwan, Hungary, or even the United States."

"Why is it so?"

"Because we have to do a year overseas before we can take up work back home."

"How does it help?"

"To increase our horizons from our immediate surroundings to the vast civilizations in all corners of the world."

"For music should know no bounds."

"That's true."

She had another sip of tea and said, "But the pity is you can't have the experiences of all these lands by being in just one. They are so different. India in itself is such a unique gathering of so much. Being in a privileged place like this you cannot have the feel of the whole of India or even the real India I'm afraid. Jacqueline and I have planned to travel a lot during the summer vacation and even after we complete our tenure at the school by the end of this year. This place is good though to meditate upon your profession."

"Have you been doing that?"

"Yes. I've had a great time with my piano. Jacqueline seems to have rediscovered her love for the violin."

He nodded but didn't say anything for a while, staring into his tea. She had finished her tea. Looking up from his cup he fixed his eyes on her face.

"I will take you to Darjeeling during the summer Rosalind."

Rosalind looked at Roy while he stared down at her rather seriously. That made her blush. Despite the smoke rising between them, he could see her cheeks turning redder than usual. This, he knew, resulted from his blurring the compartment between innocent implications and instigating insinuations.

"Thanks. I think I would love to."

"It's been years since I last visited that area."

"Are you nostalgic about it?"

"I am. I have lived there off and on. It has everything that artists need to feed upon."

"I am not so much of an artist though."

"You are a musician. A musician is an artist."

"Yes, but not much of an artist so far. Jacqueline is closer to being one. I admire her for that intensity."

He acknowledged that.

"Mr. Roy, tell me one thing."

"Ask."

"I don't even know how to put it in appropriate words."

"Try," he smiled, straightening his posture.

She thought for some more time.

"What do artists feed upon?"

He threw himself slowly back into his chair.

"What artists feed on..."

She looked at him, expecting an answer.

"On so much...Rosalind."

He took a deep puff from his cigarette. He sat forward in his chair, bringing his face much closer to hers.

"On the winds; warm or cool, on the rains, on the mountains...or the plains," he gestured by spreading out his palm.

"An artist feeds on smiles, on tears, on sounds, on emotions...on memories," he continued.

He sat back on his chair and taking another deep puff he whispered, very loudly, "An artist feeds upon images, Rosalind."

She had been sitting back too, having nearly fagged out hers.

"An image at a time or a sequence of them."

She looked at him with a faint smile on.

"I seek your permission, Rosalind."

"Permission?"

"Indeed."

"What for?"

He sat back in the chair and stretched his legs as far as he could.

"To paint that image of yours."

"That image?"

His eyes were closed.

"Yes. That image."

She said nothing. He said nothing for quite some time. He searched for that emotion on her face.

"I remember it was my second visit to the Trafford House. I had not been invited though. Of course I did not come down that day. You would have understood why... I was mesmerized...Rosalind."

He opened his eyes, sat up straight and looked hard at her.

"I could paint you just like that."

She blushed.

"You could stand by the same window. You know, Rosalind, the effect of the image is still so powerfully embedded on my mind that even if you posed like that for a painting it wouldn't be the same. You could reproduce the scene but could you bring back that air, that communication, that mildly frightened face which I couldn't see?"

She continued to look at him.

"Why do you look so queer Rosalind?"

"You could paint me any way you like. I shall be privileged." He smiled.

In the silence that followed over the next few moments, could be heard loud noises from Birdwood.

"We didn't realize the party has begun," said Rosalind.

"It's been quite a while I guess."

"Have you had dinner?"

"I have. You must go and have yours, Rosalind."

"I don't feel like. We could cook something here."

"I suggest you go and have your dinner. You may also attend the dance thereafter."

"That means you want to go home."

"On the contrary, I don't," he smiled.

"You don't?"

"Not right away," he corrected himself and they both shared a light laugh.

"I could stay here without losing anything," said he.

"Are you sure?"

"Sure."

"Let me see if I can cook something here," she said.

"You must be hungry."

"I surely am," said Rosalind as she walked into the kitchen. He lay stretched all over the armchair. When Rosalind didn't emerge out of the kitchen for a few minutes, he walked in. There she saw Rosalind standing in the middle of the kitchen exasperated.

"Why do you look so agitated?"

"I just can't make up my mind. Don't know what to cook."

"You could still attend the dinner. It has just begun."

"I don't want to go for the dinner anymore."

"I have an idea."

"Yes?"

"Let's go out."

"Where?"

"Out in the open. We could walk out of the school and have something to eat somewhere."

"Won't it be late?"

"It's never late to find something to eat in the vicinity of a boarding school. Let's go out," he asserted.

Within minutes they were walking on the dimly lit roads, in a direction opposite Birdwood in order to avoid the party goers. They walked towards the school hospital.

"One would wish that the roads were absolutely dark," Roy observed loudly.

It was a cool summer night. It was dark except for the occasional street light. Neither spoke for a long period of time. They walked along the road below the hospital and the Prep Department Field. At the exit gate they met the guard who smiled at them. They responded.

They walked out of the gate and went to the nearby shop known as Moti's Corner where a few local men were leaving after they had finished their drinks. They walked into the empty room and placed an order for omelettes, bread and fruit pudding. They sat there for almost an hour through which they drank coffee, smoked cigarettes and spoke occasionally.

"Why are we so quiet?"

"I guess it's the time and the place we are in," she replied.

"The time is appropriate, Rosalind, and so is the place. There is nothing to worry really."

There was some stiffness about them and both of them could feel it. It could be attributed to their having left behind the places they felt home at. Stepping out of the school gate made them, especially Rosalind, feel vulnerable. Here was the absence of security that is bestowed upon the inhabitants by the place they call home, even though a temporary one.

"There is nothing to worry, Rosalind," said Roy, loud enough, as if to reassure himself that there was nothing really to worry. They continued to smoke over their empty plates.

There was nothing indeed to worry. Who should worry? And why? To be seen together, in darkness? To be seen together, in a place where they had no business to be? To be seen together, in a company, the very constitution and motive of which could easily be suspected? Or was it to be seen together? May be it was to be seen at all. Perhaps it was nothing.

By the time they paid the bill and a generous tip to the attendant, they had gulped down two mugs of beer each. That was it. Nothing else could so easily have dispelled the negative notions of imagined fear. One could easily suspect that what they had felt for so long was not at all the emotion of fear; real or imagined, but an emotion of anxiety, experienced before a strange phase of togetherness.

They carried a can of chilled beer each as they left the place and walked back. On reaching the gate Roy said, "Do you want to go in from here or should we take a longer walk?"

"A longer walk definitely," she said jubilantly. They ignored the gate and walked along the Long Back, a length of road encircling the hilltop that led to the main gate of the school.

There were no street lights on the way. They walked along, sipping beer from time to time.

"Mr. Roy, it's marvelous how cool breeze can blow in these hills at the peak of the summer season."

"It is indeed. It would be the same in Darjeeling where you and I shall spend our summer vacation."

He would have liked to repeat his earlier patronizing 'I will take you to Darjeeling' remark but somehow was frightened to utter it in darkness, lest it drive them into irresistible intimacy.

She slipped her right hand into his right hip pocket and he threw his left arm around her shoulder. They walked as they sipped their beer.

"What shall we do in Darjeeling?"

"Anything you like, Rosalind. We could get lost in the tea gardens. We would live in the little huts that the travel companies have built all over those beautiful hills."

They walked along the dark road, talking intermittently.

"Mr. Roy, it is such a good time. Thank you very much."

"It might be too early to say thanks."

"But not wrong."

"Not at all. But I must be grateful to you too. I haven't felt so good in years."

They continued to walk.

"What are you thinking?"

She took a while to reply.

"I have been thinking how I should be looking in the portrait."

"You have given me complete freedom to decide that."

"I remember that," she laughed.

"Anything in particular…about the way you wish to look?"

"I was thinking about the background, the dress and…"

"Don't worry about that. I guess you've been thinking about it for long."

"Not very long. I just want it to be very different and, of course, memorable."

They flung their empty cans down the hill before they entered the main gate of the school and walked up Sergeant Tilley's Hill. She leaned against him as they walked up the tiring slope. They walked quietly as they crossed the security gate and passed through another Green Gate. They walked along the Mall, on the lower side of which lay the deserted Independence Garden.

"It's lonely here."

"It's lonely everywhere Rosalind, if you let that loneliness in."

"Do these trees ever feel that?"

"Not as long as they have darkness for company."

"Is darkness a company?"

"What else is keeping us so close?"

"Yes. Gives company to the companions."

"And is one in itself too."

"Amazing. Had never thought of it. Marvelous."

"You can talk to it; you can share anything with it. It endures everything till dawn begins to complain."

She looked at dim street lights peeping through the tall dense trees. Only faded beams fell upon the road. They reached the Arch, a few steps after which Roy said softly to her, "This path leads to the Garden City."

"I see."

They stood there. He looked at her.

"Would it be appropriate for us to walk down to the Garden City?"

"Shall I give an answer to the question or the invitation?"

"Both."

"Well, I have somewhere else to go before we go anywhere."

"Where?"

"Shall we go to the graveyard?"

"Which one?"

"The one behind the Chapel. Up there."

"You won't be scared?"

"Not at all."

"Fine. Come on then," said he.

They walked up the slope that led to the Chapel.

"I'm not sure how old the graveyard is. It is next to the War Memorial."

"Isn't that where the gateman was murdered?"

"That's true. Nearby."

They reached the gate of the Chapel, right in front of which was the War Memorial, the elegant pillar of stone, which stood brightly under the street light.

They entered the encirclement and stood in front of the stone pillar.

"It is beautiful."

He did not say anything. He just stared at her.

"Mr. Roy, let's pay a homage to those who laid down their lives to ensure freedom to others."

"Indeed."

They kneeled down in front of the pillar and she read out aloud:

To The Greater Glory of God
And
In Proud Memory of
OLD SANAWARIANS
Who Fell In The Great War
1914-1918

At the going down of the sun and in the morning
We will remember them

They got up and walked in the direction to their right and kneeled down at the corner where she read out aloud: Berry L., Byrne J., Bloodworth F., Bloodworth P., Bruce A.J., Charlton L., Cullen F.J., Cross E.M.F., Edge S.

Their name Liveth evermore

"May God bless their souls," she observed.

"Those who made the supreme sacrifice."

"For the sake of others."

They took a few steps around the pillar and kneeled down at the third corner where she read aloud the names of the martyrs: Gibbons E., Hickie C.S., Houlding H., Line C.H., Malachowski Von H., Morris A., Mc Gregor R., Ashcroft J.

They shall grow not old as we that are left grow old
Age shall not weary them nor the years condemn

"Now the last of the martyrs," she said as they walked around the mighty stone pillar to kneel down under the street light to read aloud the name inscribed at the bottom of the pillar: Nicholas D.J., Oldall E.T., Pilcher A., Richards R. E., Trowsdale C., Taylor W., Wren C., Wright G., White E.

> *This shall be written for those that come*
> *after and the people which shall be born*
> *shall praise the Lord*

"So many of them," she said.

"There are more. Those who laid down their lives in the Second Great War and the other wars in independent India. We could go there and have a look."

"But I would like to see the graveyard first."

"Yes but I'm not sure if we'd be able to read the tombstones."

"Leave the tombstones alone," said she, coming close to him and whispering into his eyes, "You could paint them in your imagination while I sing Carols for their blessed souls."

He stood there, like the erect stone pillar, looking at her.

"Mr. Roy, can we go behind the chapel?"

"We could. It's quite dark there I'm afraid."

"Yes but darkness is a great companion, isn't it?"

He smiled.

"It is indeed."

She led him through a narrow path that led to a narrow little space behind the chapel. It was not very dark there. The street light from Birdwood fell on this side of the chapel. They stood there among a few scattered stones that marked a few graves. The place was surrounded by huge walls;

the chapel wall on the one side and a huge retaining wall opposite it, that supported the path that led to Birdwood.

"Was it here that the gateman of Birdwood was murdered?"

"Must be right here. I've never been here before."

"How sad. It could have been different. Wasn't such a big deal after all."

"We live in very different times Rosalind. Those days were different. One tried to do his duty and the other did what he thought was appropriate in order to safeguard the future of his beloved and his career in the Great War and the Empire."

"But you can't murder an innocent man for that," said she.

"Most of the historical details about the incident are hearsay. One would have to do a lot of research to find out the truth."

"Would it be possible to discern some of the names written on these tombstones?" said Rosalind as she bent towards the ground.

Both of them began to search for legible inscriptions on the tombstones that were scattered on the ground. They searched in separate directions. He removed fallen leaves from top of some of the stones. He tried to decipher some alphabet by wiping away the dirt with his hands.

"Is there something in particular we should be searching for?"

He received no reply. He carried on.

"I can read a name- it is C ...R, the next two are missing."

She didn't answer. He carried on.

"I think I've got some more of it."

He received no reply still. He carried on, nonetheless.

"Rosalind," he called out and looked up. He could not see her in front of him, which is where she was supposed to be.

"Rosalind," he almost whispered but continued to look at the same spot.

He felt himself gripped by a strange feeling that made him afraid to look in other directions. He knew he could not entertain such a feeling long enough and make himself anxious as a result. He called out yet another time, "Rosalind." This time his throat seemed dry.

He stood on the same spot till he heard, "Mr. Roy."

He turned in the direction of the voice. He thought he saw a woman. She had climbed up and was seated firmly on a little wall.

Roy noted with awe that she sat upon what seemed to be a several feet high parapet with her back towards him. She had taken off the full sleeves turtle neck that she had been wearing. He gazed upon the marvelous slope of her marble back, on the one side of which he could figure out the shape of her breasts.

"Mr. Roy, can you see me?"

"Yes. I can, Rosalind," he said, trying to clear his throat.

He wanted to go further, stand against the parapet and pull her slowly upon himself.

"I would like you to paint my portrait like this."

"Yes," he said, clearing his throat, glaring upon her back, golden locks flowing down.

"Absorb the sight well. We may not be able to come here again at this time to pose for the portrait."

"Yes," he said meekly. His dusty fingers were stretched forward in anticipation of an invitation.

"Do you capture the mood? That is more important I guess."

"Yes, Rosalind." He put his fingers in his trouser pockets and leaned back on the wall, gazing at her. He was now at ease and had a smile at his painter's face.

"You should be able to reproduce the mood of the moment Mr. Roy. One can't pose in this position too often."

"I am taking it in. A young Englishwoman at the graveyard," said he.

"At the Empire graveyard."

"Apologizing to the gateman of Birdwood?"

"Sympathizing with the slain gateman. Paying tribute to his sense of duty. Paying homage to the martyrs."

"Sometime beyond midnight."

"Yes. Intimate with the past."

He walked towards her and leaned against the parapet she was sitting upon. He could smell her.

He looked up where she sat firmly on the elevated parapet with her bare back, looking away. He placed his palms on the outer part of her thighs and planted his cheek and lips on her lower back. She was warm. She smelled warm.

"Rosalind."

He took a deep breath.

"Come down."

He dragged his palms back towards her hips and moved them up till he held her firmly by her waist. He looked up her back. He marveled at the sight that was clear to him under the street light that fell from Birdwood.

"Rosalind…"

He moved his hands up the middle of her back and ran his fingers into the abundant locks that hung like watery clouds of a huge waterfall.

He felt strange about the vision of the back. It seemed to him that it did not reconcile with the vision of that night. He searched for familiarity but wasn't obliged. It was at that instant that he remembered the black mole on the upper left part, the milestone of his first sight of the maid. He felt he should greet the marker of his memory. It should have been visible despite the locks he thought. It was not. The hair may have grown longer. He parted the beautiful locks with his fingers and tried to locate the mole which was not visible. He did not believe it. He searched for it on the right side. It was not visible there either. Between the left and the right he ran his fingers, separating the hair only to behold spotless white skin of Rosalind.

Roy did not believe what he did not see. He did not believe that he did not see the jet black mole that had had a permanent place in his consciousness for the past couple of months. True to his first vision, he hung his head in despair and let his hands fall lifelessly for the woman of his enchantment was not Rosalind. And that he should know it only now, stung his heart and in that deep anguish all he could manage was a painful whisper- "Rosalind…you are not Jacqueline," as if saying to himself.

"Rosalind…how I wish you were Jacqueline," his voice cracked, his head hanging beneath her back while his fingers, like claws of a desperate beast clinched partly her warm thighs and partly the cold stone of the parapet.

Despite the overbearing disappointment, he heard his name being whispered, "Debon."

"Yes," while uttering which he placed his fingers firmly on the parapet and straightened himself firmly and asserting, said, "Rosalind." The sound 'Rosalind' assured him that it was Rosalind who was present in front of his eyes and not Jacqueline. The drowsiness left his eyes and the vision of the maiden in front of his eyes was now less mesmerizing.

"Shall I turn around?" she said, turning her head towards him. He looked at her with his mouth open.

"You might catch cold I'm afraid," was all he could say.

She smiled at him like a goddess and said, "I should have had it by now."

"What?" he said with his quivering lips.

"The cold."

She wore her turtle neck. He saw her head emerge through the round neck. She pulled her long hair out of her garment and allowed it to flow down her back. He watched in bewildered astonishment. Images existing in memory conflicted with those appearing. She put her palms on the parapet and pushed herself up till she stood straight on it.

"Help me get down."

He offered his hand.

"Both," she ordered.

He put both his arms forward.

She jumped down and stood face to face with him. She looked sternly into his flickering eyes. He was afraid she might ask 'what next.'

"Do you promise me?"

"The portrait?"

"Only, if it truly inspires you."

He nodded.

"Does it?"

"It does." He could not figure out whether he was lying. "Will you?"

"I will." He closed his eyes firmly, took a deep breath and repeated, "I will, Rosalind."

She smiled at him. He could hardly feel any sensation enough to move his lips in any way.

"Don't you think I might catch cold?" she smiled. He couldn't resist smiling.

They walked out of the deserted cemetery behind the chapel. They walked up the road that lay stretched below Birdwood and stopped on their own at the spot which stood right above the graveyard they had left a few moments ago. They could see the lofty TV tower in Kasauli. Numerous red bulbs shimmered on both its sides, from top to the bottom. Since the hill was not visible, it seemed to be a tube with glittering stars hanging from the top. Birdwood had been silent for a long time. They walked past the Ledge.

They reached the Trafford House. He walked up the wooden staircase behind her. He looked at her feet as they moved up the steps. He saw that her steps did not falter the way his were. She opened the gate at the top of the staircase and stepped in. He stood leaning at the gate.

"Come in," she said.

"Thanks Rosalind. I think I should leave now."

"Come in, it's so dark and you might catch cold."

They laughed. She laughed again, shaking her head.

"Thank you, but it's time I left."

"Fine. Good night, Mr. Roy."

They smiled at each other and he walked down the stairs.

"And…" she said, "I must thank you for the time you spared for me tonight. You must not feel any urgency about the portrait. Begin only when you have the time."

"Yes." He looked at her and smiled.

"Bye."

"Goodbye."

He heard her close the door once he had stepped into the dark. He saw the light switched off. He walked up the stone stairs. He stopped at a certain point and turned back. He faced the window where he had had the vision that had haunted him all along. He sat down and stared at it. Behind the long closed doors of his eyelids, in his personal gallery of intimate portraits, he tried to re-create the aura of the enticing vision. He shut his eyes and placed his forehead on his folded arms which rested on his knees. He did not want to allow any violation of the sight that had arrested his imagination for so long. He relished the view that he had seen at this place a long time ago and the warmth of which he thought he had frittered away. He now understood the web that Jacqueline had felt she was outside of. He felt strangled inside the web. He could see Jacqueline through it. He wanted to tear out through it and reach her. He now realized that Rosalind's behavior was not perfected pretension but unfamiliarity and normalcy. He also remembered with regret Jacqueline's failed attempts to re-ignite the warmth that had first taken shape on that dark evening across the partly revealing window pane.

His urge to light a fag, something he had not done for some time, was drowned by the sense of heavy guilt and regret. Was it due to her frustration with him that Jacqueline decided to leave for Delhi without much reason?

Within minutes he was sitting at The Ledge. It did not console him either. He felt lonely. There was not encouragement enough to take a walk to Birdwood. He finally decided to tread the familiar path down to the Garden City. He opened his door and entered his room. He did not dare to switch on the lights. He did not wish to face himself. He lit a candle and sat in the armchair. He could smell cigarette. He saw his jacket on the right arm of the large chair. He picked it up and held it in his lap. He had worn it on that long night at the Trafford House. He searched its pockets and took out two cigarette butts that had not been smoked to their ends. He held them in his palms and smelled them. One of them had been partly smoked by Jacqueline. He lit the butts by the candle flame and smoked them one by one.

After a passing nap in his chair, he got up, pulled the shawl that Jacqueline had given him on that drizzling night, lay on his bed, and, wrapping it around his face so that he could inhale her, nursing his melancholy, went to sleep.

He could not sleep. He lay in his bed. It may have been only a few minutes when he heard a soft knock on his door. He did not know how to respond to a call deep into the night. He waited for some time, till he heard it again. He was nervous but left his bed. He put his ear to the door and asked, "Who?"

"Me."

He waited patiently for that me to elaborate, but that was not to come.

"Whooo?"

"Meee."

He opened the door. He didn't believe his eyes.

"Hi. Hi. Jacqueline. How is it that…?" She stood there, smiling.

"Yes. It's me. Not a ghost."

"Surely, not a ghost. You had gone to Delhi," he said breathing uneasily.

"Yes. I changed my plan some way off. I unboarded the train and got a taxi back to Sanawar."

"Good. Thanks. But why?" Roy could hardly hide his excitement.

"No answer. The only thing I remembered was to go to a place that is neither a garden nor a city."

He smiled.

"To meet someone, who is neither a man, nor an artist," said he, as she smiled at him.

They had stood on two sides of the door till Roy was startled enough to say hurriedly, "Please come. Will you?"

"May I?"

"Yes, please. Please."

She entered the room. He closed the door.